THE YORK DIPPER

What would you risk to bring the truth to the surface?

Maria Frankland

AUTONOMY
PRESS

Autonomy Press

I dedicate this book to my home town,
and to anyone who has tragically
lost a loved one.

This book is the first in a trilogy. (The Dark Water series)

Also available:
Drowned Voices
Emergence

JOIN MY 'KEEP IN TOUCH' LIST

If you'd like to be kept in the loop about new books and special offers, join my 'keep in touch list' by visiting www.autonomypress.co.uk.

You will receive a free novella as a thank you for joining!

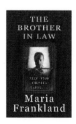

Prologue

The cold is like a million knives slicing into me. I've never felt anything like it. I try to shout, but I can't even breathe. How did I end up here? One minute I was cosy in the pub, knowing I'd had one too many, the next I was coming outside for some air, stumbling at the side of the river. Then, well, I don't know if I will ever see the light of day again.

I see the faces of my family in my mind. Again, I try to scream. Not a whimper. I'm going to die. *No, I am not.* I'm going to fight. I try to kick, to tread water. Pretend I'm a girl again, doing my level one at the local baths. One minute in the deep end. But I can't move my limbs. I'm being frozen alive.

Something is sucking me under. A force is pulling me down. My foot lodges within something hard. I hold my breath. Try to kick again. All is silent apart from the terror inside me. I really am going to die. Here, in this river where people dispose of shoes and shopping trollies. I can't move. All around me is inky black.

I see faint moonlight filtering through the surface of the water. Thoughts won't come anymore. My body is going to explode. I try, one last time, to return to the surface. To get another breath.

Instead, I choke as freezing liquid engulfs me. It fills my stomach, my lungs. I'm sinking further. This is it.

PART ONE

CHAPTER ONE

Joanne

Joanne looked around at her seven 'hens.' "I can't believe so many have dropped out. You find out who your friends are at a time like this, don't you?" Fifteen people were supposed to be coming. She had been looking forward to this evening for ages and couldn't believe how many, one by one, had let her down. Particularly after her disastrous hen party the first time around. In truth, her entire first marriage had been disastrous. Thankfully, all that was behind her.

"It's just our age," her sister-in-law-to-be laughed. "It all becomes a bit of an effort to go out once you're in your forties."

"Yeah," agreed her friend, Leah. "Not to mention the recovery time needed afterwards. I'm alright when I'm actually drinking, but nowadays, it takes me three days to get over it. Don't take it personally."

"Anyway, we're here," Wendy said. "And we're having a good time, aren't we? It's quality, not quantity."

"I guess so." Joanne noticed her mum walking carefully towards the table, balancing a tray of cocktails and shot glasses. "Mother!

What are you playing at? I'm already squiffy. I'll be neither use nor ornament after that!"

Everyone laughed as Joanne's mum placed the tray on the table. "Right girls," she said, reaching for a shot glass. "I'd like you all to raise your glasses to Joanne and Robin. Finally, she's marrying someone decent. Even I approve of him!"

"I'll take that as a compliment." Joanne necked the shot in one, pulling a face as the liquid burned the back of her throat. She'd always hated Sambuca. With it, she also tried to swallow the resentment that was bubbling up towards her mother. She had to be centre stage, no matter what the occasion. Joanne hoped she wouldn't be like that on the wedding day itself.

She was draped in L-plates and a piece of old net curtain - her mother's offering. When she had first got engaged, she'd felt self-conscious and old, especially when looking at wedding dresses amongst the twenty-somethings. Being due to turn fifty in a few months, she was aware that she looked nowhere near that age. Her life was definitely due to begin at fifty. Her dark hair flowed down her back and invited many compliments, and she had inherited her mother's green eyes and good skin. Sometimes her friends seemed envious, but they weren't up at seven, getting a five kilometre run in before work each day.

Joanne enjoyed how people acknowledged their table with a smile as they walked past. Her hens had brought balloons and streamers, so there was no mistaking what sort of celebration was going on. And even though she'd felt miffed at so many dropouts, and with her mother getting on better with her friends than she did, she couldn't deny that she'd had a great evening so far.

She watched as the rest of the hens pulled a similar face to hers whilst downing their Sambuca, then her mother started dishing out cocktail glasses. To say she had twenty-four years on Joanne, she was going strong this evening. She was going strong in general.

"Wendy - sex on the beach. Joanne - unbridled passion. Me - three in a bed." Everyone laughed.

"Mother!" Joanne exclaimed for the millionth time that evening. She was on form. Joanne looked around at the seven ladies that she had to admit, she cared most about in the world. If any one of them had said to her ten years ago that her life would look like this now, she'd have said they were mad. But they would have been right. Joanne was marrying her Mr Wonderful in a fortnight. They had met at the park and he couldn't have been any more different to her first waste of space of a husband.

Soon after splitting with him, she'd had a bit of a dalliance with a married man who'd stalked her after she'd broken things off with him. She hadn't known he was married, so it had all got messy. After him, Joanne had sworn off men forever. Until Robin had come along and swept her off her feet, or rather his labrador had - literally, so he'd bought her a coffee to apologise. From there, things had unfolded naturally.

They had a lovely church wedding planned with all their friends and family, and she couldn't wait. She took a sip of her *Unbridled Passion*. "What on earth's in that?"

"Just drink it," Wendy laughed. "It's your hen night. Do you want to go home sober?"

"I'm a long way from sober," Joanne replied. The more she got down the lethal cocktail provided by her mother, the more the pub lounge started to tilt to the left. She had drunk lots lately. This was the third hen party she was having, the first two having been organised by different circles of friends. She'd been teetotal after splitting with her ex-husband, wanting to keep a clear head whilst it all settled down and the divorce went through, particularly because he had repeatedly reappeared, either in anger or in begging mode.

As the cocktail neared its end, she accepted that the room had gone from a tilt to a spin. "I'm just going for a breath of fresh air. I'll be back in a few minutes." Joanne staggered towards the exit, the echo of laughter and *"lightweight"* roaring in her ears. She gulped in the fresh air, trying to make out shapes in the rain and the darkness, whilst deciding that when she went back inside, she was going on to pints of water.

CHAPTER TWO

Lauren

I look up from my book as Mark strides into the lounge. I was starting to wonder where he was. He's normally back from his shift by quarter past eight to tuck Alysha in. She's been asleep for over an hour now.

I watch as he chucks his police ID badge, pocketbook and keys into the dish on the sideboard. I enjoy the sense of his weight beside me as he flops onto the sofa. He's three days into a stretch of five twelve-hour shifts. I miss him. And since his promotion, he is working later than he used to.

"Sorry I'm late love. We pulled a body out of the Alder. She went in on Saturday night."

A chill creeps up the back of my neck. "Bloody hell. It was only last year there was a spate of them…"

"I know. It's awful. And this is off the record Lauren. You'll have to keep that inner journalist under wraps for now." Mark reaches for the remote. "Ugh. I've had enough police drama for one day." He flicks the TV over from *Scott and Bailey*, which I've been half watching whilst trying to read my book. In truth, I was barely concentrating on either. I was more worried about what was making him late. I always am. And my imagination often runs wild.

"What do you mean, inner journalist?" I put my book on the coffee table and swivel around to face him. "I *am* a journalist. Just like you're a police sergeant."

"Nothing official has been released yet, that's all." He pulls me closer. "Her family is only just identifying her this evening. Anyway, enough work talk. Is Alysha OK? I hate it when I don't get to see her before she goes to bed."

I nestle into him, enjoying his warmth. The heating seems to have clicked off. "Yeah. She tried to stay awake to see you, but she's had a busy day. I didn't get her from after-school club until six."

"How come you were so late?"

"Just with that new column and there was a bit of boring sports reporting to sort out. Two of the sports journalists are off, supposedly sick. Anyway, you're one to talk about me being late!"

He flicks his gaze from the TV to me then back to the TV again. "I'm sorry. I should have rung. It all got manic. Everyone going off and coming on duty, was called into a meeting." Mark's channel hopping as he speaks, which I always find irritating. I've never quite got his full attention when we're watching TV together. Whoever said men can't multitask was right.

"What about?" I look at his face illuminated in the lamplight behind us. He's a handsome man, and I feel extremely lucky to soon be marrying him. Well, in ten months, two weeks and six days. If I looked at the wedding counter on my phone, I could reel off the hours, minutes and seconds as well. We're a great team in every respect, Mark and I. Apart from the long hours we both put in with our careers.

"Just because they've pulled this woman from the same area as the ones last year. Obviously I can't say too much about it. But I'll let you know if anything becomes official."

"Don't you trust me? I won't repeat anything until I'm allowed to. You should know that."

"It's not that. It's just – if you were to slip up. I'd be in for the high jump, you know I would."

"There were five deaths there last winter. I might be a reporter, but I won't be the only person wondering if there's more to these drownings than just accidents."

"We've obviously been told we can't rule something suspicious out but then again, it's a notorious stretch of river."

"So how many women have to die before something is done to protect them? These are people's mothers, or daughters. What if it was me, or your sister?"

"Alright Lauren." He laughs, although it's his nervous laugh. He can probably tell from my expression that I'm deadly serious. "It's not my case. It's been given to Ingham. He's said we'll be stepping up the patrols at night-time this winter. Also, Yorkshire Water is supposed to be installing more lifebuoys, and fencing in the steeper places."

"The council should put CCTV up as well."

"It's funding, isn't it? We're looking at the pub's CCTV for now," Mark cuts in. "Although, it's only over the bar and outside the exit. And it only goes along the riverbank for a short distance on either side."

"What about the building next door?"

"There isn't any in there - it's been empty for ages. There's apparently no interest from anyone taking the lease on."

"I'm not surprised. It's nearly derelict." I get to my feet. "Do you want a drink?"

"When I come down." He kisses the top of my head as he stands in front of me. "I'll nip for a shower and check on Alysha."

As I hear the shower running overhead, I relax. When Mark's on shift, I never feel at ease until he's home. He's only recently been promoted to sergeant, but he's still as involved on the front line as he was when he was a constable. Even more so now that he's in a more senior job. The buck often stops with him. He's keen to climb the ranks and prove himself.

I just hope he doesn't get killed doing so. One of his colleagues was killed in a high-speed chase last year; he was only twenty-eight. I'll never forget the desolation on the face of his eight-month pregnant wife at his funeral. Another of his colleagues was knifed to death the year before, when he approached a gang who had cornered a lad.

I couldn't cope if anything happened to Mark. I wish sometimes that he had a nice, safe job in an office. I guess if he climbs higher in the police, he'll be working more at the station. I don't know how my sister-in-law Eva puts up with Mark's brother, Will, being on traffic patrol. Well, to be honest, I don't know how she puts up with him full stop. Will's made a play for me when I first met Mark, and got worse as time went on. He's left me alone since his wedding night thank God - he's finally got the message that I wouldn't touch him with a bargepole. I've never told Eva or Mark about any of it and usually manage to keep my distance from Will, well as much as it's possible to keep distance from one's brother-in-law-to-be. I've forced myself to put his previous behaviour to the back of my mind.

My gaze falls on Mark's pocketbook and for a moment, I'm tempted to see if there're any nuggets of information relating to the woman who's died in the river. I squash all thoughts back down, cross at myself for even considering having a look. We trust each other. We don't do things like that. He's supposed to keep it locked away and would kill me for even thinking about it.

I'm whisking hot chocolate in a pan when I feel the strength of Mark's arms wrap around me from behind. I crane my neck to kiss him on the cheek.

"I've missed you today," he says. "Maybe it's with that poor woman dying in the river. It's got me thinking, even more so since you said before, what if it was you or Claire? You make sure you're careful next time you're out with the girls." He turns me around to face him. "Drink was always a factor with the women we pulled out last year."

I pour the chocolate into mugs and pass him one. "I know – and I've missed you. If only we could just stay cocooned here, me, you and Alysha. Then no one would have to worry about anyone."

"Ah, but we'd soon get bored," he laughs. "We need to be out there, making the world a better place."

I nearly talk over him as I remember the plans I've made. "Now you mention it, going out, I mean, I'm out with the girls this weekend. Saturday. So don't go taking on any extra shifts."

"I'll see how things go," he replies. "Could we put your mother on standby just in case?"

"Why is it always my mother, and always me who has to ask?"

"I'm sorry love. I wish my mother was more hands on, but it's just the way she is. She was like it as a mother so she's going to be the same as a grandmother."

I sniff and turn back to rinse the pan. "You'd think her losing Dean like she did would make her value her other kids more, and her grandkids."

As I face Mark again, a cloud crosses his expression. He doesn't like talking about Dean. And Will flies into a rage if Dean is ever brought up in front of him.

"Anyway, why are you thinking you might have to work? It's your weekend off." I hope he's not copying Will, who works all the hours he can; Eva's always saying that it's not as if they need the extra money.

"We're short staffed at the station, plus we need every penny we can get to put towards the wedding."

I'm always pleased when he mentions saving for the wedding. We've been planning it for what feels like forever, and just need to pay off the balances now. We sit side by side again on the sofa and he restarts his channel hopping.

"Just leave something on," I laugh, taking a sip from my mug. "Stick a bit of news on. Or even better, talk to me. We haven't seen each other all day. We're like an old married couple before we're even married."

The local news is starting as he lands on the BBC. I want to tell him about Alysha's upcoming school trip and more importantly, how much it is going to cost, but he raises his hand, as if to shush me.

"Just a second. I want to hear this."

The woman, believed to be in her thirties, was pulled from the River Alder at nine thirty this morning after being reported missing last night. Details about her identity cannot be released until formal identification has taken place.

People are being urged to take care on its banks, particularly where stretches of the river are unfenced.

Detective Chief Inspector Jonathan Ingham told Yorkshire News that deaths in the river are a 'needless waste of life,' and so easily prevented by placing more emphasis on personal safety after an evening out, and remaining with companions. Steps are being taken by Yorkshire Water to increase the lifebuoys available and install extra safety fencing.

I frown. "What's the point in putting up lifebuoys? Once someone is in the river, they'd need someone to throw it for them. It's no good if a woman is on her own."

"Obviously," Mark replies. "But I do agree with DCI Ingham. Women shouldn't be walking around on their own in the first place. Especially after a few drinks. Which is why you should be careful."

"Women have got as much right to walk around, wherever and whenever they want as men have." I avert my gaze from the TV screen and look at him. "Unless you're agreeing with me and saying there's more to it than meets the eye? That it is more suspicious than the police seem to be letting on?"

"Lauren." Mark slings his arm around my shoulder. "We're still talking about bloody work. Let's just spend some time together."

CHAPTER THREE

Becky

B ecky had been looking forward to their meal, which she had booked for her and Seb to celebrate the start of their next chapter. She'd bought a new dress and had gone to the hairdressers to have her hair curled whilst she'd been on her lunch break. She was soon wondering why she had bothered.

Firstly Seb was late. She was on her second glass of wine by the time he arrived. "I'm sorry, hon," he said as he lurched towards her. He hadn't even had a shave. "I had to help Harvey with his car. I know exactly which wires needed connecting to get it going again."

"It's OK." Despite her annoyance, she was relieved he had turned up. There had been many a time he hadn't. And tonight they were going to discuss the holiday they were going on together next year.

Becky watched as Seb pressed the pockets on his jacket. "Shit," he said, far too loudly. "I've gone and left my wallet at Harvey's."

Becky had been starving when she'd clocked off her shift on the ward. She'd managed to get one of the nurses on nights to come in two hours early and had arranged to return the favour the following week. Her appetite was always the first thing to go when she was stressed or miserable. By the time the waitress put their food in front of them, it was non-existent. She ordered another large wine before the waitress disappeared.

Over the meal, Seb informed Becky that he was going on a lad's holiday instead of with her. And that he had decided not to move in with her after all. She couldn't believe it. Just when they'd had the mortgage approved, and the offer accepted on the house. He reckoned it was all too much, too soon, but why had he let things go so far? One minute he was hot, the next he was freezing. And he wondered why Becky was insecure with him.

The worst thing was that he couldn't understand why she was so upset. "It's only a house Bex," he said, with a nervous-looking smirk. "Can't you get one of your mates to move in with you?"

"Of all the insensitive..." Becky began. Then stopped. They'd never been on holiday together. He'd always rather go with his stupid friends. When she thought back over their relationship, Becky realised it was always her doing the legwork, the chasing, the organising, whilst he went along for the free ride - when he felt like it, that was.

Becky could see that Seb was an utter commitment-phobe and was fast becoming aware that she could no longer waste any more of her time or energy on him.

"Can we have the bill," she said to the waitress. She was close to tears and just wanted to get away.

"We're going already?"

"I'm going nowhere with you. You're a waste of space Seb. You and your mates are welcome to each other. I'll make my own way home, thank you."

"I thought you were staying at my place?"

"I've changed my mind. All you ever do is let me down."

Of course, he probably thought she was messing about, as when she stormed off, he didn't even bother going after her. Instead, he waved as she walked past the window at the front of the restaurant. Somehow she resisted the temptation to stride back inside and thump him.

What have I been doing? She thought to herself as she walked absently away from the restaurant, tugging her hood up against the driving rain. *No way can I stay with a man like him anymore.* After wandering around for a little while, hoping the rain and fresh air might clear her head, she found herself in the Yorkshire Arms, which was dead for a Saturday night.

There was a couple snogging each other's face off by the window. Becky fought the urge to yell *get a room.* There was another couple who looked as though they were having a row, sat in front of the fire, and a couple of blokes, seemingly drunk, propping up the bar. They looked as though they could have been there all day.

Becky ordered and quickly downed a glass of wine. She returned to the bar to order another one, starting to feel calmer. That was until one of the bar proppers tried engaging her in conversation. "Look," she said. "I've had a row with my boyfriend. I'm here to get drunk, alright? So back off."

"Fair enough," he had replied, raising the palms of his hands towards her. "I know where I'm not wanted."

God, if that's the best I can do, she thought as she watched his retreat, *then I might as well get drunk.* He must have been close to fifty.

And drunk Becky got. She'd done five shifts in a row and now had two days off. No way could she have faced another shift on the respiratory ward the next day, so her days off had come at a good time. By the time she was on her sixth glass of the evening, she noticed the man staring at her again. He'd obviously decided that she really was on her own. He smiled. She reached into her bag to call her friend, Caroline. She needed to tell someone what had happened with Seb. And also to look busy so the man might stop staring at her.

She felt better after talking to Caroline, who'd had to cut the call shorter than Becky would have liked; she was away for the night with her partner. Caroline had then sent Becky a text. *Sorry I couldn't talk longer. I'll give you a ring when I get back tomorrow. Chin up. I'm thinking of you. Xx*

Staring at her phone's blank screen, wondering what to do next, it lost its signal. Turning it off and on again didn't work. An initial spurt of anger at the inconvenience turned to relief, as she wouldn't know whether Seb should try getting in touch with her, or not. *Did she even care anymore?* The wine she'd drunk said she didn't.

However, she couldn't ring a taxi either. Did she even want a taxi? Did she want to go home? Might Seb have turned up there, trying to win her round? She had wanted that house they'd put the offer on so much. And she had been excitedly looking forward to their holiday with every fibre of her being. Yet it was time for Becky to accept that she would never have been able to count on Seb for anything. Despite that, she was gutted. *Why do I always go after the no-hoper time-wasters?* It wasn't as if she was getting any younger. She felt like wailing to the pub, *what's wrong with me?*

She ordered another wine, then decided to walk home, despite the fact that the weather looked to be even worse than it had been when she arrived. The barman might have called her a taxi, but she wasn't sure that she'd be able to coherently string the words together to ask him. It was about forty minutes, but the walk might sober her up and straighten out her thinking. She could not go on like she had been doing.

Without looking at the man who had been gawking at her all night, she did the walk of shame to the exit of the pub, attempting to walk in a reasonably straight line.

CHAPTER FOUR

Lauren

E ach morning I tell myself that I'll get more organised. The house looks like a bomb has dropped and I've got so much work to do today. Mark is on shift at eight and Alysha has to be dropped off by one of us at breakfast club. I'm freelance, but on some tight deadlines.

Every day, there's the madness of clean shirts for Mark, bookbag and uniform for Alysha and files for me. I always say I'll get things ready the night before, but I never do. They're long days for all of us, particularly at this time of year. The clocks have gone back and I'm struggling to adjust to darker nights and the loom of winter.

"You look tired Mark." I smile as he walks across the kitchen.

"I've been at work far too much and I didn't sleep well last night." He pauses at my side and kisses my cheek.

"I know. You kept waking me up."

"I was thinking." Mark slots bread into the toaster. "In fact, it was what kept me awake last night. Two women dying in the same stretch of the river as the women last year. You're right. It's shit."

"So what are you going to do about it?"

"I don't know. I just hope DCI Ingham does what's needed, and quickly. We can't have any more falling in. But he's become haphazard since his wife left him. I feel sorry for him but he's taken his eye off the ball. I'm not the only officer who has noticed."

"Separating from his wife is not an excuse. Not when he's dealing with life and death stuff."

"You know what we blokes are like. We go to pieces without you!" He grins.

"I don't think there's much to joke about Mark. Especially when the two are added to the women last year."

"I'm not convinced there's a connection between the recent two and the ones from last year." He butters his toast. "The only thing they've got in common is they're all women and had been drinking."

"What about their ages?" I suggest. "They've all been fairly young."

"Nah. They've been all sorts of ages. From early twenties to mid-forties."

I wrap Alysha's sandwich in foil. "That's not old. Anyway, change the subject." I nod towards Alysha as she skips into the kitchen.

"How old are you Mummy?" She holds her cup towards me. "Can I have more juice?"

"What's the magic word?" Mark takes the cup from her.

"Pleeese!"

"You know how old I am," I laugh. "Not nearly as old as Daddy."

"Will I still be five when I'm a flower girl?"

"No, you'll be six."

"Aww, that's ages away." She puts her cup next to the sink.

"It'll be here before we know it." I wish it could be. "Anyway, go and clean your teeth."

"I'll have a word with DCI Ingham," Mark continues as Alysha leaves the kitchen. "See if he might be willing to pass the case to me. Or let me take more of it on. Especially with what he's going through in his own life right now."

"Is there anything similar about the womens' appearances?" I make a mental note to do some research myself. "They've all drowned late at night too. Surely that should be a red flag?"

"Maybe. And as I say, I'll try and get more involved. That's if DCI Ingham will let me. It's his baby."

"That's a strange way to describe it." I swipe a slice of toast from his plate and laugh when he lightly taps the back of my hand. "A case investigating deaths of local women. A baby! Anyway, keep me posted."

"Handy for you, isn't it?" Mark ruffles my hair as he passes me. "Being married to a sergeant. You hear it first."

"*Nearly* married. And no, I don't hear it first. You're far too cagey." I feel a flash of guilt, recalling how close I've been once or twice to looking at his pocketbook. But I do get a sense he's not telling me everything he knows.

I call into the press association office to see if there's any new assignments for me. There isn't, thankfully, as I'm already over committed.

It's all trivial stuff that I've got on right now; an alleged infight between the directors at the local football club, a B-list celebrity break-up and a local sporting name returning to the area for her wedding. I'm always on the prowl for something meatier. Something that will get my name out there.

Within the next year or two, I want to be writing for the nationals. My surname's going to change when I get married, so if

I start getting known as a journalist before then, I'll have to start all over again. Perhaps I should change my name on reports prior to the wedding, but that somehow feels like tempting fate.

I ask my supervisor, Lindy, about the river situation. I wouldn't mind getting in on the coverage. It's all happening on our doorstep, and with what happened last year, it's bound to get picked up by the nationals.

"We only know what's been put out in the media so far," she says, without even looking at me. She's so busy and preoccupied. And always doing four different jobs at once. Right now she's talking to me, listening in to one of the copy takers, drafting an email and reading a news article. "Keep your ear to the ground though, Lauren. You're better connected than any of my other reporters." She gives me a knowing look and I know she means Mark.

He's uber professional though. I'm not sure he'll tell me anything off the record. Especially since he's only recently been promoted. I think he'd tell me more if I wasn't a journalist. I've given up trying to browbeat information from him, but I'll admit to eavesdropping occasionally when he's on the phone. We're both career driven and sometimes we just have to let the *I want to know - I can't tell you* conversation play out. Luckily, we have never let this dynamic cause any resentment within our relationship. It's how we met. Through work. When we were both on work's nights out.

The copy takers are all bashing away on their desktops as I walk back through the call centre towards the exit. It must be exciting doing their jobs, not knowing what news story might come in next. Some copy takers are rubbish, though. I get tired of having to spell words or explain terminology which they should already know.

Sometimes it's easier to type the articles myself, unless I'm out and about, and it's a piece that needs running the next morning. But I love the work I do and never tire of seeing my name beside an article in the newspaper. Particularly if it's in one of the nationals. That's happened a few times.

I leave my car at the office, deciding to take the route along the river for some fresh air. It's only a short distance to the town centre that way. There's a cosy coffee shop which I like to work in. They've got to know me in there and don't mind me hogging a table as long as I periodically buy a coffee. I'm useless at working from home. I get distracted too easily and end up cleaning the house or drinking coffee with neighbours. When it's me and my laptop in a café, I've no choice other than to get words on the page or do some research.

I tug my hat over my ears as I approach the spot where the latest woman must have fallen in. The temperature has dropped hugely. A row of flowers has been laid and police tape has sealed off a section of the footpath. About two hundred yards further on I see the pub she was drinking in before she fell to her death - The Yorkshire Arms. She was only thirty-two, the same age as me. I pause at the cordon to look at the flowers. They've been rained on overnight, and the ink has run on some of the message cards, but they're still legible.

My beautiful friend Becky. I will miss you forever. Martha. xxxxx
Rebecca. Sister. Daughter. Friend. Gone too soon. xxx
Sorry. X This one puzzles me. What for?
From all your friends on Ward 34. We are gutted. Xxx

"You're Mark's wife, aren't you?" A voice cuts into my thoughts. I look up to see Chris, a constable new to the area. I met him recently at someone's leaving party. It must be his job to guard the cordon.

"Not quite." I look up. "We get married next summer."

"I'll await my invitation them." He laughs.

I rise from the spot where I've been crouched. "Erm, we're going to the Maldives to do it."

"I was only joking. I don't know Mark all that well, anyway."

"Is he around?" I look at the bridge in the distance where a couple of police cars are parked up.

"He was earlier," he replies. "I'm not sure where he's gone."

"Are they still saying the latest woman just *fell in*?" I look at the river with autumn sunshine dancing on its surface, disguising the menace that lies beneath it. It's so calm here, almost inviting. A place to walk, hand in hand, or to sit beside with a flask of coffee, or perhaps to do a bit of writing when the weather is warmer. It's not a place to die. Yet this town centre stretch of river has snatched so many lives.

"We're still making enquiries. There are slip marks where the cordon is - it's apparently steep there. I wouldn't fancy anyones' chances of being able to clamber back out, especially in the winter." Chris follows my gaze to the river. "Other than that, I don't know much. I'd be the last to find out. I've just been told to stand here." He sounds almost resentful.

I think of Mark when he was a constable, and myself when I used to take copy. *We've all got to start somewhere.* I stop myself from these thoughts.

"At least it's finally stopped raining; it seems to have rained all weekend. In fact it looks like it's turning into a nice day." *Yes Lauren. When you don't know how to reply, talk about the weather.* "I'd best be off anyway." I smile at him before setting off on the remainder of my walk to the café.

Chapter Five

Veronica

Tricia broke her conversation off with her friend, Hazel. "How are you doing, Mum?" She'd possibly noticed that Veronica had been quiet for a while. Veronica felt guilty at the concern in her daughter's face. The last thing she wanted was to put a dampener on their night out.

"It feels odd being out, to be honest. A few of these have helped though." Veronica raised her glass in Tricia's and Hazel's direction. "Thanks for inviting me girls."

"This is the first time we've been out in years. Without..." Tricia's voice trailed off.

"Dad." Veronica finished Tricia's sentence. "It's OK, we can talk of him. I promise I won't go to pieces. I've done enough of that to last a lifetime."

"I know. I'm sorry. It's just – we're all having a nice evening and I don't want you to get upset Mum."

"Getting upset is part of things Trish. I don't try to stop that. Let it all out is what I say."

As the couple on the next table looked at them, Veronica thought she should probably keep her voice down a bit. Especially coming out with comments like *let it all out.*

Hazel laughed as she stood. "I'm with you on that – let it all out! It's my round anyway."

"I don't think I could make it to the bar." Veronica also laughed. "I couldn't walk in a straight line. You're a bad influence, you two."

"You needed an evening out Mum. You look lovely too." Tricia touched the waves she had made with her curling wand in Veronica's dark, grey-flecked hair, though the heavy rain between the taxi and the pub had flattened them somewhat. "Dad wouldn't want you moping at home all the time."

"I know. But we should have eaten before starting on this gin. If we don't go soon, I'm worried I'll get past it."

"I'll check the Indian Restaurant has got a table in an hour. They're open until about one in the morning." Tricia plucked her phone from her bag.

Veronica tried to feel sober by turning her attention to the bustling bar. It was the first time she had been out for the evening since Shaun had died ten months before. Part of her had gone with him, but there was no denying it was good to get out. After all, she was only fifty-two, not eighty-two. She didn't ever want to meet anyone else. Shaun had been the love of her life. He lived on in Tricia though – she was the image of him.

"Stop staring at me Mum."

"You're so like your dad, you know."

"So you keep saying. Snap out of it. Enjoy yourself."

"I can't. I miss him."

Hazel returned with three more gin and tonics. The drink had always made Veronica cry, and tonight was no exception. A big fat tear managed to plop into the glass Hazel had put in front of her.

"Oh Mum." Tricia's chair scraped on the wooden floor as she moved herself closer to Veronica.

"I'm sorry. We've been having such a lovely time. It's just the gin. They don't call it mother's ruin for nothing." She shrugged off her daughter's attempts to put an arm around her. "I'm nipping to the loo. I'll give my face a wash, then I'll be fine."

Veronica sat on the loo for a few minutes, trying to clear her head. Fancy crying in the middle of a pub. It was no good. There was no way her head would be clearing until she'd had some food and a good night's sleep. She was too old for this going out malarkey. She blew her nose, then flushed the loo.

Putting some make-up on and having Tricia do her hair had made her miss Shaun even more than usual. Normally he'd have either been out with her, or waiting at home for her return. He'd always say, *you look lovely honey – I'm a lucky man,* or words to that effect. Veronica couldn't believe he'd been snatched from her.

She'd pulled herself together a bit, whilst sat on the loo, but fresh tears were stabbing at her eyes as she stepped towards the sink area. The giggling girls didn't react to her – she might as well have been invisible. She tried to reapply eyeliner to her bloodshot eyes, then wondered why she was bothering. Nothing was worth bothering with anymore. Not since Shaun had died. Tricia had said a night out would make her feel better. But it hadn't. She should never have agreed to it. Veronica felt ten times worse.

She needed some air. That would sort her out. Just five minutes or so. Then she would go back inside and insist to Tricia and Hazel that they get some food.

Tricia and Hazel were deep in conversation as Veronica emerged from the toilets. They didn't seem to notice as she slipped around the edges of the room towards the exit. If Tricia had noticed, Veronica was sure she'd have wanted to come out with her and really, she just needed a few more minutes on her own.

Chapter Six

Lauren

I feel scruffy beside our immaculate wedding coordinator.

"So how many guests are we catering for?" She flicks her hair behind one shoulder. She's easily ten years younger than me and wears a smart tailored suit and perfect make-up.

My face is bare, and my hair is loosely fastened up on top of my head. Mark says he prefers my natural look though. He's always liked my green eyes and says he can't see their colour when the powder is piled on. Anyway, I had enough trouble getting Alysha ready this morning, so the idea of finding a minute to concentrate on my own appearance is laughable.

"We can accommodate a maximum of one hundred and fifty," she says.

"Let's go for that then," Mark replies. "We've both got good-sized extended families, all disgruntled that they can't come to the Maldives with us."

"Then there's all our work colleagues, Mark's in the police so has a few, and not forgetting all our friends." I look around the function room. "I think it's a great idea, having another party when we get back. I'll be able to wear my dress again."

"Perfect." The woman watches Alysha, who is bounding around all four corners of the room. I see disapproval in her eyes. There's not much damage Alysha can do in this large, empty room though.

"Excuse me. I must take this. It's work." Mark sweeps his phone up from the table and walks to the edge of the room. I strain to listen to what he's saying as the wedding woman continues to fill out a form, firing questions at me about the DJ, the food and about timings.

I'm more interested in Mark's conversation. From his tone, it sounds as though something's happened, but with the wedding co-ordinator still talking away, I'm struggling to focus on both things at once.

"I'll be there soon." He walks back towards our table. "I'll have to drop Lauren and Alysha at home first, then I'll be with you."

Irritation coils itself around me. We're at our wedding meeting and he's supposed to be having the weekend off. What could be so important?

"I'm sorry. I've got to go into work. It's urgent." He rests his hand on my shoulder. "Can we wrap this up another time?"

"There's just the small matter of the deposit." The wedding woman slides a sheet of paper towards me.

"I'll sort it." I stand up quickly, grabbing my coat from the back of the chair. "I'm really sorry about this. I'll transfer the deposit and email you to sort another meeting." I fold the piece of paper into my pocket. "It must be important for him to have to go like this. He's got a lot on at work. Alysha, come on please."

Mark is back on his phone as we walk from the function room along the thick carpet to the hotel entrance. He's striding ahead of me so quickly that Alysha and I are almost at a run to keep up. I get a warm blast as we pass the open fire in reception.

The remainder of the day looms before me. I was looking forward to spending it as a family, and I'm not sure what I'll do now. I could do some work but that will be impossible with Alysha around.

"Another woman?" He says in a loud voice, glancing back at me. "How old? What time did they find her? Was she already dead?" It's not exactly a cheery conversation. I hope no one is listening. Guests are arriving for a wedding that must be taking place this afternoon. I'm straining to hear what he's saying, so chances are, no one else will be able to make it out either.

Being that I only catch one side of his conversation, I'm not privy to the answers he gets. But I ask him anyway as we make the short drive back to the house.

"I don't know much yet Lauren. I'll find out when I get to the station. I'm sorry that I'm having to leave you and Alysha. Especially when we'd planned to do something."

"I guess the lifebuoys and fencing didn't help?" I realise how crass that sounds, the moment as I've said it.

"I don't think anything's moved there. It hasn't been sorted yet." Mark glances in the mirror at Alysha. "I'm sorry I've got to go to work sweetie pie. I'll get home before you go to bed."

"Great." I slump in my seat. "You're going to be that long?"

"Lauren. I thought you understood. When I've got to go, I've got to go."

"How can I understand? You won't tell me what's going on."

I let myself into the house and listen as the car engine dies away. "Right, what shall we do then?" Alysha slides her feet into her pink slippers. She's a very pink girl. Everything is glitter and princesses. I love that about her. I always wanted a daughter - someone I could be as close to as I am to my mum.

At least Alysha has got one grandparent who's happy to see us all. We're lucky to have my mum. I'll ring her later. I've not spoken to her for nearly a week. But first I need to ring the press office.

"Can I watch TV Mummy?"

"Just for a while. I've got some things to do and then we'll go to the park."

"Yay!" She skips into the lounge.

I walk to the kitchen, flick the switch on the kettle and press Lindy on my phone. She answers quickly, as always. "Lauren. What can I do for you?"

"Have you heard? Another woman has gone in. Into the river, I mean." I spoon coffee into the cafetière as I speak. "Last night."

"You're kidding. No, nothing's come through yet."

"I was just with Mark as he took a phone call. He's gone straight into work to help deal with it." The kettle clicks off and I fill the cafetière, only half full with the hot water, resentment prickling me that Mark isn't here.

"Another woman, you say?"

"Yep." Despite myself, I suddenly feel excited. I might get the chance to break this story.

As if reading my mind, Lindy says. "I'd like you to ring through to the copy department Lauren. Make a few notes first on exactly what you know - tell them what you can. Obviously with a little embellishment. And bring in what you know about the individual women. As quick as you can please."

There's no point me telling her that I've got Alysha to take care of so *as quick as you can,* might not be as instantaneous as she'd like it to be.

"When exactly did it happen?"

"From what I can gather from only hearing one side of Mark's conversation, it was in the early hours again."

"Well, keep your ear to the ground, won't you? We want to be providing the lowdown on this story since it's on our patch. We certainly don't want some jumped up national journalist getting their hands on it."

"I will. I really think there's more to this than women just falling in."

"Me too," Lindy says. "I think that's the reporting slant you need to take. There's been no mention of this being suspicious from the police so far though."

"I know. But I've a strong feeling about it. Someone is behind those women's deaths. And I'm going to be the one to get to the truth."

"Good. Well, you have my full support. If you need to pass any of your current assignments back to focus on this, do so. Anyway, I'll let you get on with your piece."

"I'll speak to you later."

I've only just put my mobile down when the landline rings.

"Is Mark there?"

"He's working."

"Thought he was off today. I'll ring his mobile."

Then he's gone. Will, my least favourite person. He's even more abrupt these days. No. Rude is a better word.

Alysha barely looks up from the TV as I plonk a cup of juice and a biscuit in front of her. "I've just got to sit at the kitchen table for an hour. I've some work to do and then we'll go out."

"OK Mummy." Luckily, she's an easy going girl and doesn't tantrum at a delayed promise. She's so engrossed in the TV that she's possibly forgotten all about the park, anyway.

I grab a pad and pen from the sideboard drawer, pour my coffee, and settle at the kitchen table. I fire my laptop up in case I need to look up any details. Though I've taken such an interest in the river deaths that lots of the information has etched itself into my mind. I make a few notes on what I know already, referring to news reports.

Woman One. Joanna Mason. Age forty-nine. Out on her hen night. Getting married to someone called Robin. Second time marriage.

Woman Two. Rebecca (Becky) Thorpe. Age thirty-two. Had an argument with her boyfriend and appeared to have been hitting the wine. Maybe I'm using a bit of journalistic licence here.

Woman Three. What do I know? She went into the river last night. Hang on. I check the dates. They've all been Saturdays. The early hours of Sunday morning, to be precise. Drink seems to have been involved with all of them. Each of the women seems to have been alone. I don't know the age of the woman from last night, but I've got enough facts and with a bit of speculation, enough to put a report together.

I ring through to the press office to dictate it and then add more on:

All the deaths have occurred in the early hours of a Sunday morning, and the bodies have been found along the same quarter of a mile stretch of river. Each victim has been alone at the end of a night out.

Perhaps it is not coincidence that unites these tragedies. This avenue of inquiry has not yet been pursued by the police.

After this latest fatality, pressure must be mounting on them to step up patrols on a Saturday night and to install more CCTV, like they have promised. Meanwhile, women need to be looking out for one another. This should result in whoever is responsible for their deaths being caught.

"Blimey, you're right," says the copy taker. "It's happened three times now, hasn't it? Not to mention all the other drownings there *last* winter." Copy takers don't normally comment on the content of copy, but this article has seemingly hit a nerve. "We're all women in our thirties in this office," she continues. "The drownings are happening too close to home for our liking."

"That's what I'm thinking." I chew the end of my pen. "There's no way those women are just falling in, drunk. There has to be more to it."

CHAPTER SEVEN

Lauren

It's a relief to hear the squeak of the front door and to see Mark appear in the kitchen doorway. "I'm sorry I had to rush off this morning love."

I look up from stacking the dishwasher, towards the clock. It's after nine o'clock. "OK." I try to keep the wobble out of my voice, but I *feel* wobbly. Especially with all the thinking and the research I've done today around the women, from this year and last year, who were ordinary women, just like me, going about their lives, but who've drowned in the river Alder. Mark's holding something behind his back. Suspicious as ever, I try to peer round him to see what he's hiding.

"Alysha's asleep now. She's been asking for you all day."

"I'll make it up to her. Promise. And to you. I'd been looking forward to spending the day with the two of you. Here, I got you these to say sorry." He produces a bunch of roses and a bottle of wine.

I take them from him, place them on the kitchen counter behind me and step towards him. "You don't need to be sorry. I totally understand. I just miss you sometimes."

"I know." He pulls me towards him. "One day we'll both be earning so much that we'll be able to reduce our hours. Or take early retirement."

"Will rang earlier."

"I know. He got me on my mobile."

"He was his usual self."

"You know what he's like!"

"Yeah, rude, obnoxious and arrogant. Sorry," I notice Mark's expression. "I know he's your brother, but it's true." I take two glasses from the cupboard.

"I'm just thankful I've got Claire as a sister. She makes up for him. He's not as bad as he used to be though. He's definitely mellowed since they had Heidi."

"That's about all he's got going for him. Being a reasonable dad. Just not potential brother-in-law. I'd rather keep away from him to be honest. What did he want, anyway?"

"Nothing much. Just police stuff. Anyway, get that wine cracked open. I need a glass after the day I've had."

"So what's the latest?" I pass Mark the bottle and the corkscrew.

"Another death – well you knew that anyway. Poor woman. She was pulled from the water at first light after being reported missing just after midnight."

"At first light? Why didn't they send someone straightaway?"

"They don't send the frogmen in, not in the dark, unless they're saving someone." He uncorks the wine and passes it back to me.

"God. How awful. If I were to choose how I had to die, it wouldn't be by drowning. Especially in that dirty, freezing river." I fill the glasses and pass one to Mark. "Where was she pulled from? Please don't tell me it's the same spot."

"A little further downriver." He takes a gulp from his glass. "She could have drifted though, or been dragged along by the undercurrent, as she was in the water several hours. We don't know exactly where she went in."

"Have you looked at the CCTV?"

"Of course. It's not great though. It doesn't reach far enough. I spent a couple of hours looking at it. She'd gone outside for some air. Her daughter said she was feeling the worse for wear after mixing her drinks. I've got her coming out of the Yorkshire Arms just after midnight, but then she walked out of range of the cameras."

"Her daughter? How old was the woman?" I feel like grabbing my notebook, but I'll have to just remember what he's saying to me. He'd go mad if I started writing things down.

"Fifty-two. She'd been persuaded to go out. Said it would do her good. She'd recently been widowed."

"Who the victim, or the daughter?"

Mark laughs. "Forever the journalist, aren't you? The woman. We're not really using the word victim to describe her."

I sip my wine and shudder. It's vinegary. "Well, if she's not a victim, what is she?"

"Victim suggests the involvement of a perpetrator."

"You've changed your tune. I thought you were keeping an open mind."

"According to DCI Ingham, there's nothing to suggest, at this stage anyway, that these deaths are anything other than alcohol-fuelled accidents. Have you seen how steep and slippery the bank is down there? Especially at this time of year. On all three of the nights this year, it's been chucking it down too."

"Well, it's about time you were stepping things up, if you ask me – why hasn't any fencing been put up there yet? You also said you were going to try to get hold of the case yourself."

"I have. DCI Ingham seems happy keeping hold of it, though. To be honest, I think a big case is keeping his mind off his marital woes, and yes, he's on with the fencing, don't worry. Let's change the subject shall we?" Mark steps towards me. "I could do with some down time to be honest. Let's talk about the wedding. Let's talk about baby number two." Putting his arms around my waist, his eyes light up and grinning, he adds. "Let's make baby number two."

"Easy tiger!" I laugh, "I don't mind plenty of practice making baby number two, but I've got a wedding dress to fit into next year."

We soon slip back into being who we're supposed to be, Mark and Lauren, engaged and in love, rather than Mark and Lauren, police sergeant and journalist. Those victims though, and I will call them victims, are never far from my thoughts at the moment.

I have an hour longer in bed the next morning. Half a bottle of wine has left me with a fuzzy head. Mark brings me a cup of tea and kisses me on the cheek.

"I'll take Alysha to school on my way to the station," he says. "I've done her reading book with her and she's had breakfast."

"You're a good un." I smile at him. "Don't be late home tonight if you can help it."

"I'll try not to be." He smiles. "Especially if I'm in for a repeat of last night. He winks at me, before striding towards the bedroom door, still fastening his tie as he leaves the room.

"Well done on your piece, Lauren." Lindy looks up from her computer as I walk into the Press Association office an hour later. "It's made the front page of the locals and page four and five in several of the nationals."

"Thanks," I say. "I'll take a look."

As I sit in reception, flicking through the newspapers, my mobile rings. It's Mark.

"I've been absolutely bollocked from my DCI because of your article," he states, without even saying hello first. He sounds seriously pissed off with me. It's a sharp contrast to our earlier parting.

"Why? It didn't say anything untoward. It's only facts. I'm looking at it now, in the local. I don't see why you've been bollocked."

"Lauren. It's not facts. It's opinion. It suggests that the police are inept. And with both me and my brother working for the force, it doesn't look good that we've got a family member reporting against us. Will's just rung too – he's not impressed either."

"I don't give a toss about what Will thinks. He might be *your* brother but he's nothing to me. And I'm not even your family yet, anyway," I say, huffily. "Besides, Will is in traffic, he's nothing to do with the case, is he?"

"We're used to the press badmouthing us Lauren, but believe it or not, we actually do know what we're doing with this one. You know I can't tell you everything. I'm not allowed to, even if you weren't a journalist – I signed a confidentiality contract when I started training."

"It's a free country. I can report on whatever…"

"Lauren. What I'm trying to say is that we're being criticised in black and white by someone, you. You're marrying a sergeant, me, who's involved in the case." His voice rises. "DCI Ingham has threatened to keep me completely away from anything to do with it. I've got some serious grovelling to do, especially with the mood he's been in lately. It will damage my reputation if my line manager starts taking me off cases. And it may affect Will, too. So rein it in, will you?"

Like I really care about affecting bloody Will. These days he looks at me as though I am something he has stepped in. Narcissist. I blink away memories of his and Eva's wedding night as they flood my brain. I was really drunk and told him exactly what I thought of him - it was a night where things got so out of control I can't bear to think about it.

I get on with Eva and try to keep an eye on her. She insists that there is a nice side to him and that he apparently dotes on his daughter. Alysha speaks very highly of him too not that I like her spending time around him. Wherever this nice side is, I've never seen it. But I've certainly seen the other side.

"I'm not going to stop digging around Mark. So don't ask me to. You knew what I did for a living when we met. I'm convinced these women are being purposefully drowned by someone. And I've got a professional responsibility to report the facts, and if need be help get justice for them."

"Just leave it to us love." He sighs and sounds like his anger is easing. "Like I said, I'll tell you things as soon as they become official. But I need to be able to trust you with things I tell you. Most blokes can go home and offload about work to their partners without it ending up in the local rag the next day."

"Trust me!" I slam the newspaper I'm holding onto the table in front of me. He's being patronising now. A couple of the copy takers look over at me. "I don't think trust comes into this, do you? Innocent women are dying. I'll stake the area out myself on a Saturday night if I have to. If you lot can't do your bloody jobs properly. And for your information – we're not a local rag!"

There's fury in his voice again as he replies. "Like I said, Lauren, there's a lot going on behind the scenes that you don't know about. And we don't need you going around, raising fear in people where it's not necessary."

"But it is necessary. You even told *me* to be careful!"

"That was because of your hype, Lauren. Seeing the absolute worst in things rather than at face value."

"God. I thought it was your job to investigate things."

We remain in silence for a few seconds, then he says in a gentler tone, "Look, let's not allow this to get between us. I just need you to run things you write by me before you publish them in future."

Anger is bubbling in the pit of my stomach now. "You do your job Mark and let me do mine." I hang up without saying bye to him, then make myself a coffee. I find a corner of the office to quietly fume in. I meant what I said to him. I'll investigate this myself if I have to. I begin with Facebook.

Because I like to work methodically, I start with the first death. With or without a perpetrator, they've all fallen victim to the monster that is the River Alder. It's taken so many lives over the years, especially where it runs through one of the local beauty spots.

It was only last summer when a nine-year-old boy had to be fished out. He'd been taken for a picnic and got out of his depth in a part known for its unpredictable ledges and sudden depths, creating deadly underwater currents. I'll never forget the sight of his mother, all on her own, crouched on the riverbank, waiting for the divers to find him. She must have known they weren't going to find him alive. I wanted to go and comfort her, but of course, they weren't letting anyone through the cordon. My heart broke for her. No mother should have to go through that, especially alone.

I look at the posts Joanne Mason, the first victim, wrote prior to her death. She seemed obsessed with her wedding plans, apparently looking forward to her fairytale, as she called it, after a first-time wedding on a shoestring. She's shared ideas of flowers, cars and even table settings on her Facebook page. I couldn't be bothered with all that. I tend to know what I want, find it, and whack a deposit on it.

There's many a happy photo with Robin who is, or was, her fiancé. Joanne looked well for her age, certainly not nearly fifty. There isn't a trace of grey in her long, dark hair and her eyes are a piercing shade of green. I wonder if she's used a filter on her photograph to make them look so green?

There are several posts in the hours leading up to her death. Photos shared of an increasingly drunken-looking hen party. How could her friends have let her wander away from them? I would hope mine will look after me when I'm out on my hen do. Especially if I have one too many.

There's a tremendous outpouring of messages after her death. Firstly, there's an announcement from her fiancé, Robin. If it hadn't been for the subsequent drownings, and it was only Joanne who had died, I would have him down as a suspect. I shouldn't be so judgemental, but I'm usually right to trust my gut. He does look shifty. He has thanked all the people who have posted individually.

Two weeks later, her funeral has taken place. There's another post from him. *Today I laid my gorgeous fiancé, Jo to rest. How am I ever going to live without her? xx*

The post is littered with the usual condolences, then there's been nothing written on her page since. It's always the same. Once the funeral is over, everyone gets back to normal, as though nothing ever happened.

I'm going to find out what really connects these women and what has really happened. The police might be able to protect their resources and so-called reputation by saying it's down to drunkenness, bad weather and it being a notorious stretch of river, but for me, and for the friends and family of these women, that's not good enough.

Lindy might think I get explicit information, directly from Mark, but she really couldn't be further from the truth. However, he did tell me that he'd taken a statement from the boyfriend of the next woman, Becky Thorpe. They'd apparently had a huge row, overheard by fellow diners, before Becky went to the Yorkshire Arms on her own. She'd just stormed off, and her boyfriend hadn't gone after her. Mark wouldn't or couldn't tell me what they'd been rowing about. He won't tell me anything unless it's been officially released. Luckily, I can be good at reading between the lines and listening in to his phone calls. I don't feel guilty for that, after all, I can't help what I overhear.

I recall the bouquet the boyfriend left at the scene where he had said *Sorry.* I had been struck by that because it was the only word on the card. It had been hooked onto a beautiful bunch of roses.

On Facebook, he has posted photographs of himself with Becky, as well as a quote saying, *Always tell someone how much you love them. You never know when it might be your last chance to let them know.*

I'm slightly consoled by the fact that the women were drunk. To some degree, it may have anesthetised the awful deaths they will have suffered. I can't imagine anything worse than drowning. They must have been petrified. Hopefully the freezing water stopped their hearts before they were overcome with terror and the suffocation.

I click onto Google to see if any information has emerged about the latest victim yet. It has.

Police have revealed the identity of the latest women to fall victim to the stretch of the River Alder where it runs through the city centre. Veronica Hill, aged 52, of Oswaldkirk, entered the water between 12:30 am and 1:00 am in the early hours of Sunday 15th December.

Veronica was out for the evening with her daughter and a friend. The alarm was raised by them when she hadn't been seen for some time. Her body was sadly recovered from the water at first light this morning. She is thought to have consumed a substantial amount of alcohol prior to entering the water, therefore no other enquiries are being made in connection with her death.

I click through to Facebook and type in *Veronica Hill*. It appears that her husband died recently too. There's smiling photographs of them from last year. Veronica looks like a different person in photographs which have been posted after his death. It's as though a light has gone out. From carefree and sunny last year, her face has become marked with pain and loss. News of her death must be starting to filter through. There are already three comments:

I can't believe it. Veronica, please get in touch and tell me it's not true. We were only together the other day.

Veronica, I knew you were struggling, but you could have come to me anytime.

A lovely lady now reunited with her husband. Rest in peace. x

I flick back to the news article. *No other enquiries are being made in connection to her death.*

What a cop out. How easy it is to blame alcohol. The police might even read the 'struggling' comment and try to blame suicide. Anything to deflect attention from themselves for not taking enough action.

CHAPTER Eight

Jennifer

J ennifer looked from her sister to her cousin who had been trying to talk her into staying out later. "I shouldn't even be here, you know, I should be saving for Christmas. Eight and ten year olds don't come cheap. Especially for us single mums."

"I'll get the next one," Natalie offered. "You should have said if you were short."

"Thanks sis. It's just that I've got the babysitter to pay as well." Jennifer checked her watch. "I think I'd better make this my last one. It's after midnight already. So I'll have to get the sitter a taxi home too."

Jennifer's nights out had been few and far between since Alan had left them. He'd now got himself a new girlfriend, so was looking after the kids less frequently as the weeks passed. She had almost laughed when she had first met the woman he'd left her for. Janey was like a younger version of Jennifer. Dark, shoulder length hair, and appeared to have the same style of dressing. But what Janey didn't have was the extra weight two children had inflicted on her, along with the eye wrinkles. Although, she didn't seem to have much in the way of brains. Just a high pitched voice and extra-large boobs. Jennifer hated her with a vengeance.

She missed having another adult around but didn't mind having sole charge of the children. However, just once a month, the chance to get dressed up and go out made all the difference. To be able to relax and feel young again, without having to think about fish fingers, homework or playing referee. Thankfully, they seemed reasonably unscathed by their father's departure, but then, he had pretty much left their day-to-day care to Jennifer, anyway.

"You OK?" Natalie asked, pushing a glass of wine and a packet of crisps towards Jennifer. "You've gone all quiet. I worry when you go quiet."

"Just thinking how nice it is to get out." Jennifer looked around the pub and then back to her sister. "Thanks for inviting me. I know I've had a few but you are a fab sister you know. You've really looked after me through all this break up shite."

"What are sisters for?" Natalie replied, reaching across the table for her hand. "I still think he'll come crawling back anyway – once he's got bored of his airhead."

"We're not just sisters." Jennifer sipped her wine whilst deciding to dodge the *crawling back* comment. "If we hadn't been related," she said, "I reckon we would still have been friends."

"You soppy bugger." Natalie laughed. "You must have had a few to be complimenting me like that!"

Jennifer reached into her clutch bag for her ringing phone. "Oh no, it's the babysitter. Probably ringing to see where I am!" She pressed the loudspeaker button. "Hi Kelly, what's up?"

"I'm sorry to disturb your evening, Jen, but Harry has been sick. Millie isn't looking too clever either."

"Great," Jennifer replied, envisaging a night of two pukers instead of a good night's sleep after a gallon of wine. "I'll get a taxi back. I'll be as quick as I can."

"If you could," Kelly replied. "You know I don't do sick!"

Jennifer took a large swig of wine as she dialled the taxi company. By the time she got through, she'd nearly finished her glass. As luck would have it, they were doing a nearby drop off. She hugged her sister and said her goodbyes to the rest of the group.

"Do you need me to come with you?" Natalie asked as Jennifer slid her arms into her jacket. "It sounds like you're going to have your hands full with them two."

"No. I'm not expecting you to cut your evening short! It'll be your turn one day to cope with puking kids – you enjoy yourself whilst you can."

"I'm never having kids! Well, just text me when you're in the taxi safely."

"Gosh. I can't believe you're six years younger than me sometimes. Anyone would think it was the other way around."

"Promise!"

"Will do."

Jennifer's phone beeped. *Your taxi will be outside in two minutes.*

"I'm off to wait outside Nat. I don't want anyone else jumping in it. I need to get back home, sharpish."

"Don't forget to text me. And then again when you get home."

CHAPTER NINE

Lauren

For a moment I think of ignoring the *no number* call flashing on Mark's phone. But I soon think better of it. "Hang on a minute. I'll give him a shout. Mark. It's DI Jones on the phone."

Mark steps from the en suite, water pooling at his feet on the bedroom carpet.

He takes the phone from me and puts it on loudspeaker whilst he dries himself.

"Hi Mark. I'm sorry to bother you so early, but we've had another fatality. Same spot. The police divers are there now."

"Oh erm, hang on Sir." He looks at me. "Give me a minute, will you hon?"

I try not to get too huffy as I stride towards the door, feeling more than a little put out at being dismissed in this way. As I pull the door open, Mark tugs a work shirt from the wardrobe and I know I've got another Sunday on my own with Alysha.

"You're joking," he says as I close the door. Then he lowers his voice. "That's four in as many weeks. This is starting to look terrible."

Starting to, I want to shout from the landing but stop myself. Especially with his colleague on loudspeaker. Plus, I'm not supposed to be listening. I hover around the door, poised to make a run for it if need be.

"Are you OK to come in?" His colleague's voice echoes. "I know it's your day off, but we could do with all hands on deck. We've been asked to do a press conference. The interest in this is gathering pace."

"Who's leading it?"

"DCI Ingham's on his way in, but he's hoping you will support him. Seeing as you've had some involvement with these events."

"What time?"

"Ten am. At the Associated Press Office."

My ears prick up. This is my story. I need to be there. Shit. It's Sunday. What am I going to do with Alysha? Mark never has to worry about childcare arrangements, he just does as he pleases. It's always up to me to sort Alysha out. He keeps banging on about having another baby, but it's always going to be my career that takes a back seat, not his.

"I'll be there in half an hour," he says. "Then I can get up to speed before the conference."

I realise he's coming off the phone so dart into the bathroom.

"I'm sorry Lauren," he calls from the bedroom doorway. "I've got to go into work. I'll be as quick as I can."

"Are we still going out this evening?" I say as I return to the bedroom. It's the tenth anniversary of the day we met. I bet he's forgotten.

"Of course." He says. "I'll tell them at work that I've got to be away mid-afternoon. I think it's mainly the press conference that they want me in for."

"Press conference?" I try to make my voice nonchalant.

"Yes. It's at your place, actually. At ten."

I point my feet into my jeans then drop Lindy a text. *I've just heard about another river victim. And a press conference that's due to take place at 10:00. I'll be in shortly to cover it.*

"I'm coming too. I've just let Lindy know."

"Is that a good idea? What about Alysha? It's Sunday."

"What do you mean *is that a good idea?* A press conference on a case I've been covering is happening at my primary place of work, and you think I won't be there?"

"My point is what are you going to do with Alysha?"

"*What are you going to do with Alysha?* She's your daughter just as much as mine."

There's not been a peep from her bedroom yet. She rarely surfaces until around nine am at the weekend. I've never known a child need their sleep so much. In many ways, Alysha has been such an easy child that to have another who presented more of a challenge than her would be a huge shock to the system.

"Do you think Eva would look after her? She can play with Heidi for a couple of hours."

"Not a good idea to ask. Will was working last night."

"Are you sure? I'm certain Eva said they were going out last night."

"Well, I drove past him as I was leaving the station. He looked like he was on his way in. He's still taking all the overtime he can lay his hands on."

"For this trip to Disneyland Heidi keeps going on about?"

"Yeah, as far as I know. As long as they make our wedding too."

I would be gutted if Eva and Heidi didn't come but not Will. I don't say that to Mark though. "Mum's supposed to be coming over later to babysit. Whilst we go out this evening. I'll give her a ring and see if she'll come over this morning." I rake a brush through my hair, then plait it. Mark has always said he likes my hair in a plait down my back. "She's not seen Alysha since last month, so I'm sure she won't mind."

"Sounds like a plan." He smiles at me. "Alysha will be chuffed."

At least we can ask my mum, I refrain from saying. It is hard not to feel resentful. Mark's Mum just goes through the motions with both Alysha and Heidi. She sends cards and money at Christmas and birthdays, and we all meet up for the stilted family gatherings a couple of times a year. Normally Boxing Day and Easter. She loosens up a bit once she's had a drink or three, though. The same can't be said for Will. He doesn't touch a drop of alcohol. Mark says it's because of their brother, who was killed in his late teens by a drunk driver. Will was with him when it happened. Personally, I think he should be cracked apart with a good dose of counselling, although who knows what that would bring to the surface. Maybe once, there was someone decent lurking in there but not anymore.

An hour later, I'm on my way to the press office. Mum's arrived and taken over Alysha's clothes and breakfast choices, and let me borrow her car. She's going to take Alysha to the park. I'm so lucky to have my mum. Mark annoyed me when he wouldn't wait for me or leave me the car. I want to be at the office in plenty of time to be briefed about the latest river victim. And prepare some questions for DCI Ingham. Then I'll write the piece up straight away – make sure I am the first one there with it. And I don't give a toss what trouble I get into with Mark, or him with his superiors.

I drive across the bridge, which passes over part of the infamous stretch of river. There's a large police presence and news vans have arrived already. I pause long enough to notice that more flowers have been laid. This is horrendous. I'm going to give them what-for at the conference. Four deaths in one month is not a coincidence. And the way the police seem to be batting it back is not acceptable.

The press office is busy for a Sunday morning. Normally, activity on a Sunday only comprises of getting ready for the afternoon sporting events. Lindy is setting out chairs and tables with one of the sports journalists and the copy takers.

"Morning Lauren," she says. "Glad you could make it. Have you prepared some questions for the police?"

"They're all in here." I tap the side of my head. "Though I might sit and write them down, in case I go blank. Before I do that, is there anything I can do to help?"

"You could put the kettle on. Other than that, we're pretty much sorted. We just need to wait for everyone to get here." She stops and counts the seats. "We'll sit the police at the front table – make sure you sit directly in front of them Lauren."

"No problem. I can write the piece up straight afterwards too. My mum's looking after my daughter, so I've got plenty of time."

"Good stuff." She glances out of the window. "*Look North*'s here. I didn't realise it was going to be filmed as well."

"It's a growing story now." I follow her gaze to where two men are unloading equipment from a van. "For everyone other than the police, anyway. Four lives lost this year, five last year, and the police are doing bugger all." I look to the door where DCI Ingham, Mark and a stern-faced police woman walk in. "This is going to be fun." But I say this under my breath. Mark looks straight ahead. We might as well be two strangers, not a couple who are about to get married, with a home and a daughter. I try to catch his eye as he sits, but he's looking the other way. His colleagues don't acknowledge me either, even though they both know me from work functions that I've been to with Mark. It wouldn't kill them to say hello.

DCI Ingham clears his throat as he stands. He looks absolutely exhausted - divorce clearly does not agree with him. "I'm Detective Chief Inspector Jonathan Ingham from the North Yorkshire Police Division." Behind him is a flat screen which bears the North Yorkshire police crest, our Press Association logo, and the signage from Look North. There are a few other journalists here, mostly freelance like me, as far as I can tell. It'll be a race to break the biggest and best story first. This one will probably hit the front pages of the nationals now.

"I'm leading the investigation into four fatalities which have recently occurred in a half-mile stretch of the River Alder in Alderton city centre." He speaks confidently, evidently accustomed to this sort of thing. Mark looks slightly nervous beside him. He's barely looked at me since he took his place behind the table. He's probably trying to be professional. Either that or he's worried about what questions I'll ask as soon as I get the chance.

DCI Ingham reels off the dates, names and times of each of the river deaths, as he calls them. "There has been some speculation in the media," he continues, "that another, more sinister set of circumstances may exist behind the drownings. The public can be assured that we've investigated all lines of inquiry thoroughly. Extensive post-mortem examinations and toxicology tests have been performed in each death and as a police team, the only conclusion we can come to is that each death was contributed to by a substantial intake of alcohol, adverse weather conditions, and misadventure."

"So what are you going to do about it? Are you just going to allow people to keep falling in and dying?" I turn to the direction of the male voice behind me.

"We are working closely with Yorkshire Water, who are in the process of installing extra life buoys and fencing." DCI Ingham's voice is even and authoritative. "We are also liaising with

Yorkshire Council to install CCTV cameras, in order that the area can be more closely monitored. Presently, the area is not covered much beyond the Yorkshire Arms pub."

I jump up. "This is disgraceful. I heard about your so-called safety measures nearly a month ago. Why hasn't anything been done yet?" I don't even try to disguise the contempt in my voice. "How many more women are going to lose their lives before you put your money where your mouth is?"

DCI Ingham's tone seems to be loaded with equal contempt as he answers me, though I accept I just do not like him much so might be hearing something that's not there. "I'm sure you appreciate that these sorts of works with different agencies take a little time to organise. There's budget to consider and the ordering of necessary materials."

"Under the circumstances," another reporter says, "that's not good enough."

"I've been a little shocked myself with the delay," he now says, at least having the grace to look slightly apologetic. "Because of this, I'll be personally overseeing its implementation." He sweeps his gaze over the packed room. "You can all be completely assured that the work will be carried out this week. We're approaching the Christmas period with an increased likelihood of women enjoying nights out in the city centre. We do, of course, want to do everything possible to prevent any more families losing their loved ones." He sounds genuine enough, I suppose.

Lindy speaks next. "Are you not interested in the fact that the victims have all been women?"

"That's been noted, of course. But as a police division, we believe that is coincidental," DCI Ingham replies. "The temperature of the river in the daytime, at best, is four degrees centigrade and is much colder at night. The river is also well known for its powerful and unpredictable undercurrents."

"Even more reason to put a rocket up Yorkshire Water and the Council, surely?" Lindy says.

DCI Ingham continues. "All the women have been alive at the point of submersion, we know that because of the presence of water in their lungs, therefore we have had to conclude that the alcohol they've consumed, coupled with the extremely slippery and steep riverbank, has contributed to their deaths."

"And yet, you still haven't installed fencing," someone else says. "It's utter negligence if you ask me."

"If someone predatory is prowling that area, no amount of fencing is going to stop them," I add.

Mark narrows his eyes at me as DCI Ingham replies. I thought Mark was on my side. It's not so long ago he sounded as though he at least partly agreed with me.

"We've no reason to believe that anyone is prowling the area, as you put it, but we are obviously keeping that line of enquiry in mind. When each woman has been recovered from the water, there's been no evidence of physical injury. After this fourth death, however, as a precaution, we're going to be very much stepping up the police patrol presence there, particularly at weekends, over the festive period."

"And you think that's enough?" I almost snort. "Four women with lives, families and futures before them, have lost their lives in four weeks. I think it's disgusting that extra measures haven't been put in place already." I can feel Mark's glare, but I'm not bothered. "And I think it's equally disgusting that you're not prepared to countenance any third party involvement. You should step down DCI Ingham and let someone who actually cares take over this investigation."

Under normal circumstances, I would've expected DCI Ingham to be straight back at me with a response. But he appears to be searching for words. Mark was right - he's definitely not firing on all cylinders right now - he should absolutely let the reins of the investigation go.

There's an uncomfortable silence until Mark eventually gets to his feet. His face is pinched as he stands beside DCI Ingham. "You can all be reassured," he begins, "that the possibility of third party involvement has been investigated in each case and we'll continue to explore any lead that points us in that direction. However, we're confident that we're not dealing with some river stalker, but with a series of tragic accidents."

"Some river stalker!" Lindy says, with a hint of a snort. There are flashes going off all around the room. "I don't think that's an appropriate term for what's going on here."

The stern-faced policewoman stands next. "We'll implement the additional safety measures within forty-eight hours." She looks straight into the camera. "You have our word. DCI Ingham, an experienced and time-served Detective Chief Inspector," she gestures towards him, "is overseeing this. By next weekend, there'll be CCTV, fencing, patrols and extra lifebuoys. We are monitoring the situation closely."

I grab Mark on his way out. "Are we still going out tonight? I know you're mad at me, but this is work. We have to keep it separate from home life."

"I agree with you," he replies. "But slating my line manager wasn't helpful. I'm going to have to speak to him - assure him I'm not telling you anything. I won't be surprised if he puts me on desk duty."

"I just said what needed to be said." People are filing past us towards the exit.

"I'll see you at home. And of course we're still going out. Just be careful what you report from this."

"You policeman – me journalist." I smile. "Agree to disagree? I might have to pinch the *river stalker* term though. It's too good not to quote!"

Possible River Stalker

Since October, the lives of FOUR women have been snatched by a half mile stretch of river outside the Yorkshire Arms on Carlton Bridge. The body of the latest victim was pulled from the river Alder earlier today.

I put together a photo 'gallery' of the first three women with their names, ages and dates of death captioned beside their photographs. I don't know any details about the fourth woman yet. I guess her family need to be told first.

All four women found themselves alone on the banks of the river during their evenings out – it is worth noting each of the deaths occurred in the early hours of a Sunday morning.

A more awful death cannot be imagined; falling or being pushed into dark, freezing water; being prevented or unable to climb out and quickly becoming so weak and cold that submersion and death follow.

Whilst police have offered assurances to the public that fencing, lifebuoys, CCTV and patrols will be increased, they have said that women should be vigilant and remain in groups whilst out for the evening.

The possibility of someone pushing these women to their deaths should not be discounted and pressure is mounting on the police to back up their assurances of the extra measures with immediate effect. It is not enough to blame alcohol, adverse weather and slippery riverbanks.

As the investigation continues, police are asking that all local businesses in the vicinity of the Yorkshire Arms check their CCTV for early Sunday morning footage on the dates shown.

Anyone with information should contact the police on 111 quoting reference 1179 or Crimestoppers on 0345 1111.

CHAPTER TEN

Lauren

Mum smiles as I walk into the kitchen. "How did it go?" Alysha's sat at the table with Coca-Cola and chocolate pudding.

"Hmm, I can see you're having fun with Grandma." I laugh. "Rather you than me getting her to bed later, after all that sugar." I ruffle her hair. "It went OK, I guess. Apart from me having a dig at the Detective Chief Inspector who's Mark's line manager. I don't think Mark's terribly happy with me. Is he back yet?"

"Yes, he's upstairs getting changed."

"At least he's still going out with me tonight."

"I thought the two of you had a pact. Not to let work come between you."

"We don't, sorry we do. Have a pact, I mean. It'll be fine."

"I saw you on the TV Mummy. And Daddy too." Alysha jumps off her chair and flings her arms around me.

"Have you had a nice day with Grandma?" I say, crossing my arms over her shoulders. "Have you been a good girl?"

She nods and returns to her chair, and her pudding. "Grandma's going to read me lots of stories at bedtime. She's promised."

"So they've already shown the press conference on TV?" I turn to Mum. "What did you think?"

She twists away from the sink, which she's filling with water. "Yes, it was live. I agree with you to be honest. I think there's more to it than women falling in. There's been too many for them all to be accidents. And if they were just alcohol induced accidents, you'd think at least a couple of men would have fallen in too, with what some of them drink!" She wipes the sides down. She's wonderful, my mother. She's given up her day at the drop of a hat for me.

"I know, I've thought the same." I fill a glass with water. "I can't believe the police haven't done more. It's like it's easier to blame accidental death, even though that explanation doesn't stack up now."

"That spot has been the same for years Lauren. Even when I was young. Anyone can fall in the river, but if you end up in there, you've not a great deal of chance of climbing back out. It sounds like the police are taking more notice than they ever have though."

"Well, someone knows something. And I'm going to have to prove that."

"Just be careful love. Your name and face are linked to this story, especially after being on the news earlier. If there is a stalker behind it all, which I doubt, I don't want you going anywhere near there on your own until he's caught. I honestly think they'll just be accidents though."

"Don't worry Mum, I'm OK. And I'm glad my name and face are out there. It's what I'm aiming for. Hopefully the piece I wrote earlier will be in the nationals tomorrow. You know that's what I want."

"And what I want is my daughter safe and well; career isn't everything." Mum wipes her hands. "Right, go and start getting ready. I'll bring you a cup of tea up."

I kiss her on the cheek as I walk past her. "I don't know what I'd do without you Mum."

"Let's agree *not* to talk shop this evening," Mark says after the waiter has shown us to our table. "Let's talk about other stuff. The wedding. The house. Alysha." He winks at me. "Baby number two?"

It's our favourite restaurant. A French bistro where I always have a steak and a glass of red. We came here on our first date when I was so nervous, I could hardly eat anything. Mark had been worried at the time in case I had some kind of eating disorder.

"There'll be no baby number two until well after we're married." I laugh as Mark cups his hand over mine. "I'm looking forward to wearing my slinky wedding dress in the Maldives and drinking lots of champagne."

"Your mum's been an absolute star today," Mark says. "Alysha loves having her about. We must take Alysha to see my mum too. I know, deep down, she'd like to see more of her. She just doesn't do getting close to *anyone* easily. Not anymore."

"You'd think she'd value time spent with family *more* after going through something like that. I've often wondered, do you think she'd have been better if they'd actually caught the driver?"

"Who knows, probably. At least she'd have had some closure. According to Will, the driver had been arseholed. I've probably mentioned that before to you. Which is probably why they hadn't stuck around."

"I can't imagine what you must have all gone through." Mark hardly ever mentions what happened, so I stop there, giving him space in case he wants to say more. I can't believe this subject has come up when we're supposed to be having a nice, romantic meal for two. I guess that focusing on these river deaths forces other stuff to the surface as well.

"It's more Will who went through it. He was really close to Dean. And with him when it happened."

"Yeah. I know." It might go some way towards explaining why Will's the way he is, though I don't say this to Mark. "Your mum's getting more closed up though, Mark. If it wasn't for Christmas, Easter and Mother's Day, I wonder if she'd ever make an effort to see us." This is probably the longest conversation we've ever had about his brother's death.

"She's definitely got worse since Dad died. But it's not just us, Lauren. She's the same with Claire and Will, Eva and Heidi. In fact, she's probably worse towards Will. He once said to me that he felt like she blamed him for getting off with concussion." He goes quiet for a few moments, so I speak again.

"It's such a shame that Alysha never knew either of her grandads." I think of my own dad now. I'll never forget the moment that I had to lead the police through the hallway to break the news of his accident to my mum. It had been the winter of 2010 when the whole of the UK had been in the grip of an icy blast of weather for several weeks. Our golden retriever, Monty, had fallen through the ice of the lake at the park in the suburbs. Dad had tried to rescue him but had become trapped under the ice. Monty, however, had managed to get free and had survived.

I had nightmares for ages afterwards, thinking of my poor dad, trapped in freezing water, thumping fruitlessly against thick ice that he couldn't break. It's perhaps why I feel so strongly about drowning. Why I cannot allow another woman to die in that river. If those safety measures aren't implemented by the weekend, I'm going to take action. I miss Dad so much. Monty died two years ago – at least Dad has got him back now.

"Penny for em." Mark pushes the menu towards me. "What are you having to drink?"

"I was just thinking about my dad. And Monty." I smile as Mark reaches for my hand again. "Wine. Large. And I'm having a steak."

"That's my girl."

"Life's so fragile. We have to enjoy it whilst we have it."

"Come on now. I think we've got maudlin enough for one night. Let's try to enjoy ourselves."

"I couldn't cope if anything ever happened to you."

He laughs, his eyes crinkling in the corners like they always do. "Well, it will one day. But remember what we said. I'm going to be one hundred and four when I go, and you'll be one hundred and three."

"And you're going to die two hours after me, so I don't have to be heartbroken."

"It's a deal. At least I'll get two hours to have a cuppa in peace."

We laugh together and then go quiet for a few moments. I hope we *do* live that long together. "Did DCI Ingham have much to say after the press conference?" I ask, breaking the silence.

He frowns. "I thought we were leaving work alone this evening."

"Just answer that one question, then I promise I won't mention it again. We'll get on with enjoying ourselves."

"He was OK. He said he totally gets why the public are worried that someone might be behind the deaths."

"It didn't sound like that."

"Well he does. And that's why we're stepping everything up. And he's not blaming me for anything you said luckily. The panel knew I was marrying a reporter when they offered me the sergeant role. Did you get around to writing a piece after the conference?"

"Yes, but don't worry. I've gone easy on the police. I've just said it how it is. Anyway, I thought we weren't talking shop?"

"OK. Let's leave it alone now." He reaches for my hand again across the table and kisses it.

"We should do this more often," I chew on a piece of steak and take a big sip of the delicious red wine. "I love getting dressed up and having a night out together. Mum has texted and said she's going to stay over. She's cracked open the wine too. So we don't have to rush back."

"Our daughter has driven her to drink." Mark laughs again. "Well we shouldn't look a gift horse in the mouth. We might as well go on somewhere else after here. Make a night of it."

Despite Mark's protestations, we end up in the Yorkshire Arms. I want to get a feel for the place. I haven't been in for a long time. It wouldn't be a usual pub of choice for me – I prefer wine bars. But I want to be within the walls where the women spent their final hours. I feel a huge affinity with them and can't shake the feeling that they haven't just slipped into the river. I have such a strong hunch that they've been pushed or thrown to their deaths. I'm going to come back in daylight and have a closer look at the banking. Take some photos. I tell Mark.

"Oh God, are we back onto this? Don't you think we police have already done that? It's so muddy down there, it's been difficult to get much though."

"Haven't the women shown any evidence of trying to get back out. You know, mud under finger nails or anything?"

"I can't say Lauren, you know I can't."

"Won't say, you mean."

"Look, we're doing it again. Talking about bloody work. We're supposed to be spending time together." He goes quiet then takes my hand and strokes his thumb over the top of it. "Shame we're at work tomorrow, otherwise I could have booked us into a hotel." He winks again at me.

"Shame indeed."

Two drinks later, Mark's gone to the loo. I swing my bag onto my shoulder and clip-clop in my heels from the pub to the path outside. I'm not going to move an inch from the doorway, I just want to photograph the area in the dark. It will add something to the next story I submit.

I look along the river and shudder, thinking of the poor women that have been devoured by it. What must have been going through their minds as they battled to stay alive? Were they really on their own or was someone stood there, watching them, able to help but choosing not to, as they thrashed around in the freezing cold water? Someone responsible for them being in there? There's been no sign of pre-entry injury on any of the victims – that much has been divulged by the police. The only physical injuries they have sustained have been associated with the struggle of drowning.

According to Mark, it's this lack of injury showing signs of assault that has resulted in the police not putting as much emphasis on looking for third party involvement as they might have done. I can't and won't accept this though.

I take a photograph of the water on my phone, the slight glint of city lights in the distance floating on the surface. The area is desperate for some proper lighting to be installed, along with the cameras, fencing and life buoys. There's still no sign of any of this work having begun, despite the promises made at the earlier press conference. I know it's the council and water board, who can be slow on the uptake at the best of times, but this is urgent.

Nor is there any sign of police patrolling the area. It's not Saturday, the night when all the victims have drowned so far, but still, the pub is half full of Sunday evening drinkers – it's also a popular night to go out. If there's been no movement by close of play on Tuesday, I'll be writing a scathing piece about the police, council and water board, complete with photographs for publication on Wednesday. I'm going to tell Mark as much too. That way he might put a rocket up them first.

Pointing my phone along the riverbank, I take a few steps forward. Hopefully the phone's flash will illuminate the area a little. I don't want to use the torch facility, in case I draw attention to myself. In my peripheral vision, I see movement in the dark shadows of the empty building next door to the pub. I direct my phone to it and keep pressing to take photos. I lower my phone and look. It's too dark to *see* anything, I can more *feel* the presence there.

I'm shaking but take a few steps towards the movement I saw, whilst having second thoughts and deciding to activate the torch on my phone. I should really give Mark a shout. But I kind of want to do this single-handedly. He would drag me back inside and give me a right bollocking. If he's returned to the table, he'll just think I have gone to the loo, so I am alright for a minute or two. I've got my phone in my hand and my attack alarm in my pocket. I flash the light in front of me. If anyone comes at me, I just press a button and the most horrid high-pitch noise will make them run for it. I want a photo, a photo of the man the police should be looking for. I didn't mean to walk away from the doorway of the Yorkshire Arms. But I'm not drunk and I've got all my wits about me. Still, Mark will kill me for this. So would Mum if she knew.

My heart is in my mouth as hands grasp my shoulders from behind.

"What the hell do you think you're doing Lauren?" Mark swings me around to face him. "I can't believe you'd be so stupid. Do you want to be next to end up in there?" He points at the river.

"I saw someone." I gesture in the direction of the movement, my voice a ghost on the quiet riverbank. "Over there." I'm shivering with cold and fear.

"I'll get some units here." Mark pulls his phone from his pocket. "I'm not equipped with my personal safety gear to investigate on my own. Get back inside. Now."

"I'm not leaving you here either," I reply, only just processing what Mark has said. "You must believe me though, to be taking these precautions?"

"It's probably a trick of the light or something moving in the wind." Mark brings the phone to his ear. "But still, I've got to get it checked out. I'll wait in the pub's doorway until I've got some backup."

"There's no wind for anything to move in. Nor is there any light." I walk back into the pub, glad of the warm air against my cool cheeks. Those poor women couldn't experience that feeling. Out of the cold, back into the warmth. I sink back into the seat and sip at my third glass of wine. There was someone there. I scroll through the photos I've taken, but they're too dark to make anything out. Damn.

Chapter Eleven

Lauren

This morning I remember why I rarely drink wine on a school night. Especially red. I lie, listening to Mark, Alysha and Mum downstairs, knowing I need to get up. The sun is seeping around the edge of the bedroom blind, offering a promise of one of those sparkly winter days which we don't often see. Especially lately. This winter, it just seems to rain all the time. And today, all I want to do is burrow under the duvet and stay here.

I ended up having four large glasses last night. The last one was to steady my nerves after what had happened. I'm absolutely convinced I saw movement just yards away on the riverbank. I study my photographs again, trying to make them lighter.

I'm fuming though. If the bloody police had done as they promised, when they promised it, there would've been enough light for me to prove what I saw and sensed. There was, of course, no one there by the time Mark's backup arrived. But I'm even more certain now that somebody is responsible for the deaths. Just about everyone I've spoken to agrees with me to some extent.

"Knock, knock." Mum walks into the room without waiting for an answer. She's wearing my towelling robe, and her hair in two plaits. She always plaits her hair overnight as it gives it a curl the next day. We're often mistaken for sisters, me and Mum. I hope I've got her genes and age as wonderfully as she has. Apart from when Dad died; she looked haggard for a while then. It was no wonder really – she wasn't eating or sleeping or anything much. I'd go to pieces if anything ever happened to Mark. Mum places a cup of tea on the table beside me and perches at the end of my bed, like she used to do when I was a teenager.

"You're a star Mum. Thanks for yesterday as well. Did you and Alysha enjoy putting the Christmas tree up?" I feel a pang of guilt for not doing it myself with her. But the press conference and my anniversary evening with Mark had to come first.

"Yes. Anyway, I wanted a chat before I start getting ready." I shuffle over to make more room for her on the bed. "I need to make a move soon – I've got workmen starting on the bathroom today."

"Sounds ominous. Wanting a chat, I mean."

She laughs. "Not really. But I do want to give you a telling off for going outside that pub on your own last night. I can't believe you even wanted to go in there for a drink. Of all places Lauren."

"Was it Mark who told you about me going outside?"

"Yes. And I'm glad he did."

"I'm a journalist Mum, I wanted to get a feel for it all. I can put more into what I'm reporting then."

"Not if you're the next person to fall in. Especially in the middle of December."

"You know I think people are getting pushed in Mum."

"Even more reason for you to be careful then." She loosens her plaits. "Lauren, you're my daughter – my only child. You need to look after yourself."

I laugh, then take a sip of my tea. "I'm hardly a child anymore Mum. And I'll be fine."

"You'll always be my child." She wraps her hair elastics around her wrist and her hair falls onto her shoulders. "You'll understand when Alysha gets older. I'm going to get ready." She kisses my forehead as she gets up to go. "It's still my job to worry about you. Imagine what your dad would've said."

The cup of tea and a shower have made me feel a little more human. But I'm still lying on my bed, watching TV. I can't be bothered moving.

"See you later love," Mark calls up the stairs.

"Bye Mummy," echoes Alysha.

"I'll ring you later," says Mum. "I've got to get going too."

"Bye." I call back. I've got a million and one things to do, and I'm meeting Sara for lunch. Just as I've finally figured out what I'll wear and thought about moving myself, the news bulletin grabs my attention.

This latest drowning is the fourth this year in a spate of deaths over a quarter-mile stretch of Yorkshire river. The victim has now been formally identified as forty-seven year old Jennifer Fairburn of Hestleton. Her body was recovered yesterday morning after she had been reported missing by the babysitter of her two children, aged eight and ten, following her failure to return home after an evening out.

The four drownings have a number of factors in common. All victims are female and all have occurred in the early hours of Sunday mornings. All four women have had a substantial amount of alcohol in their systems. Each one has been recorded leaving the Yorkshire Arms pub, but then have gone out of CCTV range after turning right from the pub's entrance, rather than left towards the road.

In a recent press conference, Detective Chief Inspector Jonathan Ingham of North Yorkshire Police offered assurances that the provision of extra CCTV, lighting, safety fencing and lifebuoys is imminent. This, he said, will be supplemented with extra police patrols, which will be prominent on Saturday evenings, into the early hours of Sunday morning.

Despite mounting local concern, DCI Ingham remained steadfast in his view that despite the similarities in the cases, foul play is unlikely, though he said they weren't ruling it out. All the women, he said, have entered the water from the steep and slippery riverbank after being impeded by alcohol.

Post-mortem examinations have established the deaths, in each of the cases, as having occurred after the women have entered the water; additionally, there has been no evidence of any prior injury. DCI Ingham went on to highlight the importance of women staying in their groups or pairs when out for the evening, and taking care to avoid excessive amounts of alcohol.

Anyone falling into that stretch of water, he added, *particularly at this time of year, faces little chance of being able to climb back out. At any time of year, the River Alder experiences strong undercurrents, and this, coupled with the fact the river is frequently used as a dumping ground for items like shopping trollies and household furniture, all add to the risk of becoming trapped within them, under the water.*

"Blimey." Sara smiles as I walk into the café. "You're early. What's got into you?"

"I'm hungry." I laugh. "Plus, I haven't seen my best friend for nearly three weeks." It smells divine in here. Mince pies and mulled wine.

"Has it been that long?" She laughs, pushing the menu towards me. "I'll order us a brew, you get choosing what you want for lunch – I know how long it takes for you to make your mind up."

"Before that," I say, "we have chief bridesmaid duties to discuss. Namely your dress and then there's the small matter of the hen do."

"The hen do is all in hand." Sara tucks her hair behind her ears as she follows my gaze down to where I am opening up the photos app on my phone. "Just give me a list of who you want inviting and the rest is top secret."

"Oh gosh." I raise my voice so she can hear me above the buzz of the packed café, and the piped Christmas music. "As if I'm letting *you* plan my hen do! What will you do to me?"

"You're going to have to let the control freak within you go." She waves to get the attention of one of the waitresses. "And you've got twenty seconds to decide what you want to eat."

I put my phone down and scan the menu.

Lunch does wonders for my hangover and Sara's company does wonders for my fractious state of mind, which has been obsessed with work and the river deaths. It's great to think about the wedding for a change. Sara and I have one of those friendships where it doesn't matter if we haven't seen each other for three days, three weeks or three months. We slot straight back into wherever we left off.

When one of us is feeling under par, a few hours spent together leaves us feeling positive and invigorated. As I've got older, I've learnt to trust the energies of people around me. There are those in life who utterly drain us, and those whose energy compliments our own, and whose company rejuvenates.

Luckily, I've found this in Mark too. Despite our professional differences, his presence still calms and reassures me. Getting into my thirties has equipped me to trust my gut, which is why I feel so strongly about the river deaths. I absolutely know there's more to it all than meets the eye. If only Mark was leading the investigation rather than DCI Ingham. It sounds as though he's got very little say in anything. Ingham is definitely calling the shots with this one and Mark has said himself that his personal problems are hampering his efficiency. Mark will eventually be a Detective Inspector, then hopefully a Detective Chief Inspector. I'm sure when he is, he'll listen to his sergeant's opinions and use him or her to delegate more than Ingham seems to have done. He says he's got it all under control, but has he?

Sara nudges me. "That's a serious face!"

"Sorry. I was thinking about work."

"We're supposed to be thinking about the wedding. Right. Show me these dress pictures."

After eating, as we continue scrolling through pictures of bridesmaid dresses and flower ideas, I am suddenly alerted to a sense of being watched. I look up. All around us, everyone in the café is minding their own business and enjoying time spent with one another. I rub at the steamed up window.

It looks quiet in the street outside, but in the distance, I see what looks like someone crouched behind a wheelie bin. They stay crouched as they dodge behind a fence beside the bin.

"What's the matter?" Sara follows my gaze and wipes the window at her side of the table too.

"Have you ever felt as though you're being watched?" I stare at the bin. "Someone was hiding behind that bin. Now they've gone behind the fence."

"I suppose I have a few times when we've been out clubbing." She laughs. "By some weirdo or other. Oh Lauren. You've been watching far too many of those crime dramas. Or listening to that husband-to-be of yours too much." She looks back towards me. "There's no one there!"

"There was someone hanging around near me last night." I shiver despite the warmth in here. "When I was out with Mark. It's these river deaths. I've got a bad feeling."

"I think it's given everyone the willies to be fair," Sara agrees. "I wouldn't be anyway near that river at night. Especially on my own. At least the police sound like they're now doing something."

"About time. The Yorkshire Arms has taken quite a hit too. I was in there last night with Mark. It wasn't as packed as it used to be." I don't tell her about going outside on my own. She'd have a fit.

"I can't understand why you'd want to go in there. Not with what's been going on. Anyway, what are your plans for the rest of the day?" She drops her purse into her handbag. "I need to be making tracks. I'm at work soon." And with a sly-looking grin, she says, "and I've got a hen party to organise."

"Don't I know it. Just remember, no strippers! I'd die of embarrassment." I tug my laptop from my bag. "I'm going to have an hour or two in here, then I'll pick Alysha up. I've got one or two pieces to draft and you know me, I always write well in a café."

When it's time to walk back to the car park, I take a detour over the river bridge. I feel nervous walking this way now. But it's still daylight, and there are plenty of people around. No one seems to be watching or following me and I'm beyond relieved to see work has begun. Whether the delay was the fault of the police, the council, or Yorkshire Water, at least they've finally got on with it.

A section of fencing has been put up and though I haven't got time to investigate fully, I also see a lifebuoy and a security camera have been put at either side of the water. The CCTV cameras look as though they have been hung on long poles overlooking the river from both sides. It's a start. They're supposed to be stepping up the police presence too. Hopefully Jennifer Fairburn was the last woman to lose her life in this way. Her poor children. It's only nine days until Christmas.

CHAPTER TWELVE

Olivia

Olivia watched Rick as he waited at the bar. He looked marginally better from behind. In her inebriated state, he had looked more passable from the front as the night had gone on, but there was no way she was going home with him, as Rick had suggested. She imagined that in the cold light of day, he would look very bad indeed. And she would regret it. She'd behaved in that way as a teenager; going home with just about anyone once she was wearing her beer goggles. And once upon a time, she'd had quite a reputation for it.

There was a disco on in the Yorkshire Arms that night. Olivia got up to dance on the fringe of a circle of slightly younger women. Yes, she was an idiot. She'd managed to hook up with Rick, a former work colleague. She didn't particularly like him, but she wasn't going to pass up the opportunity to get a few freebie drinks, as she was absolutely broke, and had wanted to go out. And now she was passing the time, dancing with a group of girls she didn't even know, not wanting to sit with Rick when he returned from the bar. The girls didn't appear to mind though. They all seemed well oiled too.

Really, she knew she should call it a night. But it had been a shit Christmas and New Year. Since she'd lost the baby in September and then broken up with Ben, staying out in town and getting wasted was preferable to going back to her dark and empty house. Olivia hated January at the best of times and was convinced she suffered from Seasonal Affective Disorder. She'd heard about light box treatment but could barely afford the rent, let alone to shell out for something like that. She was even toying with the idea of moving back in with her mother. Just temporarily, whilst she got back on her feet. That would be a last resort though. Once you've left home, you can't go back. Her mother had never really liked Ben either so would probably have a few *I told you so's* to impart. Olivia had never told her mum she was pregnant; in fact, she hadn't told anyone apart from Ben. Right now, she longed to ring him. Tell him how much she missed him. See if they could make another go of it. But she knew his answer would make her feel even worse.

She smelt the raw stench of Rick's sweat as he came up behind her and threaded his arms under hers. Olivia quickly turned around to face him. "I'm boiling," she said. "I'm just going to have a sip of my drink. Did you get me another one?"

"Yep. It's on the table. So…" He was slurring his words too. "How are you going to thank me? I've bought you quite a few tonight."

Olivia caught the sourness of his breath as he leaned in to kiss her. *Yuck*, she thought. I really do need to get away from him. At least he didn't know where she lived. Only where she worked. "Just nipping for a wee." She ducked under his arm and headed towards her drink to take with her to the loo. Her mother had always told her to be careful with her drinks. Especially in this day and age, when people were known to spike them. Rick didn't seem the sort though. A bit whiffy and lecherous, but not the drug 'n' rape type, but she was taking no chances.

Olivia wound her way through the gathered group of girls in the toilets. It was reasonably busy for the first weekend of January. She'd meant to do dry-January to save money and give her liver a rest, but she had felt so miserable that she had caved in on New Year's Day itself. Not that she felt any happier when she was drinking. It just helped to mask things.

There was no sign of Rick when she emerged from the toilets. He was either lost in the throng of people bobbing around to the too-loud crap they were playing, or he'd gone to the loo himself. She necked the remainder of her wine and placed the empty glass on the bar near the exit and glanced at her watch. She'd missed the last bus and couldn't afford a taxi. Perhaps she could try to get hold of her mother. Ask for a loan or a lift. Nah, it was too late. And she'd never hear the end of it, even if she managed to wake her mother at this time of night.

She walked from the pub, grateful for the slap of winter-night air and refreshing rain, after the thick sweat-laden heat of the Yorkshire Arms. She sat on a bench in the shadows so Rick wouldn't see her if he came out looking, whilst she decided what she was going to do.

Chapter Thirteen

Lauren

*G*ood morning. This is the BBC news on Monday 6th January. *Firstly, we bring you a breaking story about a fifth fatality in the River Alder at Alderton in Yorkshire.*

Following identification late last night, the victim has been named as Olivia Yates, aged twenty-eight.

CCTV footage shows her walking into the Yorkshire Arms pub with a tall, well-built man at 11:05pm and leaving at 12:35am alone.

The man in his mid-thirties, has been helping police with their enquiries and is thought to have been ruled out from any involvement in her death.

Olivia was recorded on CCTV sitting alone on a bench near to the Yorkshire Arms. She was seen getting up from the bench and walking downriver, beyond the fencing which has recently been installed. The CCTV coverage is limited there, and only captures Olivia's movements to the bend of the river.

The area has been cordoned off and is being forensically examined for footprints. It is acknowledged, however, that the area attracts heavy footfall, therefore it will be difficult to produce results that can be treated as evidence.

Despite recent local police efforts to step up security in the area, it seems people are still failing to adhere to the safety advice, which is not to be in the area alone at night. Enquiries into this death and potential links between this and other recent accidents, including five from last year, are ongoing.

Bloody hell. I rattle off four texts to Mark.

I had no idea that your stupid boss only had fencing installed to where the bend is.

And why are there only two cameras? Where are the rest of them?

What the hell is going on?

Never mind a CCTV camera, it's Ingham's head that should be on a pole after this.

And I'll be saying so when I write an article later. I think better of sending this last one and delete it. Mark replies almost straight away.

It's the council, not DCI Ingham, who are doing the fencing. You're blaming the wrong person.

He's in charge, isn't he?

It's all down to resources love. There is more work planned. They haven't finished yet.

You can't put a price on someone's life.

I'm not suggesting you can.

I really think you should have been in charge of the investigation. Not Ingham. He's messed it up.

It's not really an investigation. It's more a spate of accidents. We all have slight doubts, but officially, that's what we're treating it as for the moment.

Wake up Mark. I'll stake the place out myself if I have to. You lot are useless.

No, you will not. But I'm sure you'll write a piece about it. x
Too right!
See you at home. xx
I won't be back till later. I'm meeting Sara. My dress has come in so I'm trying it on. x
OK. Love you loads. xx
You too. xx

Before I meet Sara, I park up near the Yorkshire Arms. I want to get a few photographs of these preventative measures that have been taken. I'm incensed by the whole thing. Now I can see them up close, the measures look even more ineffective than I first thought. They haven't advanced since I walked here in December. Yes, there's the section of fencing I previously saw, but it literally only covers twenty metres, if that, and I can now see for myself, that it stops before the bend in the river and where the bank is at its steepest. It's ridiculous. Surely the police have more clout with the council than this.

Only one extra life-ring and one extra CCTV camera have been installed on both sides of the river. But the news reports were right. The river bends, and the CCTV only covers the length of the fencing to that point. Given that all the bodies so far have been pulled out further downriver, these so-called safety measures are an insult to the memory of the women who have died here. I take several photographs then head back to my car, to meet Sara.

Mark was talking some crap the other night, saying that the stretch of river is no different to an accident black spot on the M1. People know the risks and if they continue to take them, i.e. walking on a steep, slippery riverbank at night, when drunk, then they only have themselves to blame.

"You sound like your bloody boss," I had said.

As always, Sara is already there. I don't think I've ever known her to be late. Not like me. "Oooh, it's times like this, I wish I was getting married." She brushes her hand over the fabric of a dress on a mannequin. "They're all so gorgeous."

"Your turn will come." I know as soon as I say it, that's not what she wants to hear.

"Let's not go there." She frowns. She's done well mustering so much enthusiasm for my wedding, given that she ended up being ghosted by the man she was supposed to be marrying last year.

I got involved and poked my journalistic nose in when she had voiced her suspicions to me. It didn't take long, and after a bit of digging around, it turned out he was already married. It was awful telling her what I'd found out, but it was better that she'd found out before going through with a sham wedding ceremony.

There was no actual proof of their engagement to have him prosecuted for it, only the photograph of her ring, which he could have explained away as a friendship ring or something else.

In the midst of all this, he had turned up at my house just after Mark had left for a night shift and had threatened me, saying that if I didn't butt out of his business, and caused him any more hassle, he'd make me pay, one way or another. He was so menacing that I asked Eva to come and stay with me and Alysha for the night. I left it alone after that, as much as I'd wanted to tell the man's wife about his intention to marry Sara.

When Mark and I set a date to get married, I felt wretched telling Sara, but I couldn't have asked anyone else to be my chief bridesmaid. She and I have been best friends since school.

"It's been so long since I've tried this dress on that I wonder if it's still going to fit me." I feel panicky as I step into it. "What if

I've put tons of weight on?"

"It'll need taking in a bit," the seamstress says after buttoning me up. "And taking up so just the toes of your shoes can be seen. They're fabulous by the way."

I could kiss her. My dress needs taking in, not letting out. I look at myself in the full-length mirror then at Sara. "Do you still like it?" I ask her. "As much as when we chose it?"

"Lauren, you daft sod. You look absolutely stunning. I love it."

"We need to find your dress now."

Raising an eyebrow, Sara replies. "I need to find a man first."

I gasp at my insensitivity. "I meant your bridesmaid dress."

"I know silly. The look on your face was priceless though."

I spend more time trying on veils and tiaras, then Sara and I decide to have a cheeky glass of wine in the pub next door. I freeze as we leave the bridal shop. "There's someone behind my car." I hiss at her. "Just like when we went to the café last month."

Sara looks over. "I can't see anyone." Last time, she tried to wave the situation away, but now she looks worried.

I glance down the road to check for traffic before stepping out. Sara pulls me back. "Wait a minute." Her voice is a whisper now. "You can't just go charging over. If there's someone there, they'll have to come out eventually. I'm not letting you go across there. They could have a knife or anything. Shit."

I hear a sound like a rubber sole on gravel. Sara and I cling to one another as she reaches into her bag and pulls out her phone. We are both trembling. By now the woman in the bridal shop has come out to see if we're OK and what is going on. As I speak to her and Sara speaks into her phone to the police, I see a darkly dressed figure dart away from behind my car at full pelt along a side street. He's got a hood up and is over six feet tall. That's about as much as I get.

Mark rings me. "The report's just come in. Are you OK? Where are you?"

"In the Fox and Hounds." I take a gulp of my wine. "I'm alright though. Whoever it was has gone. Probably just some jerk casing my car. I'd stupidly left my iPad on the passenger seat. Is there anyone who can drop you off so you can drive us both back. We were having a glass of wine anyway, but I might need two after that!"

"I'll get DCI Ingham to drop me off shortly," he replies. "He's just come on shift to do a press release about the latest woman. Then I can drive us both home. Is Alysha in school club?"

"Yes." I take another sip of my wine, feeling rebellious for drinking on a Monday afternoon. It's part wedding dress celebration – part nerves – especially after seeing someone hanging around my car. "Hopefully, he was just after my iPad. And not me or Sara."

"I'll get some details from you when I arrive, then I'll get them circulated. We'll catch him. Are you sure you're OK?"

"Yes. Sara's with me. Try not to be long."

"We'll set off straight after his statement. He's starting now."

"I'll ask the pub to put the TV on so I can watch it. Which channel?"

"Sky News."

"Would you mind popping Sky News on for us." I smile at the landlady. "There's about to be a statement about the river deaths. It's gone national," I say to Sara, my voice still wobbling.

"Five deaths. It's no wonder. I know you're nearly married to one of them, but what the hell are the police doing? There should be patrols there night and day now. I've heard they've scaled back their usual recruitment programme as well."

"They've enough special constables they could use to patrol it."

"Would Special Constables be equipped to deal with a serial killer?" She splits open a bag of crisps in front of us.

"I couldn't eat a thing." I push them towards her. "Do you think it's a serial killer too?"

"It could be. I bloody hope not though. Hopefully we're being overdramatic. People have been falling into that river for years."

"Not this many in such a short space of time. I don't buy all this resources argument," I continue. "According to Mark, the revenue that comes in from speed cameras and fines alone is colossal."

"It's a dreadful business if you ask me." The landlady points a remote at the TV to turn the volume up. "They've not even put up fifty metres of fencing. How many more women are going to die in there?"

"No more," I say quietly. "Not if I've got anything to do with it. My fiancé is in the police and I'm a journalist. Although, I'll probably get to the bottom of it all before they do."

Sara puts her glass down. "Don't you be doing anything risky." She narrows her eyes. "I mean it."

"Of course not. I've Alysha to think about. I'd never put myself in any danger."

We listen intently as DCI Ingham makes his statement, saying absolutely nothing that he hasn't said before. To say he's got the national platform of Sky News, I'm disgusted. All he does is repeat his warning from last month about levels of drinking, staying with friends, etc. He mentions the extra security measures the council and the police have implemented and reiterates that the drowning of Olivia Yates was a needless, tragic accident.

Sara's phone rings. I gather from her responses that it's her Mum. "Hi Janice," I call out. I pick up my phone and click on Facebook. I type Olivia Yates. There is an earlier video that has been shared onto her page from a woman. I click on it.

My name is Petra Yates. I'm Olivia's mother. If anybody saw anything in the early hours of Sunday morning that could lead us to piecing together the moments before my daughter fell into the river, then please contact the police on 101.

My beautiful, caring, fun-loving girl had her whole life before her when she met her dreadful death. To the rest of you out there, please learn from this. How many more women are going to lose their lives in this way? Please look after yourselves, and each other. I don't want any other mother to have to go through this. She gulps her way through her speech through a deluge of tears.

"Poor woman." I dial the Press Association. "Lindy," I check it's her as I get through. "Am I OK to submit a piece later today through one of the copy takers. I'm going to literally take the police apart."

"What about Mark? Would it be better if someone else wrote the piece? The last thing you want is ructions at home."

"This is my story." I glance out of the pub window at my car. Whoever was there appears to be long gone. "And I'm not going to report on anything that isn't factual."

"I'll look forward to reading it."

As I hang up Mark strides in with DCI Jonathan Ingham close behind. "Hey you two. Are you OK?"

"We've had a drive around," DCI Ingham says, "and haven't seen anything untoward."

I feel like saying *so you're speaking to me today, are you,* but instead I blurt out, "I'm not happy with the measures you've put in place at the Yorkshire Arms Sir. What on earth are you playing at?"

"Lauren." Mark frowns.

"It's OK Mark." DCI Ingham smiles as he checks his watch. "I'm not going to discuss it now, Lauren. Obviously you've already been through an ordeal already today. I'm going to suggest you put any concerns about the security project in writing and mark it for my attention."

"The security project? Five women are dead, not to mention all the deaths in previous years, and you refer to it as a project?"

"Easy Lauren." Mark puts his hand on my arm. "That's another matter. Let's talk about this man you think has been hanging around, shall we?"

"I need to get back." DCI Ingham smiles at us. "I'll leave you in the capable hands of my sergeant here."

"Shush." Mark squeezes my arm as DCI Ingham walks away from our table. "He's right. Let's focus on one thing at a time. Firstly, are you having another? I'm going to get myself a coke."

"Water," we chorus. "Sara has to work this evening and I've got an article to write." I need a clear head when I'm doing any kind of writing.

"I won't ask what your article will be about," he says.

"Good. You shouldn't. And neither should Ingham."

CHAPTER FOURTEEN

Charlotte

C harlotte hadn't much felt like going out, but it was her friend Sofie's birthday and she knew she'd never hear the end of it if she blobbed. She had been feeling queasy for several days and had put it down to some chicken that she probably shouldn't have eaten. Still, a few ciders seemed to have taken the edge off, and Charlotte had felt more normal. If she'd moped around at home, she'd have been in bed by now, feeling sorry for herself. And she would have seriously pissed Sofie off.

"You're a barrel of laughs tonight." Sofie looked at her. "Come on Char. It's my birthday."

"Sorry. I was just thinking that I'm glad I feel a touch better. Anyway, how does it feel to be thirty? It sounds old if you ask me."

"You're not that far behind me." Sofie laughed. "Just over a year to go. To be honest, it doesn't feel any different to being twenty-nine."

"You'll have to start acting responsibly now," Charlotte went on.

"What do you mean?"

"I don't know. Perhaps get a mortgage and hold down a job for more than three months."

"*Get a mortgage!* I'm quite happy with how things are with me and you living in our little rented flat and having a laugh." Sofie glanced across to some men on a neighbouring table who seemed to be checking them out. "I think we've pulled Char."

"Oh, I can't be arsed with all that." Charlotte followed her gaze. That was honestly the last thing she needed. However, she knew she would have a hard time deterring Sofie from responding to them.

"Things have got boring since you started seeing Luke." Sofie necked her vodka and coke. "You've gone all sensible. You've only been seeing each other for a few months. I bet he flirts with other lasses when *he* goes out. Another drink?"

"I bet he doesn't." Charlotte just wanted her bed and couldn't be bothered with all this. "Just get me a glass of water. I'm starting to feel ropey again."

"No chance. It's Saturday night. *Water!*" Sofie rose from her chair and shimmied past the lads' table, seemingly enjoying their attention as she headed for the bar. One of them got up to join her there, whilst the three remaining lads were looking at Charlotte. She'd hardly bothered getting dressed up this evening and wished they'd stop looking at her. Suddenly, she felt awful again and her mouth started to water. Desperately, she looked around for a drink to wash the saliva away, but she and Sofie had drunk everything. Her stomach heaved and she knew if she didn't get out of there, she was going to chuck up right in front of them all.

There was a queue snaking from the toilet door so running in there wasn't an option. Instead Charlotte jumped up, managing to make it to the main exit and to the river bank, just in time.

She'd barely eaten all day. It was just regurgitated cider that pooled around her feet and soaked into the mud of the banking.

What on earth was she thinking – coming out whilst feeling like this? Although she'd spewed the cider, she still felt drunk and sank onto a nearby bench to compose herself. Sofie would probably be too busy with the lads to notice her absence.

Chapter Fifteen

Lauren

I shepherd Alysha towards the chair. "Just a trim for both of us, and my usual highlights. I've brought plenty of stuff to keep this one entertained."

Amanda, my hairdresser, laughs as Alysha pulls her tablet from her rucksack. "I can't believe how well they manage all this technology nowadays. Especially at that age."

I'm very lucky with Alysha. She sits beautifully whilst her hair is cut, telling Amanda all about school and her flower girl dress. I've had an easy time being her mum. One or two of my friends have told me horror stories about their own parenting trials and tribulations. With Mark so desperate for baby number two, I'm scared we'll get one next time that does not sleep and screams all day. I sit across the salon, half listening to Amanda and Alysha, and half paying attention to my phone. The silver-grey colour scheme in the salon and whiff of shampoo calms me. I always enjoy a trip to the hairdressers. I reach over for a glossy magazine. Normally, I wouldn't have the time to look through one of these.

"Are you doing anything exciting this weekend?" Amanda asks Alysha. "Apart from having your hair cut of course."

"I'm going to the fire station with my daddy tomorrow morning and then baking with my mummy in the afternoon."

"It sounds as though you have a very busy day to look forward to." Amanda holds the mirror behind Alysha's head. "There, you can see I've not cut too much hair off. I've just tidied it up a bit. We can see those beautiful green eyes of yours now."

"And she can see where she's going. Good girl. Mummy will swap places with you now."

Alysha accepts the lollipop she is offered then plugs her earphones in to watch whatever princess programme she's currently addicted to, whilst I get my hair done. If only mine was as quick as Alysha's. I try not to let her spend too much time being electronically babysat, but Mark is at work, Mum is busy today and needs must sometimes. I enjoy the smell of conditioner, the hum of the radio, and the latte I've been made, whilst continuing to flick through Cosmo. Meanwhile, Amanda systematically layers my hair with foils and colour.

"I saw your story in the Yorkshire Gazette last month. Well done you. I keep seeing your pieces all over the place."

"Thanks. Though I wish it had done some good." I sigh. The hairdressing salon always feel like an oasis away from reality, but I can never get too far from it all at the moment. Both Mark and I seem to be living and breathing this river case. "I don't think Mark was happy with the article, but we agreed from the get-go when we first met, that our careers would never bring us into conflict personally. Though we debate things, we would never let them come between us."

"That's the best way – there's not many couples that could cope with that." She bends another foil around a strand of hair with the tail of her comb. "And you tell it like it is – I like that. What was the headline?"

"*Local Police Fail River Death Victims,*" I sip my latte. "Everything I said was true, about them being slow to deliver on what they had promised, I mean. I had photos printed to back it all up."

"You don't need to convince me." She combs through another section of hair. "My sister's friend was one of the women who drowned."

"Really?" I replace the glass cup onto the saucer. "Who?"

"Becky. I think it was around November time when she died. Caroline, my sister, was in bits. So was Becky's boyfriend. She was only in the pub in the first place because they'd had a row."

"What about?"

"Lauren, this is completely off the record," she says, mixing the highlighting solution with her brush. "You can't repeat this."

"What is said in the salon stays in the salon." I put my finger across my lips in mock-solemn oath.

Amanda laughs and flicks her long chestnut hair behind one of her shoulders. She always wears heels and is immaculately made up when she's working. She's ten years older than me, though no one would think so.

"He'd been syphoning money out of their joint account," she begins. "A lot of money. He'd developed a gambling addiction."

"How much?"

"Thousands. Everything they had, according to Caroline. I'm not sure how much Becky knew about the money before she died, but her family got wind of it all when they were dealing with her affairs afterwards."

"Thousands! Blimey."

"According to Caroline, it was the lies that affected Becky. Right up until the last moment, he was lying through his back teeth to her. He'd backed out of a promise that they were going to go away and had booked a lad's holiday instead. And he'd called off them buying a house together."

"Do you think he's got something to do with…"

"He's been well and truly investigated," she says. "Becky went for a walk around the streets in the centre for a while and was picked up on a number of security cameras. Then obviously she ended up in the Yorkshire Arms."

"What about him?"

"Seb? He went straight to the bookies. Obviously full of remorse." Sarcasm drips from her words. "Then he went home. He can be accounted for through his IP address, all night, winning on Blackjack, according to Caroline."

"Winning?"

"Big time. Caroline told me that on one hand alone, he placed thirty grand. And he just kept winning. He's ended up with over two hundred."

"Grand? You're kidding?"

"Nope. But he's lost the love of his life."

"True."

"He could've paid back what he did Becky out of half a dozen times over. Fortunately, she never knew about the money before she died."

"Has your sister seen him since?"

"Yes. She said he was just crying. He's racked with guilt at how he treated her. And that she'd died after they'd been rowing. Caroline's been feeling really guilty as well."

"Why?"

"I've told her not to be so stupid, but she won't listen. She was texting with Becky that night whilst she was in the Yorkshire Arms. Caroline had told Becky to message and let her know she'd got home safely. She was drunk by all accounts."

"Who? Becky?"

"Yes. But she didn't. Text, I mean. Caroline was away with her boyfriend that night for her birthday. Otherwise she might have picked Becky up from the pub herself. Anyway, she fell asleep. Something she's hated herself for ever since."

"The poor lass. It's not her fault." I sip my latte.

"I've told her that. But Becky was in such a state that night about falling out with Seb. It wasn't just the fall out – it was him letting her go without trying to stop her."

"No way would Mark ever not come after me, no matter how bad a row might be."

Amanda brushes some colour onto my hair. "I think that could be said of most men. Becky talked to Caroline about it on the phone. She said she couldn't stay with someone she didn't trust. He was always distant with her and never put any effort in."

"It's got to be a two-way street, hasn't it?"

"I agree. It was the last straw for her when he changed his mind about the holiday and moving in together. And thankfully she knew nothing about the money as far as anyone knows."

"So what happened next?" I'm trying not to sound too interested. "Obviously I won't betray a confidence, but knowledge is power and if knowing more helps me to get to the truth of these deaths, then I need to know as much as possible.

Amanda rummages around in her trolley for some hair clips, and pins them to her tabard. "Caroline woke the next morning and at first thought nothing of not having got a text from Becky. But then she saw on the news they'd pulled another body out, right next to the pub Becky had been in."

"Oh my God."

"She said she just knew. I've told her that even if she'd raised the alarm that same night, there was probably nothing she could have done to change things. She'd kept in touch with her. They were texting and had a brief chat. Some bloke was trying to hit on her and Becky had wanted to try and deter him by speaking to someone on the phone. To look busy."

"What do you think happened?" I watch as Amanda clips sections of foil away from each other on my head. "Do you reckon these women are just falling in?"

"Who knows?" She picks up my empty coffee cup. "I'll get you another. I wouldn't be hanging around there on a Saturday night, let's put it that way. Aww, look at your little girl. Isn't she good?" We both look at Alysha, who is still firmly entrenched in a land of princesses. I then spend a luxurious forty minutes flicking through Prima whilst my highlights take effect. Amanda does a dry cut on another customer and Alysha barely looks up from her tablet. I'll spend some proper time with her when we leave. Right now I'm enjoying the me-time.

"How are the wedding plans coming along?" Amanda asks a short time later as she turns the shower spray on.

"Pretty well. I've had my first dress fitting. Ouch, that's a bit hot."

"Sorry. These showers can be so unpredictable. Your highlights have taken well."

"Will you be long Mummy?" It's the first peep we've had from Alysha.

"Get a packet of sweets from my bag and if you carry on being such a good girl, we'll go somewhere for hot chocolate and cake when I'm done."

"Yesss."

"That sounds nice." I can hear the smile in Amanda's voice as she washes my hair. "It's a shame I've got to stay at work instead of coming with you."

I close my eyes against the splashing water and try to ignore the crick in my neck. One day they'll invent a salon sink which doesn't half dismember you!

"He's giving me the creeps," Amanda says with a dark edge to her voice. "There's a man the other side of the road. I've been watching him for half an hour. He's staring right in here."

"What man?" I try to sit up but the sink, the soap and the spray conspire against me.

"Now that it's getting dark, it's harder to spot him." She lathers conditioner into my hair. "He's kind of slipping in and out of the shadows. I might lock the door. I've got the panic button if he comes any closer."

"Are you expecting any more customers after me?"

"No, you're my last one – I've just had a cancellation. I try to have an early finish on a Saturday, if I can, so it's worked out well as I'm going out tonight."

"I'll wait with you whilst you lock up," I say. "If there's someone hanging about, neither of us should be leaving alone in the dark."

"He's there again. Maybe we should call the police."

Amanda stops lathering, so I prop myself up in the seat on my elbows. "I can't see anyone." I turn to look at her. "I have felt someone watching me a few times over the last few weeks."

"Have you?"

"Yes. It's a creepy feeling, though I'd forgotten about it, until now. Someone was hanging around my car outside the bridal shop last month. Then there was another time I was in a café with my friend. Oh, and there was someone watching me when I was in the pub with Mark, and I went outside on my own."

"You need to be careful." She rinses off the conditioner. The water is the perfect temperature now. "Especially with the articles you're writing."

"I know. I will be."

As I return to my chair to have my hair cut, she locks the door.

CHAPTER SIXTEEN

Lauren

By the time Amanda has dried my hair, there is no sign of anyone outside.

"Do you still think we should call the police? At least report it," she says. "Or are you sure he's gone?"

"With the time they'd take to get here…" I begin. "They didn't do a lot last time, when the man was hanging around the bridal shop. Mark just came and collected me and the DCI he reports to had a drive around. That was it. Anyway, if you're going out tonight – you don't want to be waiting around here for the police."

Her car is parked right outside the salon, so I accept a lift to the end of the road where my car is. I'm taking no chances if someone is hanging around, especially as I've got Alysha with me. There doesn't seem to be any sign of him, but that doesn't stop my heart from beating ten to the dozen as Amanda sets the alarm and locks the door. I look around us, then we dash to her car.

I feel resentful that I'm having to change my behaviour because of a perceived threat, and vow to do anything I can to stop what's going on. Perhaps I really am being stalked by the person responsible for the river deaths. The thought sends a chill up my spine. I've only just allowed myself to really start believing it.

"Hi honey, I'm home," Mark calls from the hallway.

I laugh at his clichéd behaviour. "In here," I call back. "Just serving up your dinner, playing at being your wife." I smile to myself at the thought. "You timed that well. I thought I was going to have to put yours in the microwave."

Mark walks towards me, kisses me then bends down and plants a kiss in the middle of Alysha's forehead. He always kisses me when we part, and when we greet each other again. I like that about him.

"Daddy, do you like my hair?" Alysha points a fork laden with mashed potato towards her head.

"It's beautiful," Mark replies. "But if you're not careful, we'll be scraping potato out of it. Mummy's hair looks lovely too."

"Why thank you." I feel myself blush. I love it when he compliments me. "It's not like you to notice my hair."

"You never notice when I've been to the barbers." He takes a sip from his glass of water, then grins at me.

"That's different. You're a man."

"We still like to get compliments, you know."

It's nice to sit down together to eat. I often eat with Alysha when Mark's on a late, or sometimes I wait for Mark and eat with him after Alysha has gone to bed. But as I sit with my family in our warm kitchen, having shut out the world outside, I know this is how it should be. The three of us. I feel safe in here, with them.

Mark carries Alysha to bed after she falls asleep on him watching Paddington 2. When he comes back downstairs, he says, "we can put something more grown up on now."

"Or," I wink at him. "We can practice for baby number two."

"Practice?"

"Yep. That's what's on offer. Until after the wedding."

He takes my hand. "What are we waiting for?"

I've laid awake for nearly an hour, listening to the rain at the window. Mark was out like a light. He always is after we've made love. It's only half-past eleven and I really can't sleep. I lift Mark's arm that's laying heavy over my stomach. I can't put the light on and read as I'll wake him. Even if I read on my Kindle, he usually moans that the backlight disturbs him.

Yet he doesn't move as I swing my legs out of bed, tug on my gym bottoms and a jumper before heading downstairs. As I turn on the lounge light, my gaze falls on a newspaper headline I wrote last month, poking out from under the coffee table. It made it to the Daily Mail, so of course I've saved it - *Local Police Fail River Death Victims*.

I glance at the clock. 11:43 pm. It's Saturday night. A seed of an idea starts to germinate in my mind. I sit on the sofa, half trying to talk myself out of it. But deep down, I know what I must do. The police have taken little responsibility for anything that has happened so far. They're full of half-promises, without following through on any of them.

I tell myself I'm not going to put myself in any danger - I'm just going to inconspicuously park up and watch. If there's no police patrol there tonight after all that has happened, and all that has been promised, I will take photographs of the entire area and date stamp the photos, showing the police absence, ready to go in my next piece. And who knows, I might see if anyone is hanging around, lying in wait.

Deep down, I know it's utter madness but I pull on socks, boots and my coat before I can change my mind. Mark would have an absolute fit if he knew what I was doing. I would tell him that if the police did their jobs properly, I wouldn't have to do this.

Besides, I'll keep my car door locked and be ready to drive off if need be. One thing I've learnt over the years is that journalists don't get anywhere without some risk-taking.

I ease into the clearing between the Yorkshire Arms and the unused building next door. My vision is obscured by overgrown foliage, but there's still more than enough space for me to park. I turn my headlights off before I've even brought the car to a stop. As I do, I quickly turn off the engine and allow my eyes to adjust to the darkness. There's been some extra lighting installed nearby, but it's not good enough. I realise it's controlled by motion sensor rather than being on continuously, as it flicks on when someone walks by, then off again, plunging the area into blackness, apart from the weak moonlight.

From where I'm parked, I can't see the entrance of the Yorkshire Arms but I've got a reasonable view of both sides of the river. I'm sure I'll see the faces of anyone who walks past on either side, especially as it's stopped raining. I'm somewhat concealed by the bushes, so hopefully I won't get noticed. I haven't got the nerve to go any further forwards. My car doors are locked, and I can be out of here in three seconds flat if I need to be. What I can't see, however, is any police. Perhaps they're keeping out of sight to catch someone in the act. But what was assured was a police presence, to deter further incidents in the first place.

My heart is pounding in my chest. *This is what journalists do*, I tell myself. Mark's department has done the bare minimum as far as policing is concerned. I want to see if anyone is hanging around here, like I thought I saw not so long ago. If there is anything to be seen, then it will be me who will see it. And I'll break the story. I take photos for something to do whilst I wait for something to happen.

If I have to, I will come back next Saturday night and every Saturday thereafter. I know how to make sure Mark goes straight off to sleep and Mum is always happy to come and stay with me if he's on nights – I'd tell her I want the company and then sneak out after she's gone to bed. They would both slaughter me if they knew where I was.

The inky-black river is lit up beneath the moonlight. It makes the hairs stand up on the back of my neck to think of the poor souls who have slipped in there, pushed, thrown or having fallen to the most dreadful of deaths. They haven't been assaulted before going in, that much has been proven, but they've all been alive when they have. It must have been terrifying. And someone knows something.

I sit for about half an hour like this, my car thermometer registering three degrees. God knows how cold it must be in that water. I tug my coat more tightly around me and keep my gaze fixed forward, scanning left and right occasionally for any movement. I resist the urge to check my phone and continue to grip onto my camera. The glow of the backlight could draw attention to my presence. My eyes are starting to feel droopy. I rotate my shoulders and my head, then slap the sides of my face to keep myself awake. Even though I'm too cold to fall asleep, I'm certainly tired enough to now.

CHAPTER SEVENTEEN

Gemma

Gemma flicked her hair over her shoulder and laughed when her work colleague Sue offered her another drink. "Well, it would be rude not to, wouldn't it? Especially when Mike is paying."

"I can't believe he's set up a tab." Sue nodded towards their boss. "We're normally lucky to get one drink out of him. I reckon he feels guilty for delaying our works do at Christmas. Just because he's got a sad, lonely life," she went on, "he thought he'd cancel everyone else's fun too."

"At least we got that order out." Gemma thought about the extra money she'd made at Christmas and how she'd been able to treat her husband, Darren, to the Fitbit he'd wanted. "Get me – I'm holding a coherent conversation whilst I feel totally plastered!"

"Well, you don't sound coherent." Sue laughed.

"You neither!" They both dissolved in fits of laughter.

"The thing is," Sue went on. "That the more *co-here-ent* we try to be, the more pissed we sound."

Gemma noticed their boss looking over at them. As she looked away, she saw he was making his way over to their table. She nudged Sue. "Uh-oh, here he comes. Act sober."

"At least you've got tomorrow to recover ladies." He sat in the vacant chair, placed his glass before him and grinned inanely- like he fancied his chances.

Gemma attempted to straighten herself up. She'd vowed to alternate each drink with a non-alcoholic one. However, the temptation of a free bar, paid for by her normally miserable boss, had proved irresistible.

Mike had already started talking shop to Sue. *Go away,* Gemma wanted to say to him. "Excuse me," she said to both of them as her phone screen flashed on the table. She picked up her phone and saw it was Darren.

You're late back. You ok?

She stared at the screen on her phone, trying to take in the time display. She'd drunk so much vodka and coke she could hardly focus. She would get a pint of water in a minute – try to sober up a bit. Glancing up at the wall clock, she saw it was half past midnight.

Yeah I'm fine, she typed back. Slightly *drunk. Hic. Free bar and all that. xx*

He responded with a laughing emoji. *Where are you? x*

Just in the Yorkshire Arms. There's loads of us. x

I can't believe you're in there. Are you alright for getting home? x

I guess so. Unless you can come for me? Weather is awful. Xx

Sorry love, I've had a drink. xxx

No worries. I'll get a taxi soon xx

Not on your own Gem. Don't leave that place alone. Not after what's been happening. xx

Gemma stared at the screen again. That was a sobering thought. She shot Sue a sympathetic look. "Just getting some water," she said as she stood. She didn't think Sue had heard, as Mike had her well and truly cornered, looking like he had moved on from talking about work. He had, what Gemma thought, was a very lecherous expression on his face. By now, the group of work colleagues had dwindled, and those remaining were in much the same state as Gemma. The table was stacked with glasses.

Gemma lurched towards the bar. "Same again?" asked the barman.

"No, just a pint of water. I need to sober up. What's the best taxi firm to get around here?"

"The black and whites are good," he replied. "But obviously they can only pick you up around the corner, on the bridge." He tilted his head in the direction he was referring to. "Don't be leaving on your own though."

Before Gemma had got married, she'd have probably said is *that an offer,* but she kept her mouth shut and realised that she needed to text Darren back.

Getting a taxi shortly, she typed. *I'm going to try to get Sue to get in it with me. If not, there's a few others left.*

But nobody was ready to leave. Not even Sue. Gemma was dismayed to realise that she and Mike were flirting with one another. She would give her some right stick for it on Monday.

Feeling slightly panicked at the thought of leaving the pub alone, she momentarily thought of asking the barman to walk with her, just to the taxi. But then indignance took over. What was the world coming to if a grown woman couldn't leave a pub without worrying about getting murdered? Besides, there would be police all over the place out there. She'd seen them passing by the windows all evening.

"I've got a taxi coming in a minute," she said to Sue, who finally came up for air after snogging with Mike.

"Going so soon?" he said.

Gemma nodded her head before bending down to whisper into Sue's ear. "You just wait until Monday morning! I hope you know what you're doing!" Then in a louder voice, she said, "are you sure you won't come with me Sue? I can drop you off on the way."

"Nah. I'm alright here. I'll see you Monday."

"You sure will." Gemma grinned as she grabbed her coat, then waved to a few of the others as she walked towards the door.

CHAPTER EIGHTEEN

Lauren

M y gut somersaults as I become aware of a presence next to the car. I can see a shadow to my left and hear the snap of what could be a twig. Just as I reach for the keys in the ignition, I'm jolted by a thumping on the passenger side window.

"What the hell are *you* doing here?" A voice echoes in the quiet. Squinting, I wind the window down as I see DCI Ingham.

"Um. I couldn't sleep." I start the engine, freezing now. After all, no one is going to attack me when I've got a DCI at the side of me. "I came down to take some photos of the area in the dark. I thought it might enhance any more articles I write." I can't believe Ingham has caught me here. I actually feel sheepish.

"You couldn't sleep? You were dead to the world just now."

"What time is it?" I turn the heater up, but all it blows out is cold air.

"Twenty past one. Does Mark know you're here?"

"Erm, no, and I'd be grateful if it stayed that way. I only wanted some photographs."

"How long have you been here?" He didn't answer my request not to tell Mark which unnerves me.

"Long enough."

"Long enough for what?"

"Long enough to go to sleep." I shiver. "How come you're here? Finally keeping your word and doing some patrolling? Couldn't you get your minions to do it?" As soon as I've said this, I notice a familiar figure suddenly illuminated as the security lighting blinks on. Will walks in front of the car, flanked by two young girls, towards the entrance of the Yorkshire Arms. The lighting is bright enough that even at the distance we're at, I can tell he's caked in mud. They must be short staffed to be pulling Will from traffic to patrol here.

"What's *he* doing here?" The mere sight of him makes me feel even colder.

Instead of answering me, DCI Ingham tilts his radio towards his face. "Yeah. I need another officer down here. Sergeant Potts is on his way back to the station to change – he's had a tumble on the riverbank."

"Sir."

Ingham bends down again, nearly leaning into the car. "Just go home, will you. Leave us to do our jobs. You don't need me to tell you that this isn't the safest place to be. Don't let me find you here again."

"Mummy!" Alysha bounds into the bedroom. "Will you put plaits in my hair? Daddy's taking me to see the fire engines." She throws herself onto the bed beside me. "Do you want to come too?"

"Mummy looks like she needs a lie in this morning." Mark walks in behind her with a cup of tea. He places it beside me and winks. He's already fully dressed. "You didn't even stir when I got up."

"Thanks. You're a good un." I pull Alysha towards me and separate her hair to plait it. "You're both very organised this morning."

"I thought I'd leave you sleeping a while longer." He squirts deodorant under his arms. "I heard you come back to bed in the night. Were you OK?"

"Yeah." I stare at the plait I'm braiding, not wanting to look at him. "I couldn't sleep. I didn't disturb you, did I?" I'm not lying – I'm just not telling him the full truth. I hope DCI Ingham forgets about seeing me last night. Somehow, I suspect he won't.

"Nah. I didn't even hear you get up in the first place. You know what I'm like once I'm gone. It's only light that wakes me."

"So you're still off to the fire station?"

"Yeah, the one in Shelby. You don't need the car this morning, do you?"

"No, I don't think so."

"Since you're awake now, why don't you come with us? I've promised Alysha some breakfast at a cafe. I think she fancies a full English, like her dad."

"Yes Mummy. Come on."

"Do you both mind if I don't?" I smile as I look at them. My heart always swells. I am so lucky to have my little family. And before much longer we'll be married. There might even be another baby not too long after that. "It would just be nice to stay in this comfy bed and drink my tea. Besides, it's good for the two of you to spend some time together. Daddy and daughter time."

"OK Mummy. I'll take lots of photos on Daddy's phone for you."

"What – of your breakfast?"

"No silly Mummy– of the fire engines! To show you when I get back."

"Brilliant." I kiss the top of her head. "That's nearly as good as me coming with you."

As I finish her second plait, she springs up. "I'll get my coat, Daddy." She races past him.

"I'd love to have her energy this morning." I pat the side of the bed from where Alysha has just emerged.

"You do look tired." Mark takes my hand and kisses it. He's such a wonderful man, and I'm very lucky to have the life I have. He works hard for us, enabling me to chase my writing dreams as a journalist and work freelance like I do. Even when the interest I have in particular stories treads on his toes somewhat.

I probably should tell him where I went last night. Before DCI Ingham does. It will be better coming from me. But I look into his eyes and decide it can wait until he gets back. He's looking forward to some time with Alysha and I don't want to spoil it. Even if Ingham doesn't tell him, Will might. He didn't seem to see me but I'm certain that Ingham will have told him I was there. I've never heard of Will working outside traffic before – I'll have to ask Mark about it. Obviously I'll have to confess first.

After they have gone, I pull on skinny jeans and a long jumper before padding downstairs for a tea refill. I love lazy Sunday mornings. I flick the radio on and raise the kitchen blind to reveal the perfect morning beyond. Yes, it's cold, but snowdrops and crocuses are poking up in the back garden, so spring isn't that far away. It's a sight I love to see.

We are pretty much on countdown towards the wedding now. It's been great that since the new year, four weeks ago, I've been able to say *I'm getting married this year.* I'm going for my second dress fitting next month.

Steve Wright Sunday Love Songs plays its nostalgic opening tune. It's a tune that takes me back to childhood. It was always on at home when I was growing up. Dad once had a dedication played for Mum. She hasn't been able to bear listening to Steve Wright since Dad died. I fill a bowl with muesli, pour on milk, then settle at the table with my breakfast and my cup of tea.

This is the news at nine o'clock. We are just receiving reports that another body is being recovered from the River Alder in Alderton, Yorkshire. This is the seventh victim of this river since October of last year. We do not have any information to bring you at the moment, other than to confirm that the deceased is female, and is believed to have been in the water for several hours. We will bring you further information as we get it.

Oh my God. I abandon my breakfast and grab my phone from the kitchen counter behind me. I need to find out when she went in. Could it have been in that short time when I fell asleep? Or just after? Since the licensing laws changed a decade ago, the Yorkshire Arms seems to stay open for as long as everyone keeps ordering. The landlord likes a drink or ten, and since he lives above the pub, getting home isn't a problem for him. There's a DJ on in there once a month and the music doesn't stop until two am.

The only information coming through on-line is the same as what's been reported on Radio 2. I'll have a look on Facebook. Sure enough, on the 'our town' group, speculation is rife.

I think it might be a girl I work with, someone called Sue has posted. *We were in the Yorkshire Arms last night. It was a late Christmas do and our boss had given us a bar tab.*

I'm Gemma Hopkinson's husband, someone called Darren has replied. *I reported her missing just after three. Were you with her last night?*

Yes. The reply is posted straightaway. *I don't believe this. She left at about quarter to one. Said she was getting a taxi.*

Did you not think to check she'd got home safely?

I'm so sorry. We'd all had a lot to drink.

I can't believe I'm sat here, watching this get played out on Facebook. I type in. *I'm Lauren Holmes, journalist at the Press Association. Did Gemma leave the pub on her own?*

Yes.

I've been covering the story and my husband is an officer on the case. I'll get down there now and let you know what's going on.

I'll see you down there, says the husband.

I'll private message you my number, says Sue. *I'm probably still over the limit. I can't drive. God I can't believe this. I'm praying it isn't Gemma.*

The Facebook post is going to explode after this, but I'm not going to sit around watching it. Then I remember Mark's got the car. No! I hope my bike's OK to ride – I haven't had it out since last summer. I'm usually only a fair-weather cyclist. The tyres will definitely need pumping up.

I lurch around the garden shed and then around the kitchen, looking for things. As I try to locate the pump, I call the press office and hit the loudspeaker button. "I just thought I'd let you know," I say to Lindy as I point my feet into trainers and search for my cycle helmet. "I'm on my way down to the Yorkshire Arms. Woman number seven has died. I've just been speaking to her husband and friend on Facebook."

"Oh my God! Another one! It's bloody terrible. How on earth can anyone say that these are all accidents?" Lindy says. "I thought they'd put fencing up and all that. It's absolutely unbelievable!"

"There's definitely something going on, Lindy. I've said this since the first woman went in this winter." I spot my cycle helmet on top of the fridge. "Anyway, I was ringing to see if you'd be in this morning. I'm going to come straight in to the office after I've been down to the scene. I'm thinking of putting together a formal police complaint, but unsure how to go about it without rocking boats too much. I could do with your help."

"Yes. I'll start giving it some thought whilst I get myself sorted."

"There was someone hanging around the hairdressers yesterday too. I'm worried I'm being targeted now. And it's not the first time."

"You're joking. Have you let Mark know?"

"Not about yesterday. I forgot. We were having such a nice evening yesterday that I didn't want to put a dampener on it. But the police aren't doing enough Lindy. Despite what they say."

"They should be at the side of that river - morning, noon and night."

"Why isn't the area rammed full of CCTV as well? There are only two extra cameras up on poles. I've taken photos of them."

"The deaths are being covered by the nationals now, so we'll get on the ball with this."

"I'm just about to set off. I'll be in as soon as I can."

"Actually, I won't meet you at the office Lauren - I'll see you at the scene. How long will you be?"

"About half an hour. I just need to pump up my tyres."

"Shall I pick you up?"

"No, it's fine. By the time you get here and we get to the river and parked up, I'll be there."

After pumping up my tyres, I race back into the house to find my scarf and gloves. I discard my cycle helmet, opting for my woolly hat instead. The beautiful sunshine is deceiving. I'll freeze on my bike if I don't get wrapped up.

CHAPTER NINETEEN

Lauren

J ust as I'm walking through the hallway to the front door, the landline rings. I pause, debating whether I've got time to take it, especially since it's usually only salespeople or Mum that ever rings the landline. But something tells me I should.

"Is that Lauren Holmes?" The voice is female and uncertain.

"Yes. speaking." Mark always laughs at what he calls my telephone voice.

"Reporter Lauren? For the Associated Press?"

"Yes." I'm intrigued. "How can I help you?"

She seems to lower her voice. "I know something," she begins. "About the women who've drowned in the Alder." She doesn't sound like a crank. Her voice wobbles. "I've only just found out. I had to tell someone. And there's something else I need to talk to you about."

"What?"

"I need to see you in person."

"Why are you coming to me? Why not the police?"

"I can't. I'll explain. Everything. Can you meet me? I daren't say any more over the phone."

My heart is racing as I look for a pen. "Where do you want to meet? I was just on my way down to meet my colleague at the river. Another woman died last night."

"I know all about it. And all about something else you need to know. I'll meet you at the café down the road from there. The Green Teapot. I'll sit in the far right corner. How long?"

"My partner has the car. I'll have to cycle so it will take me longer to get there."

"How long will it take you?"

"Twenty minutes along the cycle path. I'll set off now."

"Please don't say anything. To anyone Lauren. Promise me."

"I won't. For now anyway. And beyond that, well, it depends on what you have to tell me."

Momentarily, I agonise about what I'm doing, briefly worrying that it is some kind of set up. It could be something to do with the man who's been watching me. But I shake the thought away, lock the house up and wheel my bike down the garden path. It crosses my mind that I should at least let Lindy know about the phone call and this meeting. There's no time though. I just need to get there. I'll get in touch with her then. The woman sounded genuine enough and clearly trusts me. And I'm meeting her in a very public place. God knows what she's going to tell me but it sounds significant.

I wave at my neighbour as I close my gate and set off down the hill. The cycle path to the city centre is quicker out of the traffic and the scenic route might calm me down. It runs between the train track and a stream. The cold air hits my face when I first set off, but before long I've warmed up and am wondering why I don't get my bike out more often. I feel like a teenager every time I ride it - young and liberated. It's something I could do with Alysha. There are lots of cycle routes around here.

I think of her and Mark and hope they're enjoying themselves. It's great that he's got contacts in the fire service to be able to take Alysha there. I wonder if he's heard about the latest fatality yet. It definitely sounds as though it is this Gemma woman who was out on a work's do. Especially if she was expected home and never made it. I shiver, despite the fact that I'm sweating under my jacket now.

I bet as she put on her makeup last night, blow dried her hair and chose what she was going to wear, that she didn't expect to drown in a dirty, freezing cold river a few hours later. Seven deaths spanning only months can't be a coincidence. And it looks like I might be about to make a breakthrough if the woman on the phone really has some information for me. I have always felt like sooner or later I would get to the bottom of it all.

Even if it comes to nothing, as a journalist, it's time for me, with Lindy's backing, to make some serious noise before this death toll gets into double figures. A campaign of some sort. There's seven families for a start who'll get behind me. Plus, I would imagine, many local women who will be scared of being out at night. There's the Police Complaints Commission too. But I'll have to talk to Mark first.

After all, it's his direct line manager, who's leading the investigation. He's full of white noise, and he's failed these women, blaming alcohol and the muddy riverbank. Personal difficulties or not, I'm going to make sure his head rolls. But I've got to try to protect Mark in all of this. I know to some extent he's between a rock and a hard place.

I really believe someone is hanging around down there – waiting for women who are leaving the pub on their own late at night. Who is it, and why? They must be taking them beyond the CCTV's range and pushing them in. There's no sign of physical or sexual attack though. None of it makes sense.

I pedal faster, knowing the woman who could make all the difference is waiting for me in the Green Teapot. Then I need to get to Lindy. I could just about get my head around the accident theory if it wasn't for knowing that I'm being watched lately. At first I thought I was imagining things. But I've seen someone, albeit hooded and at a distance, three times now.

I probably shouldn't be out like this on my own, on my bike. I could kick myself for not taking Lindy up on her offer of a lift. I try to shake the thought away. I'm beyond curious at what the woman on the phone is about to tell me and wonder again why she's come to me, and not the police. I guess I'll find out soon enough.

Gemma might have gone into that river last night, right under my nose – just yards from me. The thought makes me feel sick.

I can't believe I fell asleep. Unless it happened after I'd gone. No one was patrolling when I first got there, but obviously DCI Ingham had turned up later. There should be more than one officer on patrol though. If they need to go off to the loo or take any sort of break, then the area is left unsupervised. Maybe that's when the killer is going for it. It could even have happened before I got there. If I'd got out of my car, it could have been me. I shiver again.

As I get further along the cycle path, I'm struck by how quiet it is along here. The council could do with spending some money on chopping it back. The path itself is clear though. It's normally a popular dog walking route. Yet, this morning, it's deserted. I push on, feeling a little vulnerable. I should have probably gone the main road way. I wonder about turning back, but I'm well over the half-way point. And anyway, I haven't got time to go back now. I'm running late as it is after pumping my tyres up.

In the distance, I see movement in the long grass. Probably an animal of some sort. It's far enough away from the track for me to get past it, I think. I hope. My heart hammers inside my chest. *Why did I come this way?* I stare at the cloudless sky and think of Alysha and Mark, in a bid to quell my foreboding. In another five minutes, tops, I'll be back on the road. I'm nearing where I thought I saw movement. I see it again. Close now. It's not an animal. I pedal frantically. I'll get past.

There's no chance of keeping going as something hard and heavy is hurled at my front wheel. Instinctively, I brake to minimise the impact and skid to a stop. I scream as I'm suddenly yanked backwards from my bike and winded as my back connects heavily with the ground. My hat has slipped over my face and being winded, I struggle to sit up and uncover my eyes.

"No!" I whimper. "Please don't hurt me. I've got a little girl at home."

I sense my assailant is crouched behind me, gasping for a breath I try to stand as he suddenly wraps his arm around my throat. He doesn't speak. If I don't fight, I'm going to die. My body seems to have gone into shock. I've frozen. I've always said I'd kick anyone where it hurts in these circumstances, but this man's grip on me is rock solid. He's dragging me through the overgrown bushes and grass towards the stream. Adrenaline courses through me. I start kicking and thrashing around within his grasp. This will not be the day someone murders me.

"Help. Someone help me!" I'm shocked at the sudden power of my voice. *God please help me.* I silently pray a dog walker will materialise and come to my aid. "Help!" As the man clamps a hand over my mouth, I sink my teeth into it, tasting salt as his skin punctures. He yowls and momentarily lets me go. I attempt to scrabble to my feet but he's back on me, pinning me to the floor, still from behind. Maybe he wants to rape me. Being raped is better than being dead. I wriggle around beneath him, but he's too strong. I try to turn and look at him but he's got too tight a hold on the back of my neck. At least if he rapes me it might buy some time for someone to come along before he kills me.

I watch as his thin fingers curl themselves around a small rock to the side of my head. He's going to – I feel the weight come crashing down on my head, then again and again. I feel sick and dizzy as I realise I'm being dragged along the floor again. I can't move. I can't open my eyes. I choose to let my body go limp. Maybe he'll think I'm dead and leave me here. He grips the back of my neck and drags me further. Then I gasp at the ice cold water and realise my head is being immersed in the stream. He's going to drown me.

As I kick and splutter, his grip becomes tighter. I can feel the stones at the bottom of the stream crushing against my face. Images of Alysha and Mark seep into my mind. I'm never going to see them again. I'm going to miss Alysha growing up. I'm never going to get married. And my mum… I try to breathe and instead fill my chest with water. I feel like I'm going to explode. His grip on me loosens. All becomes silent and black.

PART TWO

CHAPTER TWENTY

Mark

I laugh at Alysha as we step into the hallway. "You can't still be hungry. Not after that massive piece of cake. Hang your coat up and see if Mummy will do you some lunch."

I've missed Lauren this morning, though it's been nice to spend time with Alysha. Will doesn't know what he's missing out on as a father. Eva's confided in me several times he does little with them these days. He's too busy doing overtime. I probably should have taken Heidi along with us this morning. She is my niece, after all and Eva often looks after Alysha. I slide my arms out of my coat and sling it over the bannister.

"I think Mummy's in the kitchen love. I can hear the radio. Probably why she's not heard us come in."

Alysha kicks her shoes off and runs into the kitchen. "Mummy, we've got some pictures to show..." She turns in the doorway and looks back to me. "Mummy's not here." She pushes the lounge door open. "Not here either."

"She'll be upstairs then. Let's go and find her. Lauren!" I begin up the stairs, Alysha is hot on my heels. "Mummy looked tired this morning. Maybe she's gone back to sleep." Together we look in all the rooms.

"She must have gone to work Daddy. You'll have to make my lunch instead." She grins at me.

I ruffle her hair. "Come on then. What would you like? A cauliflower sandwich?"

"Noooo!"

"Broccoli on toast?"

"Noooo!"

"Carrots and custard it is then."

"Noooo!"

I butter some bread and peel slices of bacon from the pack. I flick the kettle on before turning up the radio, to drown out the loud princess whatever music coming from the lounge. I'll let Alysha have half an hour, and certainly no more than an hour of TV. She'd watch it all day if we let her.

By then hopefully Lauren will be back and we can all go out together. I slide my phone from my jeans, surprised that she hasn't texted me to let me know where she's gone. I thought she was just having a quiet one at home whilst we were out.

We're back hon. Let me know what you're up to. Thought we could all do something nice this afty. Love you. Xx

I get the notification straight back to say it's delivered, but quarter of an hour later, Alysha and I have eaten our butties and Lauren hasn't responded. I'm always laughing at her for never being more than two seconds away from her phone. I guess we're all like that to some extent nowadays, but it's not like her not to reply straight away. It's not even as though she would be driving, as I've got the car. That's a good point. Where on earth is she?

As I stack plates and cups into the dishwasher, my attention is captured by the radio.

This is the BBC News at one. We can now bring you more information about reports of a seventh body that has been pulled from the River Alder in Yorkshire.

The victim is thirty-four-year-old Gemma Hopkinson, who was last seen by friends at 12:45 am. This latest death follows intense speculation that the multiple deaths, occurring in the last two months, are something other than accidental. So far police are attributing alcohol and wintery riverside conditions to the drownings, and have implemented extra safety measures. These measures include additional police patrols, extra lighting, and additional CCTV in and around the area.

The news moves onto the usual bolitics politics that's around at the moment, another MP and his mistress, instead of real political issues like police underfunding. I dry my hands and look at my phone again. *Why hasn't anyone let me know about this latest woman?* I'm supposed to be part of the investigation team, even if I'm not on duty until tomorrow. DCI Ingham is off as well today so it might be a Detective Inspector from another team that has stepped in this morning.

In any case, it explains why Lauren's not here, so I relax. I'm surprised she hasn't let me know about it though. No doubt, she'll have her journalist nose on, sniffing for sinister circumstances. I can see where she's coming from. Especially now. I couldn't so much at the start.

It is a lot of deaths. It's just that, as DCI Ingham has said, there's been no injuries and nothing at all to suggest anything other than *misadventure.*

Serves her right for being so smashed, he said after the third one. A young student, I think. DCI Ingham never touches a drop of alcohol, so has never been very understanding about those who do. I've always kept it quiet when I've gone in nursing a hangover. I wouldn't get much sympathy from him. He's lucky really that we have all cut him a bit of slack whilst he's been going through his split and everything.

Still, I thought his comment about the student was overly harsh. All I could think was it was someone's daughter or someone's sister. The other women are wives and mothers too. He can be heartless, Ingham. He's definitely not someone I'd socialise with. He has a very old-school way of policing. I mentioned it, in passing to Will, who said he agreed with DCI Ingham. I know Will's seen all sorts of alcohol-related stuff, especially in his job in traffic, but it shocked me when he sided with him.

DCI Ingham made similar comments about the next woman as well, something about police resources being wasted on women who can't control themselves. I had to speak up then – ask him to keep his comments to himself. He hadn't liked that. From being someone who was once supportive about helping me climb the ranks in the force, he became hostile and stopped giving me as much top level knowledge in conversations we had.

He acts like he cannot stand Lauren. He never passes up an opportunity to try to discredit her and her work, but then he's been funny with everyone lately. Luckily, I get on with everyone else I work with. But as my mum used to say when I was a kid, there'll always be someone, wherever you go in life, that you won't get along with.

Over the last couple of months I've stopped being one of the first to know what is going on, or even the second, which I should be as a sergeant. Instead, I become privy to things at the same time as the constables, sometimes even the Special Constables. Which is possibly why I'm finding out about this latest death, from Radio Two. I'm not impressed. And I'm more than anxious that Lauren's not been in touch about it. Nor has she texted back yet. I glance at my phone on the kitchen table and swipe at it before pressing Lauren. It just rings out. She must be busy. Now I know how she feels when I'm late back. And Eva. It must be worse for her, especially knowing that Will's often doing over a hundred, chasing after drunk and drugged up drivers speeding along the motorway.

I'm not sure what to do with myself. As I glance around the lounge door, I see Alysha is asleep, her arms around a cushion. I must have tired her out this morning. I smile as I go in and turn the TV down. Then, out of the corner of my eye, I notice a police car pull up next to our garden wall. It must be something to do with this latest death. They've probably come to pick me up. They're out of luck though, whilst I've got Alysha, unless I can get hold of Lauren. DI Jones and Chris Canvey, a fairly new PC, get out of the car and make their way up my drive. He's great is DI Jones. I've always got on with him.

"I don't know." I laugh as I swing the front door open. "Can't a man even have a Sunday off?"

I'm taken aback at their expressions. I've never seen Chris look so serious. He's normally a good laugh – he certainly was at our last work's do. To say he was new to our division, he soon came out of his shell after a few pints.

"Can we come in Mark?" DI Jones steps towards me.

"Course you can. Come through to the kitchen mate." I beckon towards the lounge door. "We can't go in there. My daughter is wacked after a morning at the fire station and has fallen asleep." I turn to them as I open the kitchen door. "Lauren's out so I'll be glad of some sensible adult conversation. Or is it about the latest death at the river?"

They follow me into the kitchen, not saying a word. They're making me nervous. "Am I in trouble or something? Has Lauren been writing something she shouldn't have?"

They look at each other, still not speaking. They're really making me nervous now.

"Take a seat." I flick the radio's off switch. "Can I get either of you a brew? The kettle's just boiled."

"I wish this was a social call Mark," DI Jones begins, looking down at his hands. "Is anyone else here with you or is it just you and your daughter?"

"Well, I've been trying to get hold of Lauren. She should be back soon." I study their grave faces. "What is it?"

"Can you get someone else to be here with you?"

"Lauren's Mum, I guess, or my sister. But like I say, Lauren shouldn't be long. I'm not sure where she is though. Anyway, tell me what's wrong. I don't want to wait until someone else gets here. I need to know."

DI Jones squints in the sunshine, which bleeds through the blinds. "We've got some dreadful news, I'm afraid Mark."

Chris moves the chair he's sat on, next to mine and places a hand on my arm.

"This isn't about the woman you've pulled from the river, is it?" I'm confused. Obviously it's not Lauren. She was in bed with me last night and I brought her a cup of tea this morning. "What is it?" I think of my sister, then my brother's wife, Eva, then my mother-in-law flashes through my mind. It's not them though. They've already named the woman who drowned last night. So what is it? Could something be up with my mum? But she doesn't live around here.

"We've found a body," DI Jones begins, his words slicing into my jumbled thoughts. "We were alerted by a dog walker. We got a report of a woman who had been assaulted on the cycle path which runs into town. Her injuries suggest she'd been beaten around the head and held in the stream until she drowned."

"Drowned?" I stare at them. Another death. Is that eight now? Who? A multitude of possibilities cascade through my mind. "Do I know her?"

Chris swallows. They look at each other again. *No! No!* I scream silently inside my head. I don't want them to say what they're about to tell me. I can already read it on their faces. They're not going to say it. I'm not going to let them.

CHAPTER TWENTY ONE

D I Jones's voice is soft as he looks at me. "It's Lauren, Mark. I'm so very, very sorry."

"No. No. It can't be. There's a mistake. There has to be. I only saw her a few hours ago. She'll be home soon."

"I'm so sorry Mark. I'd give anything for it not to be her."

"It's not her. There's no way. I'll ring her now. You'll see."

"Obviously we need you to formally identify her," DI Jones adds. "But we've no doubt it's her. Her rucksack was on the ground near her bike."

"It can't be her." I straighten up in my seat. "It must be someone who looks like her. She never rides her bike when it's cold. She's a right wimp. If you check, you'll find she's at her mum's or something."

"It's her rucksack," DI Jones repeats. "It had her phone and her identification inside."

"Someone must have taken it. Or she might have lost it and they were returning it for her." I rise from my chair. "I'm going to check the shed now for her bike."

"Mark. I've seen her body myself. We would tell you if we weren't sure." Chris puts his hand on my shoulder. "Is there someone we can contact? You can't be here on your own."

With trembling hands, I use my thumb to unlock my contacts, I slide the phone across the table towards him. "My sister, Claire."

"Is she local?"

I nod. *It can't be Lauren.* There has to be some mistake.

Chris presses the screen and raises the phone to his ear. I sit staring at the table. I feel as though I'm having an out of body experience. In a moment, I'll wake up in bed with Lauren's long legs wrapped around me. She always warms her feet on me in winter. It should annoy me but I find it endearing, really.

"No, it's not Mark. I'm just using his phone," Chris says after a few moments. "I'm PC Chris Canvey, I work with Mark. I'm with him now. Is this Claire, his sister?"

I can hear her voice on the other end of the phone in the silence of the kitchen. "Yes. Is everything alright?"

"I'm afraid not. Can you come over to your brother's house straightaway?"

"What's up? Is he there? Mark, I mean?" I can hear the panic in her voice. "Can I speak to him?"

"How long will it take you to get here?" Chris asks. I understand why he can't tell her anything yet. Not when she's about to drive. Tears are cascading down my face and dripping off the end of my nose. I never cry. I think the last time was when Alysha was born.

"Tell me what's the matter." Claire's tone is more urgent now.

"I can't, I'm afraid. Not over the phone."

"Is Mark alright?"

"It's Lauren," I call out, surprised at the voice that no longer sounds like mine. "Just get here sis."

"I'm on my way," I hear her say.

"Lauren's mum, Brenda," I whisper. "Has anyone spoken to her? She needs to know what you think you've found."

"We haven't told her yet." Chris passes the phone back to me. "We obviously needed to speak to you first."

"When did you find this person who you *think* is Lauren?"

"About an hour and a half ago. We don't think she'd been there very long."

I wretch as the bacon sandwich decides to make a reappearance. I lurch to the kitchen sink just in time to puke my guts up. "She can't be dead." I howl in anguish as I wash it all down the sink. "We're getting married soon. We've got a little girl asleep in there." I can't get my words out. I can barely breathe.

DI Jones comes up behind me and puts his hands on my shoulders. "I know, I know. Come and sit down."

"She's been taken to the hospital mortuary to be examined by the police pathologist." Chris says gently, looking as though he's going to cry too. "Our priority now is to catch the bastard who did this to her."

I drop my head into my hands and close my eyes. This really can't be happening. I think of Alysha, sleeping in the next room. "What the hell am I going to tell my daughter?" Tears are dripping all over the table and my shoulders are shaking. "What am I going to do?"

"You'll have all the support in the world from the force," DI Jones lets a long breath out. "For now, just take things one moment at a time. When you're ready, we'll need to ask you a few questions, but there's no rush."

"Her mother needs to know." I raise my eyes from the table towards DI Jones. "She's going to be absolutely devastated."

"Where does she live?"

"Not far away. A ten minute drive."

"Do you want to tell her yourself?"

"I can't do it. I just can't."

"What about her dad?"

"He's dead."

"Any brothers or sisters?"

I shake my head, sobbing harder. "She's an only child. Her mother. It's going to kill her."

"If you give us the address," DI Jones says. "We'll drive round. Shall we bring her back here?"

I can't think straight. "You're asking me too many questions. I don't know what to do." My voice is a wail. I need to keep it down. Alysha has to stay asleep. Oblivious for now.

"We won't go anywhere until your sister gets here," Chris says. "Is there someone who can take care of your daughter today? Give you a chance to process things before you tell her?"

I think for a moment. "I'll get Claire to sort something out," I say. "My brother and his wife might come for her. Whilst I work out how I'm going to tell her. How on earth do you tell a five-year-old that her mother has been murdered?"

"If that's what it is," DI Jones replies. "It's looking like murder, but the post-mortem could reveal something else."

"Like what?"

I hear car doors bang outside, then footsteps in the hallway. Claire and my brother walk into the kitchen. "I picked Will up," Claire says. "It sounded serious."

"So what happened?" Will sits at the table in between DI Jones and Chris. Even though he's in traffic, they all cross paths now and then. As my older brother, I'm sure he'll step up for a change and take control of the situation for me. He'll flag up the huge mistake they've made. It won't be Lauren. She's too savvy to go and get herself *murdered*.

"I'm afraid we've found Lauren's body on the cycle path by the stream." DI Jones looks from Will to Claire. "It appears she's been the victim of a dreadful assault."

"Body! You mean she's…" Claire stiffens and looks at me in horror.

I rise from my chair and fling myself at her, sobbing into her shoulder. Now that my sister's here, I have someone to lean on. I can fall to pieces.

"When? How?" Will stares at DI Jones. I'm not sure why Claire brought him. He's made no secret of not being overly keen on Lauren and had started making excuses why he couldn't make the wedding. But still, he's my brother, and I need him to sort this out. His face twists into an expression I remember from years ago. "Are you sure it's her?"

DI Jones nods as he pushes the kitchen chair back with a scrape. He tilts his head towards Chris. "We've seen her ourselves. I'm so sorry to have to bring this news to you all. We'll be back shortly. We're going to have to let Lauren's mum know."

"Bring her back with you." I raise my head from my sister's shoulder and step back. "She can't be on her own at a time like this." Lauren would want me to look after her. Even if I can't think straight enough to look after myself at the moment.

"Where's Alysha?" Will asks.

"Sleeping in the lounge," DI Jones replies.

"She could wake up at any moment." Fresh tears leak from my eyes as I contemplate telling her. The thought then crosses my mind that if I hadn't taken her to the fire station today, she would have been with Lauren instead. And so would I, and it would never have happened.

"Why don't I drop her off with Eva?" Will stands. "You need to let things sink in."

I know he's making sense. Her cousin Heidi is two years older and they adore each other. "But what if she hears what's happened some other way?"

"I'll ask Eva to keep an eye on her and Heidi. No internet. No radio. She's better off out of this."

"He's right Mark." Chris joins DI Jones at the door. "You need looking after first. We'll be back soon."

"Here." Claire slides a tumbler of something or other in front of me. "Get that down you. You're in shock." Then she disappears upstairs to get a bag ready for Alysha whilst I sit at the kitchen table, shivering.

"Shock isn't the word," I say through chattering teeth to Will. "It doesn't feel real." I sniff it, then neck the brandy in one, feeling immediately nauseous but then warmed inside. I can't breathe for a few seconds, wondering whether the brandy is going to come back up again.

"It won't sink in for a while."

"I'm convinced they've made a mistake. Until I see her with my own eyes."

"I'll see how Claire's getting on." Will strides to the kitchen door. "She can wait with you whilst I drop Alysha off. Then I'll be straight back to go with you."

"Go with me? Where?"

"To identify Lauren."

To identify Lauren. No, this is not happening. It can't be.

Claire comes back into the kitchen and squeezes Will's arm as she passes him. She sits in front of me and picks up her glass of brandy.

"You promise Eva won't say anything to Alysha?" I say as he opens the kitchen door. "It has to come from me."

"Of course. We'll take good care of her."

"I don't want to see Alysha before you go. I'll break down, I know I will. Just tell her I've had to go to work. Don't let her come in here."

CHAPTER TWENTY TWO

B renda's voice in the hallway reassures me in a strange sort of way. "What is it? What aren't you telling me?" She sounds like an older Lauren. She's always sorted us out. Me and Lauren. Silly arguments, worries about big bills, times when Alysha has been poorly. Maybe she can sort this one out too. Help unravel this awful mistake that has been made.

I stiffen as the lounge door opens. We've reconvened in here now Alysha has gone with Will. The news Brenda is about to hear can only come from me. I would give anything not to have to impart it. Anything.

"Sit down Brenda," I say, with a calmness I don't feel. I'm going to be the one to blow her world apart. I don't know if she is strong enough to take this.

"What's happened? Where's Lauren? And Alysha? Have they gone out? Why have the police picked me up? What on earth's going on?"

"Brenda, we've had some news that I don't believe myself yet…"

"What?" She stares at me. "What is it Mark? Is Lauren alright?"

"I'm afraid not." I can't tell her. I can't say the words. "She's…"

"What! Where is she?"

I should just leave her in blissful ignorance, like I'm trying to do with Alysha. Instead, I can't speak, and the sobs break out of me with a force I never knew existed.

"They're saying she's dead," Claire steps towards Brenda. "Someone has attacked her."

"Dead!" For a few moments, all is silent. Then a wail rips through the room like I've never heard in my life. "My Lauren," she shrieks. "No, no, no, no, no, no!" Claire catches her as she slumps against the wall, looking as though she might faint. "She was only on the phone to me yesterday. There has to be some mistake."

"I can't see her. I just can't." Brenda's wails pierce the air. It will be a relief in a way to leave the house – the pain of a mother who has just been told that her only child has been murdered is agonising to see, and I can't deal with it.

Claire rushes towards her and envelops her in a hug. "No one expects you to Brenda." She turns to me. "Are you sure you can do this Mark?"

"I'm going to have to. Can you come with me?" Claire's the only person capable of holding me together when I'm falling apart.

"I think I should stay with Brenda." She looks pointedly at Will, who's just returned. "You can go with Mark, can't you?"

"I can't," he replies. "It would be better if you did."

They argue back and forth over who's not going to come with me for several moments until I snap. "It's fine. I'll go alone."

"You will not." Claire nudges Will. "I'm best staying with Brenda, Will, *you* need to support our brother. It's not as if anyone ever asks much of you."

"Fine," he concedes. Really, I'd rather he didn't bother, but arguing with Claire is pointless.

"It feels strange travelling in the back of a police car," says Will. "And so slowly. I'm normally chasing some crank up the M62."

DI Jones and Chris don't respond. They both just stare ahead. I glance at my brother. How dare he try and make small talk at a time like this? He witters away some more – he always does when he's feeling nervous about something. He's doing my head in.

But I'm in no fit state to drive, so I have little choice other than to be driven there. At least, according to Will, Alysha is none the wiser about what's happened. I want it keeping that way for as long as possible. She was surprised at being awoken and then dropped off to play with her cousin apparently, but she's fairly used to Lauren and me both having to work at the drop of a hat.

If only I could allow her to stay in her little bubble of normality. Life as we knew it is over. Fresh tears roll down my cheeks as I realise Lauren's not going to walk towards me in her wedding dress, she's never going to become Mrs Potts and baby number two will never be born. Some sicko has brutally taken her life and when I find out who it is, I'll...

My brother doesn't seem able to sit still. He winds the window down, then up again. He takes his phone out, then puts it away again. He sighs. He looks at me, then looks away. Takes his phone out again. Jiggles his leg up and down in a way that makes me feel like smacking him. His voice cuts into silence. "We're here."

"I can see that."

"God this is going to be grim," he says. "I've seen plenty of injury and death whilst I'm working, but this will be something else."

"Shut up Will. Try to find a little sensitivity, can't you?" He's always been the same.

We walk in behind DI Jones and Chris towards the reception desk. I'm taken aback at how the world seems to be going on as normal. I even hear someone laugh. I want to shout at them. *How dare you laugh? My fiancée has been murdered. Don't you know what I'm going through?* We're asked to take a seat and wait for the mortuary technician.

"Do you want some tea, Mark?"

I shake my head. "Tea? Maybe another brandy."

I stare at the TV screen fastened to the wall. Sky news. The newsreel pans across the bottom of the screen. *Double Yorkshire tragedy in Alderton. Seventh victim pulled from the River Alder. Dog walker finds beaten and drowned body in a stream a short distance from the River Alder. The deaths are not thought to be connected.* I sit, silently watching it as it pans along the bottom of the screen once again. The shrill ringing of a phone startles me. Will too. He jumps up as he pulls a nineties looking Nokia from his pocket, and springs away from our group.

"Mark Potts." I jump at the sound of my name. "I'm Kevin Sanderson, the duty mortuary technician." He stands before me, dressed from head to foot in blue, looking more like a porter. "I understand you're here to formally identify the body of your fiancée before we begin the post-mortem process. You're on her records as her next of kin."

"That's right." My voice sounds strangely calm. "There's no one else anyway. To identify her, I mean. Only her mother. And she's distraught. My sister's looking after her." I look around for Will. He's still on the phone and seems to be having a very heated conversation.

"If you'd like to follow me." We all walk behind him, in silence for several minutes until we reach the sign saying Mortuary. I've been in here on police business on several occasions. This is surreal. I keep thinking I'm somehow imagining or dreaming what is going on right now. Will suddenly appears. I'm relieved. I can't do this on my own.

"Who were you speaking to?"

"Just something to do with work. They've got my money wrong."

"What's with the phone?" I can't believe I'm having a normal conversation.

"It's an old one. Just while I get my screen fixed."

The technician rings the doorbell. "Come in," a shrill voice instructs over the intercom and a buzzer sounds. We all file in and drop to seats in the dimly lit waiting room. Before long, a woman dressed in normal clothes has joined us.

"I'm sorry you're having to go through this." She says after the introductions have been made.

"We just need you to look at the lady we believe is Lauren," DI Jones adds, "and confirm whether it is her or not."

I'm still clinging to the hope that it won't be. That she'll be holed up in some café somewhere, bashing out an article or out shopping with a girlfriend, having lost track of time. No way am I about to see my beautiful, fun-loving, full-of-life Lauren, laid out on a mortuary slab.

"Then I'll need to ask you a few questions," DI Jones says. "If you confirm it *is* Lauren, that is."

"When you're ready." The woman beckons to a door. "If you go through that door and then through the door facing you, you'll be able to view through the window. Take your time. There's absolutely no rush."

"I'm going to wait here Mark," Will says.

"I thought you were going to come in with me?" Typical Will. Right at the last minute, he lets me down.

"I'll be with you," DI Jones says. "You're not on your own."

"Right, let's get on with it then." My heart is thumping as I stand and walk towards the door. Slowly, I reach for the handle, then turn to DI Jones. "I can't do this."

"We've got you." He puts his hand on my shoulder.

As soon as I see her through the window, I have to turn and barge past the woman and DI Jones. I get to the visitor toilet in time to barf again. The brandy burns my throat as it comes back up. I try to compose myself so I can go back into the room. Tears are flowing down my face again. I didn't think I could cry this hard.

Chris and DI Jones stand together, waiting for me by the window. After a moment, I force myself to look. Lauren's covered up to her neck with a sheet. Some of the blood's been wiped away, but I can see the back of her head is matted with it. Her lips are blue with a trace of froth around them.

"She only had her hair done yesterday," I remark. Don't we say the daftest things sometimes? "I told her it looked nice. Thank God I did. I don't usually notice."

DI Jones points at the window. "Is the person on the other side of this window, Lauren Frances Holmes, your fiancée?"

"Yes." My voice sounds as though it belongs to someone else. "It's Lauren."

"I'm so sorry Mark." Chris's voice is deafening in the quiet room.

All is quiet between us for several moments. I keep expecting her to sit up and laugh at us for being so serious. Tell us it's all been a big joke. I can't take my eyes off her. This might be the last time I'm ever going to see her face. In the soft lighting, it looks like she still has colour in her cheeks. What am I going to say to

Alysha? My life feels as over as Lauren's is. I want to go with her. Who the hell has done this to her?

"Can I sit with her? I mean, in the room?"

"I'm afraid not Mark." DI Jones's voice is soft in the stillness. "She's yet to have a post-mortem examination. Then you'll be able to sit with her."

"Who the hell has done this to her?" I echo my thoughts.

"That's what we intend to find out," DI Jones replies. "Mark, I know it's awful timing, but are you up to answering just a few questions? Nothing heavy or formal. We could just sit in the hospital foyer."

"Well, I've nothing else to do, have I? Apart from drive myself insane with grief. Though I don't know how anything I might say could point you in the right direction."

DI Jones buzzes for us to be let out.

"I need some air." I stride ahead of the others towards the exit. "Or else I'll be sick again."

I flop onto a bench outside the revolving doors, watching as people come in and go out. People going about their normal business, visiting loved ones, being able to spend time with them. Perhaps getting the chance to say goodbye. Lauren is dead. I absolutely can't believe it.

A few minutes pass before the others come through the revolving doors. Will hands me a cold bottle of water, which I gratefully take a large glug from. He sits beside me, and DI Jones and Chris sit on the bench facing ours. DI Jones pulls a notepad and pen from his top pocket.

"OK Mark," he says. "Just answer everything as best you can. Then we can get on with finding whoever did this. So firstly, what time did you last see Lauren?"

"Just before nine o'clock this morning. At home. I left her in bed after taking her a cup of tea. Then I went out. With our daughter."

"Can anyone verify this?"

"Why? I'm not under suspicion, am I?"

"Of course not," DI Jones says gently. "But you know we have to ask."

"Half of Alderton Fire Service saw me – I'd arranged to take Alysha there to see the fire engines – she had a ride on one. Then there was the lady in Bridge Café. We went in there for breakfast. I wanted to give Lauren a morning to herself. She seemed really tired."

"Did you see anyone else?"

"Only Lauren. Before I left, I mean."

"Do you know what her plans were this morning?"

"Just to stay at home and blob out, as far as I knew. She often enjoys spending family time on a Sunday. That's what I thought we were going to do when I got back home with Alysha."

"Do you know of any friends she might have decided to visit?"

"She's got several friends. And if she'd arranged anything, she never mentioned it. But then, she doesn't always."

"We'll be checking her phone for calls and messages."

"Have you got it?"

"Yes. It was in her rucksack. And we'll need her laptop too. It's just a formality, as you know. I'll get you to sign for everything. And we'll return it as quickly as we can." He clears his throat. "Do you know whether Lauren had any enemies?"

"She wouldn't hurt a fly."

"Is there anything she might have been involved with?" he continues. "A situation where she might have rubbed someone up the wrong way?"

I think of her work. "Nothing out of the ordinary. The main thing she was working on was the river deaths. So no."

DI Jones writes something in his notebook. "We'll be speaking to her employers. The Press Association is the main one, isn't it?"

"She's actually freelance, so they're not her employers. But they're the people who pay her most for her work."

"She was good at her job, wasn't she?" Chris's face relaxes into a smile. "I've seen her in action a few times since I started this job."

"Haven't we all?" There's an edge to Will's voice which I ignore. I have not got the energy to lock horns with him.

I think of Lauren in action. A formidable sight. And I'm never going to see it again. "I can't imagine who could have got the better of her. It's not that long since she went on a self-defence course."

"Do you know of anyone she might have spoken to or involved in her plans over the last few days?"

"She never said anything to me. There's her best friend Sara though – I think she's had lunch with her recently. And then there's her mum. And she went to get her hair done yesterday."

"Do you know where?"

"It's somewhere on the main street. She's been going there for years."

"That shouldn't be too hard to pin down. Get in touch if you think of anything else that might be relevant."

"I just want to get my hands on the bastard who did this to her. We will get him, won't we?"

"Of course we will."

Throughout the conversation with DI Jones, I realised I've spoken about Lauren as though she is still here. As though I'm going back home to her. Suddenly I gasp as I duck into the back of the police car, it hits me like an iron fist twisting my guts. This is really happening. The woman I love has gone forever.

"You OK? You're not going to puke again, are you?" Will looks at me as we make the short journey back home. Home. What is home ever going to be now?

"I just can't believe it. None of it seems real. I can't get that image of her just now, out of my head."

"I'm sorry I couldn't come in with you. It's just..." He does actually look genuinely apologetic.

"It's fine. Without having seen her there, I would never have accepted she was dead. God, what I'd give to turn the clock back a few hours." We pass the bridge crossing the river deaths spot. There's a collection of flowers building for the woman who drowned there last night. I think of the other family going through the same thing we are.

I wonder if flowers will be laid for Lauren. I'll have to take some. I need to see where it happened and what is being done. But that can wait until tomorrow. I want to get back and see Brenda. The only family Lauren had apart from us. Then I must tell Alysha.

Brenda darts from the lounge as I enter the house. "Tell me it's not her Mark." Her face looks raw with crying.

I see Lauren in her face more now than ever before as I shake my head. "I wish, more than anything, that I could tell you that." I fall into her arms and cry with her. "What are we going to do?"

"I don't know." Her voice is a squeak in the hallway. Claire comes out of the lounge and puts her arms around both of us.

"I'll put the kettle on." Will strides past us. "Make myself useful."

DI Jones and Chris don't stay long. They have a look around the house then, seemingly satisfied, take Lauren's laptop with them.

Saying he has a shift tomorrow and refusing to cancel it, Will returns home. The three of us spend the rest of the day barely able to move. Crying. Speculating. Forcing a sandwich down. Thinking. Crying some more. Necking an occasional brandy. In the end, it's the brandy that helps me to sleep for a few hours. Brenda resorts to a sleeping tablet.

CHAPTER TWENTY THREE

I slide my hand across the mattress towards Lauren. We never wear anything in bed, preferring to sleep skin to skin. I always sleep well when she's beside me. I reach to draw her into my arms, then it hits me like a train.

She's dead. I identified her body yesterday. Someone attacked and drowned her. A sob gathers in my throat as I sit up in the darkness, the light from the en-suite partially lighting up the bedroom. The towel she used yesterday is in a heap on the floor and her dressing gown hangs on the back of the door. I look at my watch. 6:07 am. This time yesterday we were curled up together. Tears leak from my eyes and run down the sides of my head. I can't just lie here. I've never felt pain like it in my life.

If I could have only known what was going to happen. Was she targeted? Or was it a random attack? I have to know. But first, I need to tell Alysha before she finds out another way. Lauren's death has been reported in the news, but today they will actually name and show photos of her in an attempt to bring witnesses forward. I think of Alysha, in my brother's spare room, sleeping in still blissful ignorance. And I'm soon to go around there and ruin her life.

Eva pulls me in for a hug as soon as I walk in. It's only 8 o'clock. The sleeping tablet must have completely knocked Brenda out, so I've left her sleeping. "I can't believe it Mark. I just can't believe it. How are you doing?"

"It hasn't sunk in properly yet," I reply as fresh tears bubble up. "I don't know if it ever will."

"You must be devastated. I'm devastated for you."

"Where's Will?"

"Where do you think? I did ask him to take the day off."

"I guess carrying on as normal is his way of dealing with things."

"It doesn't make it the right way, though."

"Alysha doesn't know anything yet, does she? It's news she should only hear from me."

"I agree. No, she doesn't know a thing. It was difficult to act normal yesterday after I found out. I barely stopped crying all day and had to tell the girls I was full of cold to explain my red eyes." Eva relaxes her hold on me. "It's all starting to come through on the news now, so you do need to tell her."

"I'll go up now. Oh God Eva. What the hell am I going to say? How can I tell her she's never going to see her mummy again?"

"Do you want me to come up with you?"

"Thanks. But no. This should just be me and her."

"Just be honest with her Mark. And don't try to hold it all together. It's OK to cry in front of her."

I stare at Alysha for a few moments, knowing that as soon as I wake her, I'm going to shatter her world as she knows it. She looks peaceful and content with her arms around a borrowed teddy bear.

This is a conversation no father and daughter should ever have to have.

"Alysha, wake up, it's Daddy." I sit on the edge of the bed beside her after gently shaking her arm.

"Huh. Is it school time?"

"No, not today."

She sits up. "But it's Monday." She looks around the bedroom. "Why did I sleep here all night?"

"Alysha." I take her hands in mine. "I've got something really terrible to tell you."

She rubs her eyes and looks at me, wide-eyed now.

"It's Mummy." I tighten my grip on her hands.

"Where is she?"

I swallow. As soon as the words leave me, there will be no taking them back. "Alysha. Mummy. She's…" I can't say it. I just can't say it.

"Where is she Daddy?"

The earnestness in her voice breaks my heart. I've just got to say it. "I'm afraid she's died sweetheart. She's gone to heaven."

She frowns, looking like Lauren. "When is she coming back? Will she pick me up from school?"

"No Alysha. When people die, they go forever."

"How did she get there?"

"She was very badly hurt yesterday. When she went out on her bike." I can't tell her the exact truth. Not yet.

"I want to go and see her." Alysha swings her legs out of bed. "Where are my clothes? We'll bring her back."

"Come here." I scoop her onto my knee. "Daddy needs a big cuddle and I'm sure Alysha does too. We've got to look after each other."

"But I want Mummy to look after me too. When can I talk to her?"

"I'm not sure she understands," I say to Eva when I go back downstairs. "She's getting dressed."

"It's a lot for a five-year-old to take in." Eva passes me a cup of coffee. "Do you want to leave her with me again today? You're not going to be able to do much with her, you need to look after yourself."

"I know, but it should be me, looking after her."

"Mark. I'm her auntie. She'll be fine with me and Heidi. It's probably for the best to keep some sense of normality for her. It's going to be anything but normal at your house."

Guilt tugs at my belly, but I know she's right. "Are you sure you're alright with that?"

"I'll let Heidi stay off school too. Try to give them as nice a day as possible. I'll keep talking to her about Lauren – perhaps I could find a book in the library about losing someone."

"I really appreciate this Eva." Heat prickles at the back of my eyes again as I sink into a chair. "I don't know what I'm going to do."

"Just keep breathing and putting one foot in front of the other."

"But I don't want to do that without Lauren. I don't want to do anything without her."

The car is littered with Lauren's hair grips and crisp packets, and her jacket is still on the back seat where it was thrown. I can almost smell her in here and I can't cope. I don't know if I can do this. If it wasn't for Alysha, I would tie rocks to my feet and jump in that bloody river myself. Be with Lauren. Together forever. Like we were supposed to be.

As I reverse out of Eva and Will's drive, the local news comes on the radio.

The woman whose body was discovered on the Alderway cycle path yesterday has been named as local woman and mother of one, Lauren Holmes. She was thirty-two and worked as a freelance journalist. Miss Holmes is thought to have been cycling along the path when she was grabbed and attacked by someone lying in wait. It is not yet known whether she was targeted or if she was a victim of circumstance.

Anyone with any information is asked to contact police on 101, quoting reference 1402. We will bring you more as we get it, but women are once again being urged to take extra care until the assailant is found.

I arrive back home, relieved when I see my sister's car, glad that she's still here. I couldn't face an empty house. No way. Before I get out of the car, I pull my phone from the glove box, ignoring Lauren's notebook which falls out with it. I'll look at it later. I can't bear to see words she has written.

I've got several Facebook notifications.

Lindy Taylor *Mark. I can't believe it. I want to help you catch whoever did this. Get in touch as soon as you're up to it.*

Sara Hollins *I've just heard the news. Please tell me they've made a mistake.*

Amanda Johnson *Mark, we haven't met. I'm Lauren's hairdresser. I only saw her on Saturday. I'm so, so sorry. Please let me know if there's anything I can do.*

I'll look at the rest of them later. I can't face them right now. I check the texts from DI Jones and Chris.

Again – I'm sorry mate. Hope you're being well looked after. Take as much time off as you need and I'll be in touch later.

How are you doing this morning? We're doing some house to house today. I'll keep you informed.

I slip the phone into my pocket. I'm aware that messages and support might be the thing that keeps me going through this. And Alysha. It's going to be a long, long road.

"Have you eaten?" Claire's buttering toast as I walk into the kitchen.

"I'll try to get a slice down." My stomach is churning, but I know I'm going to make myself ill if I don't look after myself. Plus, I've got Alysha to think of. "Is Brenda still about?"

"She took a taxi home to get some things. I'd have taken her but wanted to be here when you came back." Claire says. "She won't be long."

"How is she?"

"The poor love's barely stopped crying. I heard her up and down, out of bed all night. She said even the sleeping tablet couldn't knock her out properly. You seem to be holding up OK Mark. I'm proud of you."

"Appearances can be deceiving. I'm all over the place inside."

"I'm here for you. I'm not going anywhere. I'll stay here as long as you want me to."

"I appreciate it sis." Thank God I've got Claire. If Will had been my only sibling, I'd be in trouble right now. I don't often think about him, but my other older brother Dean enters my head. I remember feeling the pain when he was killed. But it was nothing like this.

"How did Alysha take it? That is where you've been?"

"Yeah. I don't think she really understands. She seems to think heaven is a party or something. How can a five-year-old understand that she's never going to see her mother again? Especially when she only saw her yesterday."

CHAPTER TWENTY FOUR

B renda looks dreadful when she returns. As soon as she sees me, tears stream from her eyes. Her road will be as long as mine. In fact, I don't think either of us could ever reach the end.

After Brenda has been back for an hour, the house feels like it's shrinking around me. If I don't get out of here, it's going to crush me within it. And if I'm honest, I'm struggling to manage Brenda's grief alongside my own. Claire offers to come with me but I need some space. If I'm on my own, I can be with Lauren. In my head, anyway.

I decide to retrace the route that Lauren made yesterday. I tug my bike from the shed and set off in the direction of the cycle path. It's unthinkable that twenty-four hours ago, she was riding up this same path. We used to enjoy it together in the summer. I always cycled behind so I could look at her bum and made sure to tell her that. She'd try to act all indignant, but secretly she liked it. I enjoyed watching her long hair billow out behind her. What I wouldn't give to be following her now. I really don't know how

I'm going to get through this. She fills my every thought and every fibre of my being.

I've been in the force since my early twenties, but approaching the cordon and seeing the two white tents engulfs me in shock. There's a forensic expert, laying and lifting markers whilst taking photographs. "Stay where you are," she orders me as I'm about to duck under the cordon.

"I'm Sergeant Potts." I pull my ID from my coat. "I'm the victim's fiancé."

"Then you should know better than anyone that you can't come in here." She nods to the police officer who is stood a few yards away, at the other side of the cordon.

"Did you say you're her fiancé?" He approaches me. I don't recognise him.

"Yes. Mark Potts. Have they got anything yet on the bastard who did this to her?"

"DI Jones is leading the inquiry. You'll have to ask him." He holds his hand out. "PC Ryder. I'm new. Scott. I'm sorry for your loss. It's bloody awful."

His words swim in the air as I look all around where I am stood. This time yesterday she was still alive. If only I hadn't gone out. I stare at the tent that's over and around the stream. Where some evil nutcase held her head underwater. She had said recently that drowning must be the worst way to die. She'll have fought to the end, my Lauren. I know she would have. It would have taken some strength to overpower her.

"Thanks."

I continue on to the press office, wondering if this is where Lauren was heading yesterday. Perhaps she'd found out about the latest river death beforehand – was that why she was going into work?

It's the first question I ask Lindy as she ushers me into a side office. I brush off her hug and ignore her tears as we sit facing each other.

"We were meeting at the river." She wipes her cheeks with her hand. "You know Lauren. She wanted to cover the story from the sharp edge and get some photos. Her mission had become to prove someone had pushed or chucked those women in."

"I can't even think about the river deaths at the moment. Who has done this to her?" I let a long sigh out as I fight my own tears. This was Lauren's domain. She was passionate about her job and once told me about the excited buzz of energy she felt all around her when here, in the press office. She had told me loads of times how lucky she felt to be doing the job she loved.

"When I tell you what I've got to tell you," Lindy says. "You'll probably agree that Lauren's death is connected to the river deaths."

"Whatever you're going to say isn't going to bring her back though, is it?"

"I'd do anything if I could," Lindy says softly. "It's such a waste."

"So what is it you wanted to tell me?" I ask.

"I've had a lady called Amanda on the phone this morning. Lauren's hairdresser. Lauren was there on Saturday."

"I know."

"There was apparently a man hanging about whilst Lauren and Alysha were there."

A cold hand of fear grips my throat. Thoughts whirl. Why hadn't she said something? Is Alysha in danger too? My fear turns to dread. Between us all, we mustn't let Alysha out of our sight. "What's the name of the hairdressers?"

"*Tangled*, I think. But that's not all. Lauren told Amanda that there was a man hanging around the bridal shop when she was there last week and again when she was in a café with one of her friends last month. She said that Lauren seemed unnerved by it all when she was there on Saturday. She actually gave Lauren and Alysha a lift back to their car. It was only parked at the end of the street."

"It's not like Lauren to not have mentioned it to me. I knew about the bridal shop incident but not the café or the hairdressers. She actually reported that one."

"You know what she's like, what she *was* like, God I can't stop talking about her as if she's still here."

"I know what you mean. I have to talk about her in the present. To refer to her as if she's gone is like admitting it. And I can't. I don't want to." I look down at the notes I have made. "It sounds as though it's this man that we're looking for. I'll pass the information on."

"How's Alysha coping?"

"I told her this morning. I don't think she understands. Not yet."

"Poor little mite. If there's anything at all I can do…"

"She's staying with my brother and sister-in-law. I feel guilty, but she's better off with them for a day or two." Her face floats into my mind from when I broke the news to her. "They've got a daughter only slightly older, so at least she's got her for distraction. I can barely look after myself."

"I hope you're taking some proper time off."

"I haven't thought that far ahead." I really can't. "Although to be honest, I think I'll give myself a few days. Then I want to be helping to catch him if they haven't got him by then already. Have you let the station know yet about the man that's been hanging around her?"

"No. I thought I'd mention it to you first."

"Right. I'll pass it on." I write it down. *Amanda. Tangled Hairdressers. Main Street.* "Let her know, if you don't mind, that DCI Ingham will get in touch to take a statement. I'll get the CCTV looked at by someone too."

I'm back in police mode and it's a welcome distraction from reality. As I pass through the press office, two or three of the copy takers look at me. Nobody speaks – I don't give them chance, which they are probably grateful for. What could anyone possibly say to me? *Sorry for your loss?* The wave of sympathy that emits from them as I pass by their desks almost takes my breath away.

I jump on my bike and within ten minutes, I'm locking it up outside the station.

"Mark!" The desk sergeant, Anthony, looks up as I walk to the desk. "What are you doing here?"

"I've come to see DI Jones, I've got some info on Lauren's murder." It feels horrendous using the word murder, but that's what it is. "Can you buzz me in?" "I've only got my ID on me, not my keycard. I wasn't expecting to be coming in today."

"Yes. Of course. I think he's at the back desk."

The heavy door clicks behind me; DI Jones and DCI Ingham look as shocked as Anthony did when I walked in.

"Mark," DI Jones begins. "You should be with your family. Not here."

"Lauren was my family. Are there any results yet from the post-mortem?"

"No, as you know, these things can take at least a couple of days."

"Any leads?"

"We're following up on a few things."

"Like what."

"Mark," says DCI Ingham. "Honestly. You've got enough on your plate. Leave us to sort it. We'll keep you in the loop."

I stare at him, aware that the dark rims around his eyes are probably similar to mine. I have felt sorry for DCI Ingham with his marriage split, but no pain could possibly equal what I am going through - at least he has a chance of getting his wife back. "I've been speaking to Lauren's colleague, Lindy, at the press office. She says someone has been following her."

"Following who?"

"Lauren."

"Lindy, surname?" says DCI Ingham. "I can follow this up."

"Don't you want to know what she's told me first?"

"You shouldn't be here Mark. You should be taking time off. Honestly, we're on it. I'll speak to this Lindy now. Get a statement. You get yourself home."

"No chance. There's been someone hanging around her hairdressers too. *Tangled* on Main Street. We need to look at the CCTV." I pull up a chair and sit before them at the desk. "So long as the nutter who did this to Lauren is out there, I'll be here, making sure we catch him."

"Why don't you leave it to us Mark?" DCI Ingham doesn't look happy, but I don't care. I've seen him make a right cock up of the river investigation due to his lack of focus. He's not doing the same thing with the inquiry into what has happened to Lauren.

"Look. I'm another pair of hands on the job." I'm trying to appease him, knowing he can force me to take compassionate leave if he deems me to be ineffective. "Being at work. Having something to concentrate on. It will help me deal with everything. And I've got an interest in finding him. So I'm back."

His eyes dart to his mobile, which lights up before him. Swiping it up, he darts towards the door. "I've got to take this."

CHAPTER TWENTY FIVE

It's Tuesday morning, forty-eight hours since I lost the love of my life. Day has turned into night and back into day again. I'm still breathing. Life is continuing, though I don't really want it to. Brenda stayed in the spare room again last night – Lauren was her world and I think it makes the loss easier for her to bear, being in her daughter's home.

All life has drained from her face though, and when I looked at her yesterday, I wondered whether she would ever smile again. Whether any of us will. I should probably bring Alysha home. Helping to look after her might give Brenda a sense of purpose. However, Alysha seems to be doing well enough with Eva and Heidi, and I don't feel like I can deal with her. I'm out of my depth. I know that sounds selfish. I'm working on it and I'll sort it out. Lauren would be furious with me for palming our daughter off like this. Right now, all that concerns me is bringing the psycho who did this to justice.

Claire's still here, spending each night sleeping on our sofa. She doesn't say much and doesn't need to. I need her here. She's always kept me grounded and calmed me down. She has an energy that I haven't found in many people, and we've always been close as brother and sister. To the exclusion of Will, usually. Maybe it's because we're much closer in age than to Will. He and Dean were born close together. Then a few years elapsed before me, then Claire.

As I lie in our bed, the smell of Lauren lingering on the pillow, I realise I've got a funeral to plan and a wedding to cancel. The two simultaneous realisations almost wind me. I sit up. I can't just lie here, thinking. I need to get moving. At times, it feels as though the grief could overwhelm me. Then it ebbs away with a momentary distraction before returning.

The petrol tank's nearly empty when I start up the car. Lauren's always left it to me to fill up. And put oil in it. And check the tyres. I pull the glove box compartment open, looking for the fuel account card, and pull Lauren's notebook out instead. It's twice I've stumbled upon it now – it's like she wants me to see it.

I knew she was interested and meticulous in reporting on the river deaths, however, I didn't realise she had become this involved. A page in her notebook has been dedicated to each of the women, detailing as much as she'd found out about them, their home, their background, work and their family. She has followed these pages with a list summarising her findings.

-All female.

-Age range spanning from twenty to fifty two.

-According to circumstances and Facebook, each victim was substantially drunk.

-All have occurred in the colder months on the same small stretch of the River Alder.

-All deaths have happened in early Sunday morning hours, soon after midnight.

-Victims have been reported missing quickly.

-Drownings have taken place following a visit to the Yorkshire Arms.

-They have all been 'petite' women, with shoulder length dark hair and green eyes.

We've known all of this as a police force, but seeing it as a list, in black and white, somehow makes me go cold, particularly the last item on Lauren's list, the importance of which, seems to have been overlooked by us. To be honest, as a sergeant, I've had to be guided by DCI Ingham, as he's been leading the inquiry. If I was a Detective Chief Inspector, and if the buck stopped with me, I would have handled things very, very differently. Definitely. There are other common themes that Lauren didn't know about. I grab a pen from the side pocket of the driver's side and add.

-All victims had water in lungs and were therefore alive at the point of entry into the water.

-No victims had any prior injuries or evidence of struggle.

-All toxicology reports have shown very high levels of alcohol.

-Heavy rain was present on all the night when the victims died.

It seems likely after talking to her hairdresser and Lindy, she was targeted personally, suggesting that because she was onto the killer of all the women, they wanted her out of the way, either so they could carry on, or to get away with what they've done so far.

I wish she had told me about being watched on the other two occasions. I would have taken it seriously – she'd still be here with me now. I wouldn't have let her out of my sight. As a police force, we've been too quick to attribute the deaths to circumstantial accidents. It's been like DCI Ingham has not got the energy to look any further for answers, or perhaps it's down to budget – I don't know. He's reminded me of a lone wolf lately- rather than conversing with colleagues, and operating as head of a team, he's shut himself away in his office and taken several decisions on his own. I suppose he eventually ensured the safety life buoys, lighting, fencing and CCTV were installed. I know the council can be slow, but it took months.

Lauren's death has firmly put our Yorkshire town on the map. The other deaths were non-violent, which marks her out as different, but the fact it's another drowning and in such close proximity to the River Alder, has meant that questions are now being asked and speculation is rife.

After filling up at the petrol station, my next stop is work. I park up and go straight in – this time I've got my swipe-card.

"You should take some time off," Haley, one of the administrators says to me. "I can't imagine what you must be going through."

"When that monster is caught, I will," I reply, knowing I probably won't. If I stop, I'll only think. If I think, I'll probably have a meltdown. No - I've got to stay strong and focused.

"Mark." DI Jones pokes his head out from his office. "I thought I heard your voice. Are you still hellbent on continuing to work even when you can have compassionate leave for as long as you need it?"

"Do you know if DCI Ingham is in today?" I walk into DI Jones's office, ignoring his question about leave. I need to be here.

"No, not today. Can I help instead?"

"Yes. It's about the river death investigation, which I tried to talk to you about yesterday."

"That's DCI Ingham's investigation. I'm heading up the one regarding Lauren."

"I know. Though I think we should link them. He didn't seem to listen to me yesterday. DCI Ingham, I mean. Do you know if he followed up what I said about the hairdresser?"

"I'm not sure to be honest Mark. But I'm positive he will have done. Tell me what you know."

I slide a piece of paper across the table. I've already rung Scarlet Poppy Bridal shop and found out when Lauren went in for her dress fitting. They were lovely to me on the phone and offered to refund the dress in full if I didn't want to keep it. I can't even contemplate that right now. I also phoned Sara and found out the time, date and location of their last lunch meeting.

I've written the dates, times and contact names for the café, shop and hairdressers. "I know it's a long shot," I say. "But can we see if these locations and surrounding areas are covered by CCTV? If she was being watched because she was on to some maniac that's going around pushing women to their deaths in the river, then it must be plausible that he wanted her shutting up. It can't just be coincidence, can it?"

"I agree. And because I'm leading the inquiry into Lauren, I can get onto this CCTV without treading on anyone's toes."

"I don't give a rat's arse about DCI Ingham." I raise my voice. "I'm sorry Sir, but all I care about now is finding the man who killed my fiancée."

"Excuse me one second," he says, as his computer bleeps.

I watch as he studies the screen, frowning as he reads.

"It's the post-mortem report."

"Lauren?"

"Yes, just give me a moment. It's pretty much as we expected." I watch his eyes as he scans down. "The cause of death was drowning. She had extensive injuries to the back of her head, where fragments of stone were found, suggesting she was attacked with a rock of some description. She also suffered extreme lacerations and contusions elsewhere on her body. There is no evidence of any sexual assault. However," he looks at me. "Mark, I don't know if this is going to come to you as a shock or not."

"What?"

"Lauren was in the very early stages of pregnancy."

I was just about coping, I think. Or perhaps I was numb, in shock. But as soon as I heard the words *early stages of pregnancy*, that was it. I wanted a second child more than anything. So did Lauren; she just didn't want to be, as she saw it, fat and frumpy when we got married. I'd adored her when she was expecting Alysha, though. I thought she was the sexiest woman alive, and she positively glowed with good health.

I drive home in a daze from the station after the news, consumed with sorrow about our robbed future.

"Where've you been?" Claire pokes her head out from the kitchen.

"Nowhere. My head aches. I'm off for a lie down."

"That's what Brenda's doing too. She's exhausted. I've a few calls to make so let me know if you need anything."

I can't tell anyone else about the pregnancy. Not yet. I need to make sense of it myself first. I'm not even sure I should tell Brenda – it will only pile on even more heartache, but I guess she has the right to know. I'll tell them later.

"Do you want something to eat bro?" Claire calls from the landing. "You've been in there for hours."

I rub my eyes and glance at my watch, realising I must have fallen asleep. It's nine o'clock. "No thanks. I'm knackered. I'll just stay here for now." I wish she hadn't woken me up. I never want to wake up. I just want to be with Lauren.

Every time I wake, I have a few seconds of blissful ignorance, then the situation steamrolls over me. *Lauren has been murdered, and she was carrying our second child.* I lay, staring into the dark, imagining what could have been. She would have been shocked but excited. We wanted more children, just not for another year or so. I bet it would have been a son. The name we'd had for a boy before we got Alysha was Oliver.

Oliver Mark Potts. Our son. He would have probably been blonde like Alysha, although her hair is darkening now. It'll end up the same as ours. Both Lauren and I have light brown hair, which goes blonde at the front in the summer. There I go again. Thinking about her like she's still here. Oliver would have had green eyes like his mum, and God, I would have been so proud. A son and a daughter and my Lauren. Our wedding day is four months away. There were twelve people due to fly out with us and we've been saving for two years. It's only three weeks since we bought the rings and organised our photographer over in the Maldives.

We had our entire lives in front of us before some bastard killed her. At the thought of it being taken away, an anger flares in me, dispelling the sorrow briefly before it returns. Now that I've seen exactly where she died and know of the injuries she suffered, I keep imagining how it must have been for her at the end. She will have fought tooth and nail to stay alive, but he will have been too strong for her.

We always seemed to know what each other was thinking and feeling, and right now, I just feel the terror that must have been coursing through her as her body gave way to the inevitable. I would have gone in her place – I would do anything to bring her back. Lauren and my children are the most precious people in the world, and I have let them down.

CHAPTER TWENTY SIX

A clock in the distance strikes midnight. My mind has being going around and around for three hours. My pillow is soaked with tears. I close my eyes and will sleep to rescue me. It doesn't.

I remember when we met; Lauren was in the last year of her uni degree and I'd just joined the force. It was someone's leaving do or someone's birthday at work; I can't remember which. And Lauren was out with some friends. We got talking at the bar and there was an instant spark. She kept looking over at me, then I noticed her friends were too. I saw her writing something down and as they were leaving, she pressed a piece of paper into my hand with her phone number on it. My colleagues made fun of me for the rest of the night but I was over the moon. It sounds clichéd, but we became inseparable very quickly. The copper and the journalist.

We had to quickly make the decision to keep our work out of our relationship as much as possible - with me being bound by confidentiality and her, well, always sniffing around for information. We've always worked hard and had some brilliant holidays prior to finding out she was expecting Alysha. We've done a fly-drive in America, had a Nordic cruise, and camped in the South of France twice, South Africa and Italy. India and Australia were our big dream trips to come.

We were out together one evening for a Valentine's Day meal; she refused a glass of wine and ate like a sparrow. Then she told me she was feeling a bit off colour and her period was late. As soon as the meal was over, I frogmarched her to the late night chemist and we were both beside ourselves with happiness when the result was positive. Now we would have a little one to share our adventures with. I was never scared of becoming a dad and always thought I'd want four kids; one would be lonely, two would fight, with three, one would get left out, so four seemed like the ideal number. Lauren wasn't so sure though. More practical than me. Which is why I'm so surprised that she was pregnant again. The thought slaps me hard once more and I throw my head back against the pillows a few times. This is awful, just lying here. I can't stop thinking about everything – it's all caving me in, but neither have I got the energy to move.

I hear someone, Brenda, get up to go to the bathroom and listen as she blows her nose and fills a glass with water. It must be killing her too – I know I should make more effort to look after and support her, and Alysha obviously, but right now, I can't think straight.

"Mark." I hear a tapping on my bedroom door. "I've made you a cuppa."

"Just leave it by the door sis." I sit up in the emerging dawn. "Thanks."

"You OK? You've been in this room for sixteen hours. Do you want some food? Or some company?"

"No. No thanks. I'm fine. Just knackered. And I need to think."

"Well, I'm downstairs if you need me."

A short time later, Brenda comes to the door. "Mark, are you going to get Alysha today? I'd like to see her."

"I don't know." I should, but I'm too down.

"You can't lock yourself in there forever. That little girl needs her daddy."

"You could always go to their house and see her."

"It's you, she needs. And her familiar surroundings."

I feel resentful. I will not allow anyone, not even Brenda, to tell me what to do with my own daughter. And there's no point me collecting Alysha when I can't meet her needs properly. Although I suppose I have Claire and Brenda here. It's going to break Brenda's heart when she finds out that Lauren was expecting again. "I'll be out soon."

"It's not going to do you any good staying in your room like this. You know that, don't you?"

What I do know is that nothing is going to do me any good. Unless someone can wave a magic wand and bring the love of my life and my unborn baby back.

I've hit a brick wall today. I can't seem to move myself. I've never felt this low, ever. Part of me wants to be swallowed up by death myself so I can be with her. Then I feel unbelievably guilty for feeling like this. I can't see a way forward without her and can't get images of the violent way she died out of my mind. I should have been there to help her.

Claire and Brenda keep trying to coax me out of the bedroom, rattling the door on its hinges when they realise I've locked it.

"What on earth is up with you?" Claire calls out.

"Um you, know, my wife-to-be has just been murdered."

"Mark, get a shower. Let's go and pick Alysha up - get out of here for a while."

I ignore her. Brenda returns a short time after and announces that she's left a sandwich next to my door. Hopefully it contains cyanide.

Then Will's voice. "Mark. Let me in. Come on."

Then another voice. "Daddy." The one that finally brings me back to my senses. After nearly twenty-four hours of being holed up in my bedroom, I know I've got to get sorted.

"I'll be downstairs when I've had a shower," I call out. I get a glimpse of myself as I look in the mirror. I've already lost weight and have a two-day-old beard emerging. I haven't even showered since Sunday morning, when Lauren was still here. I can imagine life becoming like that now. Not feeling an urge to shave or shower. There's no purpose in anything. My life has divided itself into two time zones - before Lauren was robbed from me and after.

Chapter Twenty Seven

D I Jones stands in front of his captive audience of police personnel. "So, I've been looking carefully at the two cases, and I have to conclude that there are many coincidences that must be considered. He then reels off pretty much everything that was in Lauren's notebook and everything I added to it, whilst referring to a list he has made on the whiteboard.

All around the room on the foam backed noticeboards, there are photographs of each of the river victims, with key information about them all. On the last board, there is a photograph of my beautiful, smiling Lauren, looking full of life. I bite my lip at the irony. He sweeps his gaze around the room, now named the 'incident room.' "Personally, I believe there's every likelihood that we could be dealing with a serial killer."

There's silence for a few moments then a voice breaks the tension.

"Do we know anything about him?"

"I don't know if we can make assumptions that it's a 'him' just yet. I'm waiting on some DNA reports from the post-mortem on Lauren Holmes." My heart lurches as he says her name. He looks across at me, as though making sure I'm alright before carrying on. "There's been no DNA found on the women from the river that hasn't been accounted for. The funerals have taken place of all but the last two. I'm also going to be looking at more CCTV footage soon."

"Of what?" DCI Ingham frowns at DI Jones. "And why is it, that this is the first I'm hearing about it? I'm leading the river enquiry - I should have been briefed."

"It's because you haven't been on shift." DI Jones frowns back. "One or two more things came to light that I needed to deal with as well."

"And if there is someone out there…" Chris begins.

A female police officer adds, "We need to get him locked up before he goes after his next victim."

"I'm not at all happy with this." Hutton, a sergeant from South Team says, his voice booming around the incident room. "It's taken eight deaths this winter before we're seriously looking for someone?" He looks from DI Jones to DCI Ingham. "Not to mention the deaths last winter. This could be a Police Complaints Commission job Sir. I've got a missus, a sister, a mum…"

"Most of us have."

"Lucky you." Bitterness trickles through my words. "I haven't got a missus anymore, which is why I want this bastard caught. Hopefully it'll be me doing the catching – he'll be meeting the same fate as my Lauren did, if I do."

"You shouldn't even be at work," DCI Ingham says, his voice bearing a stern edge. "And you certainly shouldn't be anywhere near this case any more. You have too much emotional involvement."

"Of course I have! Which makes me far more use than you." The words are escaping me before I've chance to consider what I'm saying. "It took my fianceé to flag up incompetence in handling the case through the media before you sorted any safety measures around that river. Even then, you've only implemented half measures!"

"How dare you speak to me like that Sergeant?"

"How dare you suggest that I shouldn't be anywhere near this case? I'll do a far better job than has been done so far."

Everyone is staring at me but I don't care. And I don't care about his marital woes either. To slate a DCI, especially publicly, is unheard of. Usually it's Ma'am or Sir, bowing and scraping.

"Alright Mark, calm down." DI Jones's voice is steady. "I'm inclined to agree with DCI Ingham though. You should be taking some time off and spending it with your family."

"My family is lying in a hospital mortuary," I snarl. "Because of him." I point at DCI Ingham. If he'd only done what he was supposed to do. He kept saying that the new measures were in hand and that he was chasing things up. He should've been on the phone to that council office every single day.

I want to have a closer look at all the evidence that's been taken from around the riverbank too, when I get the chance. I bet all that's been brushed under the carpet. I know Ingham's had stuff going on at home but there's no excuse for this sort of thing. Not when you're a DCI. If you're not up to the job, you pass it on.

"I don't have to listen to this." DCI Ingham stands, his chair scraping the floor. "In all my years on the force, I've never heard such disrespect for my judgement."

"*Judgement!*" I almost laugh. "Is that what you call it?"

"Mark. That's enough. Anymore and you'll be up for a disciplinary"

I know DI Jones is right but glare as Ingham marches away. As the door bangs after him, the female officer, Paula, I think her name is, speaks. "We can't blame DCI Ingham. It is a dreadful stretch of river. There's been multiple deaths in the Alder over the years, not just recently. We all know about the sudden depths and the undercurrent. It was fair that he deemed the drownings to be accidental."

"That's as may be," the other policewoman replies. "But it doesn't explain why all the fencing and the other stuff has only just been sorted."

"He has been waiting on the various contractors and services to do their bit." DI Jones is addressing us all but is looking directly at me. "And DCI Ingham did have a point about respect. Whatever anyone is thinking or feeling, he is a Detective Chief Inspector with many years of experience."

"Ingham has been a bit of a prat for a while," Chris says in the staff room after the meeting. "I heard him having words with someone in his office earlier. When I was walking past. Don't let him get to you Mark."

"He's not been right since he split with his wife last year," Paula adds. "It sounded like a messy one. My husband works with Sue, who used to live next door to the Inghams. She and I really hit it off when I went to their work's Christmas do with him - she was telling me all about Ingham's break-up."

I glance around. There are only police constables, special constables and me around, so she is safe to talk.

"Blimey." Chris stirs his tea. "Talk about Chinese whispers. It's like my sister's, friend's, brother-in-law's uncle. So, what's the lowdown then?"

I think of the gossip that I could go home and tell Lauren if she was still alive. The realisation that she's not there hits me again like a thunderclap. It's the only reason I've ever listened to gossip. To tell Lauren. Obviously, only when it's not something that's confidential and pertinent to an investigation.

I try not to listen to them talking, but it's hard not to. I feel more normal being here, at the station anyway. It's my domain, apart from being at home. And I can't bear being there, amongst the grief and the reminders. Lauren's stuff is everywhere.

Paula sits on the corner sofa, her coffee in front of her and a banana on her lap. "The neighbour, Sue, heard loads of shouting all the time. She's an alcoholic, his wife, that is. A functioning one anyway." She peels the top off her banana as she speaks. "Ingham apparently couldn't handle it any more. You've got to feel sorry for him really. Especially when he caught his wife in their bed with some bloke she'd met at an AA meeting. They were both leathered and had fallen asleep. Ingham threw them into the garden with no clothes on and Ingham himself left soon after that. I'm still in touch with Sue - she reckons she still sees him at the front door from time to time. She reckons Ingham wants them to try again."

The staff room is quiet as everyone listens in. "So that's why he was on leave in the summer for so long," she adds.

I was given some of his caseload last summer. I didn't know why he was off at the time and didn't ask. It wasn't really any of my business. To me, he's just a work colleague who I've got to show respect to, because he's a superior officer.

"Anyway," Paula continues. "Sue was friendly with Ingham's wife too. Divorce had been on the cards for a while. He'd not liked her having a drink, not even a glass of wine when they first got together – he was really controlling."

"I can imagine," I say. And I can. He has to be in charge.

"His wife hid her drink problem from him. Sue had a good idea about it, being at home through the day and chatting to her. If Ingham suspected her of drinking, she said he would slap her about a bit. I'm not sure I believed that though."

"Really?" Chris puts his cup on the table. "Our Detective Chief Inspector! Knocking his wife about? Never!"

"That will do."

There's a silence as we all turn to the booming voice at the doorway. DI Jones stands there. "I've been listening long enough to you lot. I'm not having it. If you want to keep your badges, have some respect. Mark, I need a word." He turns and his footsteps thud along the corridor.

Everyone looks mildly sheepish. I get up.

"I'll tell you the rest later," Paula mouths at me.

"I don't know what all that was about," DI Jones begins, gesturing to the seat in front of his desk.

"I wasn't really listening to be honest. I've enough crap swirling around my head without getting involved in police station gossip." I sink onto the chair. "Have there been any developments yet?"

"I got hold of the CCTV. I wanted you to look at it with me. See if you recognise the person. But first, if you want to stay on the case, I need assurances there will be no more outbursts towards DCI Ingham."

"Yes Sir." I know I'll have to watch myself at the moment.

"Good. Otherwise you're suspended. And that's the last thing I want to happen."

I nod. "Where've you recovered it from?"

"All of the places you told me about."

"That's good." I can't believe I'm using the word good in relation to this. Nothing is good anymore.

"I've been lucky." He goes on. "None of it has been hard to get hold of. The hairdresser had it ready for me. Plus, I've got local authority CCTV for the street outside the bridal shop and the café too. Because you gave me good estimates of the times Lauren was there, I haven't had to trawl through as much as I might have had to."

"So there's someone actually there, on all three films? Hanging around?"

"It looks that way. I'll show you the one from hairdressers first."

I watch as a tall, wiry figure in a hood stands on the corner outside the salon. He's not there long before he crosses the road. He definitely looks to be hanging around, waiting for something, or in this case, someone. The image is a bit grainy and will need forensic examination.

"Look, he goes out of shot." DI Jones tilts the screen so we can see it better. "Then he comes back again."

"Does it show his face at all?"

"Unfortunately not. None of them do. Maybe he knew where the cameras were. But I'd swear it's the same guy." He clicks his mouse. "Look. This one's outside the bridal shop."

I watch as our car comes into view on the screen. There's someone crouched behind it.

"I'll forward this bit." DI Jones clicks the mouse again. "There's nothing much to see. He's pretty much like that for about seven minutes. At least it seems as though it is a man we are looking for."

I watch as Lauren and Sara leave the shop, and Lauren points towards our car. It's bittersweet to see her alive on the video, large as life. I can't believe she's gone. I swallow. I will not cry. I have a job to do. The man in the CCTV moves as though he is doing up his shoe and then darts around the corner.

"Do you recognise him?" DI Jones's voice startles me somewhat. I was miles away. I'm finding that over the last few days, I can't focus on anything.

I peer at the now-stilled picture. "To be honest, in that hood and wearing those non-descript clothes, he could be anyone. But it's the same guy as before. Same build and height."

"With some sort of interest in Lauren." DI Jones takes a sip from the water bottle beside him. "Here's the first CCTV footage. It's from last month outside Bridge Street Café."

This time the man is trying to conceal himself around a corner. Then he walks up and down at the other side of the street. I hate the bastard. He's brutally snatched Lauren's life and ruined mine and Alysha's too.

"Surely we can get his face from that." I point at the screen. "He was facing the camera for a few seconds there."

"I've looked at that already. He's too far away to be in focus. I've tried to zoom in on his face and you just can't make anything out. But I'll pass it through. The tech team might be able to do something with it. How old do you think he looks?"

"Joggers. Hoodie. And is he wearing trainers?"

"I can't tell." DI Jones leans towards the screen.

"Given his dress, I'd say he's probably at the younger end of the spectrum."

"Possibly." DI Jones turns the screen back towards himself. "There's no doubt though that your fiancée was being stalked and it's very important that we find this man. I reckon he'll have a lot to tell us about how she died. I'll get this image circulated and ask for info about those dates, times and locations."

"I've just remembered something else."

"Go on."

"Did you hear about a week last Sunday, when I was out with Lauren at the Yorkshire Arms? She'd nipped outside to take a couple of pictures in the dark, forever the journalist – she wanted them to go with her articles." I sag at the memory. If only I could turn the clock back. "Anyway, she swore blind there was someone hanging around then too. I even rang for back up but there was no one there by the time it arrived."

"Yes, someone mentioned it to me. By the sounds of it, there probably *was* someone there. He'll have scarpered. And, as we've already found out, we didn't have cameras covering the area then. We have now, but obviously it's too late."

"When can you get those pictures out? I just want him caught."

"I know. So do I. But Mark, you look knackered. Sorry to be so blunt." DI Jones leans back in his executive chair, hands clasped behind his head. "You need to go home and get some rest."

"I need to be at work. I've had plenty of rest. I was in bed from four o clock in the afternoon yesterday, till nearly lunchtime today. I couldn't face anyone." My eyes fall on a framed picture of him with a woman and two young boys. *Lucky sod,* I think. What I'd give to have Lauren back here. "Your family?"

"Yes." He comes from around his desk and slaps me on the shoulder. "You're doing great. In fact, a little too great. But you should be with your family."

"You're sounding like Ingham now."

"*DCI* Ingham." He states, his frown serving as a reminder of what he said a few moments ago. "We've got your best interests at heart, that's all. Me *and* DCI Ingham. What you're having to deal with is unimaginable to most people and we want to support you. And if that means taking time off…"

"It's not time off I need. I keep saying this. I want to keep busy and help get this maniac off the streets. The thought of catching him is what's keeping me going."

"I understand. I really do. Just don't push yourself too hard."

I don't see how he can understand. His wife hasn't been murdered. "I've got time with my family tomorrow. We've got an appointment with the funeral director. I'm absolutely dreading it."

CHAPTER TWENTY EIGHT

I get only a few seconds of normality each day when I first wake up. Then I remember. This is my fourth day of waking without Lauren. I keep looking for her in the night, moving to her side of the bed, feeling for her warmth. Not being able to find her anymore is a living hell.

Alysha is back in her bed, which is where she should be, and what Lauren would want. Eva is bringing Heidi over here whilst I go with Brenda, Claire and Will to see the funeral director. Both girls are having the week off school.

I've never been involved in planning a funeral before. When my brother Dean died twenty years ago, my parents did all the organising. I imagine him looking after Lauren now, wherever they may be. I wonder if they know who each other is if there's such a thing as the afterlife - I hope there is. I can't bear to think of her light just being snuffed out and her not existing somewhere else. Wherever she is, I hope she's waiting for me.

We're offered tea and a seat around a large mahogany desk in a side room. A portly woman closes the door and eases herself behind the desk. "I'm Tracey," she says, shaking our hands one by one as we introduce ourselves and inform her of our individual relationships to Lauren. This is an awful place to be, but it's probably doing everybody good to get out of that house. None of us seem to know what to say to each other.

"Let me begin," Tracey says, "by offering my deepest condolences for such a tragic loss. It's never easy losing a loved one but at such a young age…"

I place my elbows onto the shiny desk and lean forward. I feel slightly faint. I've not had any breakfast, and it stinks of lilies and furniture polish in here.

"Have you seen the news reports?" Brenda dabs at her eyes. I've been struck by how much of Lauren there is in Brenda. So much so, I can hardly bear to look at her. They've got the same green eyes, the same laugh and even the same tone of voice. Lauren can't have been much like her dad.

"Yes, I have. I can't imagine what you're all going through. I hope that we can begin to bring you some comfort through her funeral service."

"Has Brenda explained that Lauren hasn't been released yet? She's still undergoing investigations."

"Yes. I know. And as soon as she's ready, we'll bring her here. OK. I'm going to start by getting some details from you. What was her full name?"

Brenda and I speak at the same time.

"Lauren Frances Holmes."

"Date of birth?"

"Second of July nineteen eighty eight."

"It was Sunday when she passed away, wasn't it?"

"Passed away makes it sound peaceful." Hot tears stab at the back of my eyes.

"I know. Forgive me. It's just the term we use."

There's a soft knock at the door, followed by the woman on the front desk coming in to place a tray of tea and biscuits on the table. I immediately reach for one, knowing I need to get something in me. She then gives steaming mugs to us all.

"Right." Tracey's manner is far too brisk and business-like for my liking. "We can get all the basic funeral details now and then it's one less thing to do once her body is released."

I hate her described as a body. I spoon sugar into my tea. I never normally have sugar. Claire looks at me with a raised eyebrow.

"Will you be wanting a burial or a cremation?"

"Cremation," Brenda replies.

Tracey looks at me as though checking for my agreement.

"That's fine by me." Lauren and I had once discussed this, and where we wanted our ashes scattering. I thought that was going to be many years in the future though.

"She was pregnant," I say, a golf ball forming in my throat. "That needs to be acknowledged in the service. It wasn't just one life. It was two."

"I didn't know that." Tracey writes something down. "How awful. How far along was she?"

"None of us knew." I keep my gaze down. I know I shouldn't be breaking this news like this. I hold my breath, awaiting the onslaught.

"Why haven't you said anything?" Claire grasps my hand. "When did you find out?"

"The other day. It came to light with the post mortem results."

"Do you not think I had the right to know?" Brenda's face is white and twisted into a sorrowful and angry expression I've never seen before.

"I'm sorry Brenda." Tears are dripping down my face yet again. "Things are horrendous enough. I didn't know how to tell you."

We sit in silence, staring at one another.

"I'll leave you all alone for a few minutes," Tracey rises from behind the desk and walks to the door. "Call me when you're ready to resume. No rush."

"You should have let Brenda know about the baby." Will's voice sounds loud in this quiet room. "She's spot on. She had a right to know."

"Did *you* know? You sound like you did." Claire swings around in her chair to face him.

"I heard. I'm a cop too, aren't I?" He takes a sip of his tea. "Look, what difference does it make now? Yes, she was pregnant, yes it's all awful..."

"Shut up Will." I slam my cup onto the tray. "You've got the sensitivity of a sledgehammer. Brenda..." I reach for her hand. "I'm sorry. I was going to tell you. I just wasn't thinking straight."

Luckily, she squeezes my hand. "I'm sorry Mark. I'm not blaming you. I'm just devastated. It's horrendous enough to lose my daughter. But a grandchild as well?" She closes her eyes and tears spill from them. "It's like a bad dream."

Part of me is glad that I've imparted this news in a more 'controlled' environment. Brenda's reaction has probably been more contained than it would have been at home. She would have probably paced the house for at least a day, weeping and wailing. Though equally, with Alysha around, maybe she would have tempered herself.

"I don't want Alysha to know anything about the baby. Not until she's older. It will be too much now. The loss she's already dealing with is more than enough for any five-year-old." Brenda nods her approval of this. She dabs at each eye in turn, then blows her nose loudly. I frown at Will, who grimaces. "Right," I say. "Are we ready to continue this meeting?"

"Is everyone OK to carry on?" Tracey asks as she lowers herself back into her seat.

"I guess so." Claire looks around at the rest of us.

"I'm dreadfully sorry for you all," Tracey says again. She's good at her job, I'll give her that. "It's an absolute tragedy that you've lost two lives here. And there's no reason why the baby cannot be mentioned in the service."

"I'm not sure I want everyone knowing."

"It's not just your decision." Brenda scowls at me.

"The celebrant from the crematorium will be in touch once we've brought Lauren here, and they'll discuss that with you. In the meantime, be thinking about the songs you want played and the readings and any poems you may want reading out, before you meet."

Songs. Readings. I can't bear to go there right now.

"I need to ask you a few more questions." She points her pen over a form. "Would you like Lauren embalming?"

"Erm. I don't know. What difference will that make?" Brenda asks.

"It just stops Mother Nature taking hold quite so fast," Tracey explains, looking around at each of us in turn. "Really, I need a decision on that today."

"I guess that sounds best," I reply. "Are you alright with that Brenda?"

"I suppose so."

Tracey writes on her sheet. "We do that as soon as she gets here. And at the same time, we can dress her in something you want her to be wearing for her final journey."

That's nearly the final straw. And then I remember her recent trip to the bridal shop. Her wedding dress. The golf ball in my throat turns to a melon. I'll run it by Brenda later. I daren't make any suggestions that will look like I'm trying to take over. "Can we get back to you on that? We'll have a think about it."

Brenda gives me a small nod, which makes me feel as though she's half forgiven me for not telling her about the baby. Though, Will is right, to a point. Knowing. or not knowing about the baby changes nothing. We were probably best not knowing. It's only increased the heartache.

We choose flowers, organise a press announcement and talk about times we can visit her in the Chapel of Rest once she's released. Then Tracey slides a brochure towards me which takes my breath away. "If you could just choose which one you would like. The wood and the lining. There's also a choice between silver and brass handles."

The pictures before me swim in front of my eyes. I swallow. "I can't do this." I push the brochure in front of Brenda who stares, horror similar to mine in her eyes.

"How can I choose my daughter's coffin?" She weeps openly and Tracey pushes the box of tissues towards her.

"If it was for me, I'd choose the white one with silver handles," Claire says, calm as always. "Just write that on the form for now. We can change our minds later if need be, can't we?"

"I've still got our wedding to cancel." I'm utterly drained as we leave the warmth of the funeral home for the wintery street a short time later.

Claire looks at Will. "If you give us a list of who to contact Mark, me and Will can do the necessary with that."

"Yeah." Will strides in front of us. "I'm doing some extra shifts so I'll get Eva onto it. We'll do it between us."

"She had a wedding organiser, some folder with everything in." I think of her now, poring over it. I called her *bridezilla* once or twice. She wasn't amused.

"Do you want to go home or shall we take a detour for a pint?" I look at Claire, Will and Brenda, hoping they'll agree. I never normally drink in the daytime, but I need something to settle me down after that meeting. "Oh hang on, what's this about. It's a withheld number."

"Mark, DI Jones here. I need to see you straightaway. Are you free?"

"Well, erm, I've just had a meeting with the funeral director so I'm feeling a bit fragile. I was just about to go for a pint with my family."

"I tell you what. Tell me where you'll be, and I'll come to see you. I've something I really need to tell you about."

My stomach churns with both hunger and anxiety. I'll try to have some crisps with my pint. Hopefully, I'll be able to keep it all down. What now? "Is it about Lauren?"

"No. Well, kind of. Where are you going to be?"

I glance across the road. "The Black Horse," I say, making mental calculations. It'll take him about fifteen minutes to get here if he's coming from the station.

Claire gets a round in and we sit, waiting for DI Jones. "That's good." She sips at her wine. "I think we deserve these after that meeting."

"I can't believe what we're having to do." Brenda's tears haven't stopped since we left the funeral director. The man behind the bar seems to take it in his stride though. Being across the road from the funeral home, he's probably used to it. "This isn't the normal order of things. No parent should have to bury their child. Not to mention their grandchild. I'm devastated. Bloody devastated."

Claire puts her arm around her. "I know."

"You've been a godsend, you have," Brenda rubs the top of Claire's hand. "How you've looked after us all. "

"It's all part of the job description."

I look at my sister, feeling a rush of warmth I don't often feel. Lauren adored her and would be really glad of her being around for us.

"How are you doing after that Mark?" Claire looks at me.

"I don't know. Numb. Unreal. Like it's all happening to someone else." I follow Will's gaze to the door where DI Jones has just appeared.

"Hello again." Will shuffles his chair towards me to make space for DI Jones. "Can I get you anything to drink?"

"Not for me thanks." He looks at my pint.

"Not on duty sir." I smile despite my misery and nerves.

"I'm not judging you Mark." DI Jones sits down next to Will. "I'd be here too in your situation. And I'd probably have a damn sight more than one pint. How are you feeling today?"

"Pretty crap. Especially after having just been to set the ball rolling with the funeral arrangements. But I'm lucky to have these guys around me." I take another swig of my pint. "Anyway. I've been on tenterhooks waiting for you to get here. What do you need to speak to me about. Is it alright in front of my family, or do you need me on my own?"

"No, you can all hear this. I wanted to get to you before the news broke."

"What news?"

He takes a deep breath. "A woman has just had a miraculous escape after she was attacked in exactly the same way as Lauren."

"What? Where?" My voice rings out in the silence of the pub. At 11:45 am on a Wednesday morning, we are literally the only ones here apart from the man behind the bar.

"In the same place. A passer-by heard some commotion."

"The same place?" Will speaks now. "Is it not still cordoned off?"

"No, they had concluded the search. We'd taken as much evidence as we could." DI Jones looked pained as he continues. "The woman's been taken to hospital. She's been bashed around the head several times with a rock, just like Lauren was. Then she had her head held in the stream. She was probably moments away from death when a dog walker disturbed her attacker. He bloody got away though."

"A man?"

"Yes. The dog walker reckons he got a good look at the assailant's face and says he would recognise him if he saw him again."

"Are you going to get him to put an e-fit together?"

"Yes. I thought we'd do a reconstruction as well. We're so close to getting him."

"I'm not sure a reconstruction would work," Will says. I want to remind him he's a mere traffic cop, but that would sound pathetic.

"They usually bring good results in." DI Jones looks straight at me. "We'll have him soon, I promise."

"You'll have to let me deal with him." Fury engulfs me. Why the hell is this man still out there, doing what he wants to women? Our force must be a laughing stock to other forces around the country.

"You wouldn't be allowed near him Mark. You're too connected to the case."

"How is she? The woman?"

"She was still unconscious when she arrived at the hospital. I've seen her. She's a bit of a mess and bloody lucky to still be with us. I'll be speaking to her as soon as she's up to it."

"There are no cameras around there, are there?"

"On the cycle path? No. But I've got officers looking at the CCTV in the surrounding area. I've no doubt in my mind that it's the same person who killed Lauren and possibly the eight women in the river."

"They should bring back capital punishment for men like him," Claire says.

"He should just be drowned. Same as he's done to all those women. It would cost the state a lot less to finish him off, rather than the taxpayer funding a court trial and a lifelong prison sentence." I've never heard such venom in Brenda's voice. "Did you know Lauren was expecting another child?" Brenda looks at DI Jones.

"Yes. I unfortunately was the one to tell Mark. I'm sorry."

"How come you've known for however many days, whilst I, her mother, have only just found out? Why didn't anyone tell me?"

"Erm, I'm sorry. I told Mark."

"Look, Brenda." I don't know if she's ever going to let this go. "I've said I'm sorry. You know now. I should have told you. I was just so far up my own arse. Don't you remember how much time I stayed in the bedroom? I was in bits. I still am."

"I'm sorry for all of you." DI Jones rises from his seat. "I'm going to have to get back Mark, but I wanted to let you know in person. It's going to be in the next news bulletins."

"Is there any word on Lauren?" I think of her lying in the hospital mortuary. "The undertakers have said they will collect her when she can be released."

"Nothing yet. It might be they want to keep her there, to make comparisons with this other lady now. I'll try and find out what's going on."

"Thanks. I just want her out of that mortuary." I can't bear to think of my fiancee lying alone in a fridge. She hated being cold. "I feel like she'll be better looked after at the funeral home."

Chapter Twenty Nine

C hris drops a newspaper onto the table that sits between the two sofas in the staffroom. "It's all over the news."

There's a photograph of Lauren smiling up from the front page and the headline *Manhunt for the Yorkshire Dipper.*

"The Yorkshire Dipper!" I want to be angry, though Lauren would probably approve of this headline. To me, it's making light of all the tragedy that's taken place. Bloody newspapers! "Is there any news on the latest woman?"

"She's been put into an induced coma and is in intensive care," Paula says. "Until the swelling on her brain goes down. Apparently she has some lung damage that they're monitoring, but it sounds as though she'll pull though."

I reach for the paper. The dog walker who saved the woman has helped produce an e-fit. I look into the eyes of the monster who killed Lauren and feel sick. He's wearing a hoodie like the man we've seen on the CCTV and there's a familiarity in his face that I can't put my finger on. He could be someone I've dealt with in the past. I stare at the image until it blurs in front of my eyes. I then decide that if I stop looking at it, a memory might just return to me of its own accord.

"DI Jones has called a meeting in the incident room," Paula strides into the staff room and flicks the switch on the kettle. "I've heard a rumour as well that Ingham's been pulled off the case completely."

"Who told you that?" The plastic sofa squeaks as Chris leans back on it.

"Tina in the office. But that's between us and these four walls."

"Why?"

She walks back to the doorway and glances along the corridor outside. "Partly to do with his head not being where it should be." Tina was in the room when he was told to take some time off. She had to take the minutes of the meeting. "He admitted that his marriage break-up has interfered with work. Apparently."

"What was it you were saying about Ingham the other day Paula? Before DI Jones caught us bitching."

"I can't remember." Paula squints in the overhead fluorescent light. "What was I on about?"

"Why his marriage broke up. Something to do with Ingham's next-door neighbour being friends with his wife."

"Oh yes, after he caught his wife *at it.* Can't blame her really! But she drank a lot, according to Sue, and he's got issues with alcohol."

"Ingham - no," I say. "He can't have. I've never seen him have a drink at any of the work's dos. Not that he's ever stayed that long. He only ever shows his face and leaves."

"It's not that he's got a drink problem. It's the other way around." Paula goes on. "His mother was a drunk, and walked out when he was thirteen. He didn't see her again and found out when he was in his twenties that she'd died from liver failure.

"That's rough."

"Pat, his wife, told their neighbour that she was taking the brunt of things. She tried to stop drinking completely, but used drink as a crutch when times were difficult."

"Plenty of people too. But they must have thought something of each other to stay together so long." Chris stands and the rest of us follow suit.

"Who knows? Sounds a toxic marriage. In all sorts of ways."

"He seems straight down the line, though." From what I've gathered about Chris, he always sees the best in people. "You wouldn't have guessed he had all this marriage problem stuff swirling around inside him."

"I don't care what he's had going on at home. He messed up with this investigation." Everyone looks at me. "If it wasn't for him, perhaps some of those women might still be alive and I wouldn't be having to cancel my wedding and plan my fiancée's funeral instead." For the time being, until they catch the maniac, Ingham can have the full force of my anger and all the blame. "I'm glad he's been kicked off the case. He wants sacking if you ask me. At least now, the person responsible might be caught before anyone else is killed."

Tina puts her head around the door. We're all just stood looking at each other. "The meeting's starting. I've been asked to come and get you all." She puts her hand on my arm as we file past her. "How are you doing? I've been thinking about you these last few days. I can't believe you're even here."

"I need to keep busy. And if I can help catch this nutter before he gets someone else…"

"I know." We walk towards the incident room. "It's still touch and go for that other woman. I don't think it's safe for any woman to be out on her own."

"Mark." Chris catches my arm before we go in. "I know how bitter you feel towards Ingham and I don't blame you. But things not happening as quick as they did, it's down to all of us, not just him."

I stare at him. "How do you work that one out? He was in charge of the investigation."

"Well for the first couple, it was probably safe to assume they were accidents. I admit he could have done more but he was away, wasn't he... when the sixth one happened."

"I can't remember."

"I dropped him at the station for some police federation conference."

Tina curls her head around the door of the incident room. "We're ready to start."

"Right!" DI Jones leans his elbows on the table. "First, I want to communicate that women, and it seems to be just women, in this area, are at serious risk until we catch this man." He points to the e-fit. "We need to relay that information to everyone, and we have to be patrolling the at-risk areas. And second. I've cancelled everyone's leave, which at this time of year, is minimal anyway, and I'm asking for as much extra staffing as possible until we get him. Some of it will be paid. Some of it will have to be taken in lieu – just keep a record of what you work on the system."

There's some shuffling of feet and muttering in the room.

DI Jones ignores it and carries on. "The river deaths inquiry has now been joined with this one. I'm now leading the entire investigation and would ask you all, for your continued support and effort. As you know," he looks at me. "This awful series of deaths has impacted on one of our own. We have to get this man off the streets."

"It should never have got to this," Paula mutters, looking around the room at all the photographs of the women.

"There have been some discrepancies in the inquiry so far, admittedly." DI Jones scratches his head. "Along with me taking over the day-to-day, DCI Towers will be overseeing everything. We're very much in the firing line for our perceived failings up to now." He sweeps his gaze over us all. "It could easily end up in the hands of the Police Complaints Commission. So all I can do now, is offer my full commitment to this inquiry and implore you all to get behind me and do the same. I can't undo what's happened already, but I can make it my absolute priority to do what needs to be done from here on in."

"DCI bloody Ingham's head should roll for what he's done." I squint in the sunlight that's seeping through the blinds. I've got to blame someone. "Or more for what he hasn't done."

DI Jones's expression remains calm. "I'll speak to you privately Mark if that's OK. Right, if I could have everyone's attention please. We need to be building a clear picture of who it is we're looking for. I know it's overly pixelated, but we can see from the still image here that he dresses in hoodies, baggy clothes and trainers."

"So it's someone fairly young, Sir?"

"No, according to our dog walker, he's in his forties at least - he has brown eyes and dark hair."

"Well, that's a bit nondescript. It sums up about a third of the men in Yorkshire."

DI Jones continues, whilst referring to the e-fit and CCTV still of the man on the board. "We're looking for someone of about six foot, medium build and pock-marked skin. The dog walker reckons he would recognise him again and when the second lady comes around, she'll hopefully be able to provide more information."

"If she comes around," Paula says.

DI Jones ignores her. "So, I'm going to give all of you individual responsibilities." I listen peripherally as he doles out door-to-door zones, poster and social media campaigns and patrolling areas.

He designates two officers to take over sitting in shifts at the hospital, and two officers to speak again to the families of the river victims. The second of these tasks is to establish any further commonalities and also find out the likelihood of a complaint being made by the victims' families and hopefully mitigate against them.

He gives me the job of getting the TV re-construction organised. "These yield excellent results usually," he says. "And this case is becoming so high profile now, that lots of people will tune in to watch. Can you get on with that ASAP?"

"That's not exactly a big job," I argue. "It'll take me, what? Two hours tops."

"It's a very important task and with respect Mark, you shouldn't even be here."

"I'm pig sick of people saying that to me. Look at me. I'm holding up. And whilst there's breath in my body, I'm going to help catch him. I want to be involved with the visits to the families. I need to keep busy."

"I don't think that's a good idea."

"Why not?" The entire room is watching our ping pong discussion. "It would help me," I continue. "And I can help them. After all, we are going through the same thing."

DI Jones looks at Chris and Hutton, the officers he has given the visitations to. Neither of them says anything, which in police code means it's fine to go ahead. "OK," he says after a brief pause. "After you've sorted the reconstruction, that's most important, then you can help with visitations. But I don't want you asking the questions. You should be the one who takes notes. And if it becomes too much, it's fine. Take time off if you need to."

"I will. And thanks Sir. I need to be working on this."

After the meeting concludes, I follow DI Jones to his office.

"You've every right to have a grudge with DCI Ingham," he begins.

"A grudge doesn't cover it, to be honest with you. If he'd only done what he was supposed to have done straight away, then God knows how many lives could have been saved." I think back to his dismissal whenever I made suggestions. "He knew best all along. That's not what policing is about – we're a team, aren't we?"

DI Jones sighs. He looks as tired as me. It's the first time I've seen him with the shadow of a beard – he's obviously flat out with this. I, on the other hand, have four days' worth of beard. What's the point of shaving or anything anymore? Lauren's not here.

"You must remember Mark, in front of your fellow police officers and work colleagues, you need to remain respectful of rank. If I've to remind you of this again, I will pull you from all involvement in this case and send you home. Am I clear?"

"Yes, Sir."

"Good. Now the only thing I can say, and I'm not defending DCI Ingham, is that he's not been himself. You know yourself, what mental anguish takes out of you."

"But he's been dealing with people's lives, Sir. He could have delegated. I was his Sergeant when he was in charge of the river inquiry. He wouldn't let me in, apart from the surface aspects of the case. If he was having problems, then he should have had time off to sort them out, instead of doing a cack-handed job here."

"That's what he's doing now. Having time off, that is. Obviously, there'll be an internal investigation into perceived failings with the case and with not realising that DCI Ingham was struggling so much."

"But it's too late." Nothing is ever going to bring Lauren back. Under normal circumstances I would sympathise with a colleague in distress but these are not normal circumstances.

"Mark. Trust me. I'm with you on this. And I'm blown away by your commitment to your work. Particularly with what you're going through. I understand your need to keep going and to know you are contributing to catching this man. And like I said earlier – I need as much manpower as possible right now."

"I'm not going anywhere. I might take a little time off when we get to Lauren's funeral…"

My voice trails off. Lauren's funeral. I hate that word. It's real. The melon returns to my throat and for a second, I feel like I might break down in front of DI Jones.

"Are you OK? Silly question. Course you're not. How could you be?"

I need to distract myself. "The reconstruction," I begin. "What do I need to do?"

"Tina's got the number. After you've contacted them, it's just a matter of following their procedure. They'll take all the facts from you, times, location etc and ask for photographs. They'll then set up and stage the reconstruction."

"Do they have actors for that or would I have to sort something out?"

"Either."

"My sister-in-law has a look of Lauren. Their hair is a similar length and colour. My family are all wanting to do something useful. Wanting to help."

"We need to get it out as soon as we can. There were four days between what he did to Lauren and this latest attack."

"There were gaps with the river drownings, weren't there. On average, two a month. So are we telling the people putting the reconstruction together that the river deaths are definitely linked to Lauren and the woman who's in hospital?"

"I think we're correct to link the two cases. But equally, we need to keep our minds open. And DCI Ingham could've been right all along in treating the drownings as accidents. It is a terrible stretch of river. And as we know, there have been plenty of accidental deaths there over the years. The attacks on Lauren and Denise could have happened in isolation."

"I would be more inclined to agree with you if it wasn't for Lauren having been stalked before she died. And he *was* hanging around the river that night I took her to the Yorkshire Arms. The e-fit also aligns with the CCTV. It's just a shame we've nothing close up of him."

"Do you know Mark?" DI Jones leans back in his chair and clasps his hands behind his head. He has a slight smile on his face. "I can't believe how well you're coping."

"I'm not coping as well as you think, Sir. I just want him caught. Before he does it to someone else's wife or mother."

CHAPTER THIRTY

Joanne's Family

I stand behind Chris and Hutton as Chris knocks on the door. We've agreed that it is not necessary to say who I am; that my fiancée has been murdered. Lauren had a different surname to me, so the connection won't be made. Besides, all the families we're visiting will be absorbed with their own grief. They don't need to be made aware about mine, and I have been ordered by DI Jones to keep a professional distance.

I just need to be part of things. To feel as though I'm doing something useful. At least at work, I've got some semblance of normality. At home, I'm the grieving husband and must support everyone else too. Besides, I'm finding it tough being around Lauren's things. She's everywhere at the house and I can't stand it.

We've rung ahead and made an appointment to see Joanne Mason's mum and fiancé. They already know that we're now investigating what looks like a serial killing rather than an accident, plus linking what happened to Lauren and the other woman, Denise, to the river deaths. A man answers the door.

"Robin Gilmore? I'm Sergeant Robert Hutton. We spoke on the phone a little while ago. These are my colleagues, PC Chris

Canvey and Sergeant Mark Potts."

The man looks shattered. But there's an anger in his face as he looks us over. I want to tell him I know how he feels. But obviously I can't.

"Come in." His voice is hard to read. We follow him through to a room where a woman rises from a chair as we walk in. "Though I don't know what you're doing here."

"Sit down," she says. "Can I get you all some tea?"

I want to say yes, but Hutton politely declines before I can say anything. In a strange way, it's a comfort to be around people going through the same thing as I am. I sit in an armchair nearest the lounge door whilst Hutton and Chris sit side by side on the two-seater sofa. The woman sits back down and Robin joins her, bolt upright. The room is stuffed with mahogany furniture and dust particles dance in the sunlight which streams through the window.

"Myself and my colleague, PC Chris Canvey, are going to ask you a few questions, if that's OK?" Hutton gestures to himself, then to Chris and me. "Sergeant Potts will take notes."

"You must be Joanne's mum, Carol, is it?" Chris smiles at her. I can see the resemblance. He nods towards a sideboard where many photographs, which must be of Joanne at an entire range of life stages smile back at us.

"Yes. Thank you. I don't think she liked being told we were alike though."

"So what can we do for you?" Robin sits back on the sofa and stares at Hutton with a chill in his eyes. "I don't see what we can tell you that we haven't told you before."

"It's brought it all back to be honest," Carol says. "Just when after three months of counselling, I was starting to feel a fraction more acceptance, I'm back to where I started."

"Me too." Robin follows my gaze to what looks like a fairly recent photograph of him and Joanne stood together, looking like they're at a party. "That was our engagement party," he explains. "We would've been married by now. But that aside, I'm bloody furious that you weren't out there earlier, looking for whoever did this to her."

Carol places a hand on his arm. "It wouldn't have brought her back love."

I nod, a torrent of emotion running through me as I busy myself in rummaging for a pen in my jacket and taking out my pocketbook.

"Your daughter, your fiancée," Hutton nods at each of them. "As you know, was the first in a spate of similar incidents."

We never refer to them as accidents anymore. They've become incidents now.

"Yes, we know." Robin speaks through gritted teeth. "And when all this is over with, you lot are going to be held to account."

"Robin, you're not doing any good. Just let the man speak."

"At the time..." Hutton goes on, "everything did point to Joanne's death being an accident –she was on her hen party, known to have been drinking, and there was a lack of any injuries."

"She was on her hen party." Robin screws his face up. "Of course she was drunk."

"You don't need me to tell you how well-known that area is for people under the influence falling in."

"So why weren't fences put up sooner?"

"Joanne was the first of seven women. However, because of those numbers of women, in such a brief space of time, and with the deaths from last year, we believe they can no longer be treated as accidents."

"Especially when we factor in the two most recent incidents which have happened on the nearby cycle path," Chris adds and my body slumps with the realisation that he's referring to Lauren.

"Which is why we're here to talk to you again," Hutton says. "To go over things and to make sure that you can't remember anything else, no matter how insignificant you might feel it sounds."

I notice that Robin's fists are bunched at his sides. "I can't fucking believe this," he says. "Why are you back here, putting us through this again, having us rake it all up?"

"It was five months ago," Carol adds. "I'm sure I've told you everything I know."

"All I've got," says Robin, his voice calmer now. "Is the memory of telling her she looked beautiful at eight pm before she left the house and then getting the phone call from Carol after they'd realised she'd gone." His fists uncurl and his body slumps. "I don't know what more I can tell you."

"Was she in contact with you at all during the evening?"

"Yeah, a couple of times." There's a ghost of a smile on his face, which surprises me after his anger only a moment ago. I guess that's what grief does to you. "Mostly to report on her mother's youthful behaviour. They were like sisters, these two."

Carol wipes a tear away. "We'd had a lot to drink that night. But there was plenty to celebrate. She had the whole of the rest of her life to live for. I'm sorry. I'm off again. I'm sick of crying. I don't cry all the time anymore, but the tears are never very far away."

Tears well up in my eyes too. I want to ask her. *How long until you start to feel better? How long does grief feel like a physical pain?* Get a grip Mark. This is feeling too close to the bone. Perhaps DI Jones was right. Perhaps I should be at home grieving with my family for Lauren, instead of immersing myself in the grief of a family who have gone through the exact same thing. Only at least Joanne wasn't savagely beaten around the head before she drowned. I can only pray Lauren's death was quick. I fight to regain my composure.

Hutton's voice cuts into my thoughts. "Did anyone talk to Joanne that night? A man, maybe? Or to all of you, as a group."

"Not really," Carol replies. "There were seven of us. It would've been a brave man who would have approached us lot. We were quite rowdy."

"We are really sorry to be taking you through things again," Hutton goes on. "We're visiting all the families, in your situation. When the deaths originally occurred, it looked like the victims had fallen in. Now it's looking like something else. If you can remember anything at all about the evening, it would really help us."

"I really wish I could," Carol says. "We were all laughing at her when she went out for some air. Calling her a lightweight." Her smile quickly fades. "I'm her mother. I should have been looking after her. Not letting her go outside alone."

"We've been through this." Robin touches her arm now. "You've got to forgive yourself. Someone must have already been outside, you said."

"We'd have noticed if she'd been followed out – we all watched her leave the building," Carol says. "But I'm not sure how long it was before we noticed she hadn't come back in. We were all so drunk." She hangs her head. "God, I feel so guilty."

"So then what happened?" My voice is so soft, I don't even realise I've spoken. I'm supposed to be keeping quiet and taking notes, but I'm forever a police sergeant. I can't help it. The families we are meeting will think I'm a right weirdo if I'm completely silent. I don't want to give myself away though. It would complicate the whole situation if they know who I am – it would detract the focus from them.

"We still didn't act straightaway." Carol glances at the photograph of Joanne that I was looking at earlier. "We wasted time ringing her mobile and looking around inside and outside the pub. But we went straight up to the road, thinking she'd have gone towards the lights. Not into the darkness. Then I rang Robin to see if he'd heard from her."

"I hadn't heard a thing. I started trying to ring her too," Robin looks out of the window, squinting in the light. "But her phone was going straight to voicemail."

"How much time do you think passed between you last seeing her and calling the police?"

"At least twenty minutes." Carol wrings her hands. "It's horrendous enough having lost her, but to know I could have stopped it…"

"Stop it Carol. She was a grown woman." Robin stands and walks towards the window, his voice regaining its hard edge. "Look, is this really necessary? I don't see what good it'll do now. And look what it's doing to Joanne's mother."

"Whoever is behind these now eight deaths and nearly a ninth one needs bringing to justice." I'm struggling to conceal the emotion in my voice.

"As you know," Hutton says gently. "Joanne is now part of a murder investigation. We have to make sure no more families go through what you're suffering."

I haven't written anything in my notebook yet. I feel as though I'm inhabiting another person's body today. I don't think I have quite grasped what's happened yet. All I know is I would give anything, *anything,* to have Lauren waiting for me at home, waiting to pummel information from me for her next article, waiting to give me a hug, waiting for our wedding day.

"She might have been a grown woman," Carol sniffs. "But she will always, always be my girl. You will catch him, won't you? If someone did push her in. Then let me at him."

"I meant what I said earlier." Robin looks at each of us in turn. "You lot are going to pay when all this is over."

CHAPTER THIRTY ONE

Becky's Family

A dishevelled man opens the door to us.

"Seb?" Chris says. "I'm PC Chris Canvey and these are my colleagues Sergeant Hutton and Sergeant Potts."

"Hi." He runs his fingers through his hair. "Do you want to come in?"

"If that's OK?" Hutton steps forward. "We won't take up too much of your time."

He holds the door ajar. "Becky's friend, Caroline, is here, like you asked. I dropped her a message after you rang."

We follow him in. The front door opens straight into a sparse lounge where a blonde woman perches on the edge of an armchair. We make our introductions as Seb leans against a sideboard and gestures for us to sit down. He's as cool as a cucumber. In fact, he looks like he's stoned.

"I can't believe this has turned into a murder case." Caroline sinks into her armchair. "As if things haven't been bad enough."

"You spoke to Becky that night, didn't you?" I say. "We've had a look at her phone records and text messages."

"I was worried about her." Caroline shoots Seb a look. "She was in a terrible state and getting drunker and drunker. To be honest, she seemed that drunk, I thought it was likely she *could* have fallen."

Seb looks sheepish. "If I could only change things." The tone of his voice doesn't authenticate his words. "Sometimes you don't know what you've got until it's not there anymore, do you?"

I want to tell him I know what he means, although I did know what I had with Lauren. I hope there was never a day that passed when she didn't know how much I loved her. I don't know how Seb lives with himself, given that they'd been rowing before Becky died. At least I got to kiss Lauren that morning and bring her a cup of tea.

"I was a bit of a lad," Seb goes on. "All she wanted was for us to move in and to go on holiday. I wasn't ready to commit. You know how it is. And I had financial stuff going on. I let her down."

"Right until the very last minute." Caroline's voice is hard and her face is even harder. "You might as well have pushed her in that river yourself. And we won't even get started on the money side of things."

"I didn't ask you here to hear this crap." Seb stuffs his hands deeper into his pockets. "We're supposed to be helping. See if we can come up with anything new."

"The only thing that's new is that you're finally showing remorse for something. Though I suspect you're mostly feeling sorry for yourself."

Caroline is certainly still venomous towards him, even though it's been months since Becky died. Seb has been proven not to be involved in her death. All he's guilty of, as far as I can see, is being dishonest and spineless.

"I tried ringing her the next morning." Caroline's voice is lower now. "She wasn't answering. I thought she'd be nursing a hangover. My partner, Nick, was going barmy with me for interfering, as he saw it, but I think I knew, in my gut, that something had happened. Especially when I heard where a body had been recovered."

"Were you and Seb in contact at all throughout that time?"

"No. We've never exactly been friends, have we?" She glances at him before continuing. The air between Seb and Caroline is crackling with tension. "It was only when she wasn't answering her phone the next day that I sent Seb a message."

Hutton clears his throat. "We've established that Seb was here, and active online all night. Which means he isn't under investigation."

"Are you aware of any enemies Becky might have had?" I've still hardly written anything in my notebook.

"Apart from him?" Caroline gestures towards Seb. "He was her biggest enemy."

"Alright Caroline. Give it a rest. My ex-wife?" Seb's tone is still non-committal, as though he can't be arsed. "Her ex-boyfriend? Some lass she used to work with but didn't get on with? Everyone has enemies, don't they? We don't all go pushing each other into rivers though."

"I mentioned that someone was trying to hit on her that night, haven't I?" Caroline presses her hands together as she speaks.

"Not to me, you haven't." Seb stares at her, with more interest in his voice now.

"We'll check it at the station." Hutton looks at me as if to ensure I'm writing something down. "Can you tell us any more?"

"It's probably nothing. She was very drunk. She mentioned that some weirdo was trying to chat her up at the bar and then kept leering at her after that. She said if he carried on, she would empty his pint over his head."

"Was that whilst you were on the phone to her?"

"Yes. She was that way out though."

"What do you mean?"

Caroline shrugs. "Drunk. Angry. In a bit of a man-hating state of mind."

"Did she say any more about him?"

"Not a lot. She said a couple of times, *he's still looking.* And once she called him a hoodie, whatever that's supposed to mean. I guess he must have been wearing one."

I look at Chris and scribble it down. "That's really useful. We'll follow it up." It's the word *hoodie.* Again. A moment of silence hangs between us all.

"Is that it?" Seb's voice breaks it. "Cos if you don't mind, I've things to be getting on with."

"You're all heart, aren't you Seb?" Caroline stands. "You'd have made Becky's life a misery if you'd bought that house together." She walks to the door and looks back at Hutton and Chris. "You've got my number," she says. "Please keep me posted. But don't ask me to come here again."

I'm wrung out. I can't do much more today. For the first time since Lauren was killed, I want to be at home.

CHAPTER THIRTY TWO

I return to the kitchen, having taken Alysha some toast.

"Is that Mark?"

"Speaking." I'm going to have to try and get some toast down myself as well. My appetite has gone to pieces over the last few days. I can hardly believe it's only been seven days, it feels like seven weeks. Claire turns from the sink where she's washing up and mouths, '*who is it?*'

"It's Tracey from the funeral home here. I'm just letting you know that we've had a call from the hospital and Lauren's ready for us to collect."

She makes it sound as though Lauren's waiting for them. This fills me with fresh misery. I still can't believe I'm never going to hear her laugh again or feel her hand within mine. We've sometimes had to spend a few days apart due to work or having to attend a course, but now I'm starting to physically ache for her. It's like a punch in the stomach. This is the longest time we've been apart since we met, and it's as though she's taken a piece of me with her. I think of the van marked Private Ambulance, which she'll be travelling in, one of the last journeys she'll make.

"Will I be able to see her?" I've already identified her, but suddenly I need to see her face. Perhaps I should be remembering her as she was, but I know I'll regret it if I don't see her again. Besides, part of me still expects her to come bounding through the door. I know, from my police training, that seeing the body can help with acceptance. *The body*. How can I describe her as a body? Tears stab at my eyes. I just want the pain to go away. It's agony.

"Yes. We'll have her ready for you. There's the embalming process we spoke about, that will take us a little while to sort out. And is there anything you'd like her to be wearing?"

"Her wedding dress." My voice cracks as I speak. Brenda agreed with me when I suggested it. She hasn't even seen Lauren wear it. Brenda was going to attend the second fitting with her.

"It's the only way I'll get to see her in it." Tears are dripping from my eyes as I struggle to get the words out. Claire peels off her rubber gloves and walks over to me. She squeezes my shoulder. I'm so glad she's here. I couldn't bear to be on my own.

"We'll call you when she's ready." Part of me likes how Tracey speaks of Lauren as though she's still with us. I want to keep her here for as long as we can. "Then you can come and see her."

"Oh Mark." Claire sits opposite me and takes one of my tear-soaked hands. "I'd give anything to take some of this pain away. To wave a magic wand and bring her back. I hate to see you having to go through this."

I squeeze her hand. "You've been amazing sis. You've been here all week looking after me and Brenda. Eva and Will have helped with Alysha, well Eva has anyway – Will's mostly been working. I don't know what I'd had done without you all. I wouldn't have been able to keep going to work, that's for sure."

"Well, you know what I think about that." Claire takes a sip of her coffee. "You should be taking time off. Though I do understand. We all have our different ways of coping with things. But according to Eva, Will's been working more hours than ever."

"Why? It's not as if they need the money, *is it?* I thought the extra hours were so he could save to take them to Disneyland." A sudden fury rises within me. "Will must be made of steel - how can he even think about a holiday at a time like this? I've not heard from him since the meeting for the funeral. Not even a text. Have you?"

"He's messaged me to check on you. Eva reckons it's all brought memories back from Dean being killed," Claire says softly. "Don't you remember how much he suffered? Especially with being there when Dean was hit."

"With the concussion he had, I'm surprised he has much memory of it. If he hadn't been knocked out, he'd probably have given a better description of the driver."

I hear Alysha's laugh from the other side of the wall. It's good to hear. Whatever she's watching has distracted her from our reality. I can hear Brenda moving about upstairs at last. She's been getting up later and later each day this week. I've heard her up and down all night, every night since Lauren died. It's been the worst week of my life, and hers too, no doubt.

"We'll be able to see Lauren later on tomorrow. That's if you want to." I look at Claire, hoping she'll offer to come with me.

"I'm not sure I can face it Mark. Seeing her, I mean. I'll come with you though - maybe stay in the waiting room. You do understand, don't you?"

"Course I do. I'll have to pick her wedding dress up and take it to the funeral home. I reckon she'd want to be wearing it."

Claire makes an attempt at a smile through her welling tears. "Yeah. She'd want to get her money's worth from it, if I knew Lauren at all. Typical Yorkshire woman."

"Yeah." There's a moment's silence.

"Do you want me to come with you to pick it up? I could do with getting out of the house to be honest."

"I don't know Claire. I can't really take Alysha along, can I?"

"We can drop her off with Eva. I thought that was the plan anyway."

"No. Eva's filming the reconstruction later this morning. I'm dreading seeing it to be honest."

"I know. Me too. Will's got Heidi at home, hasn't he?"

"At least he's having a day off for a change. OK. Can you drop Alysha off for me then?"

"You've hardly spent any time with her Mark. It might do you both good to have that journey together in the car."

I'm struggling with Alysha, but I can't tell Claire. What we've told her about her mother doesn't seem to have gone in, she still thinks her mum will be back, and I'm finding it difficult to cope with her being chatty and normal. Plus, she's too much of a reminder of Lauren. I'm keeping Brenda at arm's length too, for the same reason. It's all something I've got to deal with, but not yet.

"I'll spend some time with her later." I slide my jacket off the back of the dining chair and put it on. "Eva will be more pleased to see you than me, I reckon. She'll be nervous. If she's still there, that is. They're not filming until later this morning. You can calm her down much better than I can."

"I'm surprised Eva wanted to do the reenactment. I imagine it'll be one of the hardest things she will ever have to do."

"We talked about it yesterday. I rang her from the station." I drop the mug I've been drinking from into the washing-up bowl. "She was pleased to help to be honest, and said she'd rather pose as Lauren than have a stranger do it. She's going to use her own bike as we haven't been given Lauren's back yet."

"It's going to be awful for her."

"I know. There's an actor who's going to be dressed up like Lauren's killer. He's going to have to yank her off her bike then drag her towards the stream."

"Well, whatever happens, it raises the profile, doesn't it?"

"But it doesn't bring Lauren back." I throw my uneaten slice of toast in the bin and fill my water bottle from the tap. "I'm going to get this wedding dress sorted out."

"Can I help you?" A woman pokes her head out from another room as the door of the bridal shop beeps.

"Mark Potts. I'm here to pick up the dress of Lauren Holmes."

"Ah yes." Her expression darkens. "Come through. I'm so terribly sorry to hear about Lauren." She reaches out and touches my arm. "It's such a tragic waste. You must be devastated."

"You could say that." I just want to get on with this and out of here, away from this sympathy – I can't stand it. "Anyway, it might sound odd to you, but the funeral home where she's going, have asked me what she'd want to wear. I could only think of her wedding dress."

The young woman's eyes appear to fill with tears. She looks away and busies herself with her computer. "That's one of the most beautiful things I've ever heard. And the saddest. How are you doing? And your little girl?"

"She's too young to understand. She's spent a lot of time with my brother's family since it happened. I'm just taking it hour by hour. Well, minute by minute really."

She sniffs and seems to compose herself. Her tone changes and becomes more matter of fact. "Right - Lauren came in last month for her first fitting. Following that, the seamstress took up the dress an inch. I'll just check she's brought it back. Have a seat."

I sink into a pink chair at the edge of a mass of white satin and polythene. To me, they all look the same. I imagine Lauren coming in here with Sara and picking out her dress. To me, she'd have looked gorgeous in anything. She shouldn't be dead. She shouldn't be dead. She. Shouldn't. Be. Dead. By the time the shop assistant returns, five minutes later, I've got my old friends, the tears, for company. I'm supposed to be a tough-as-old-boots police officer, but I'm a whimpering wreck.

"I'm sorry." I wipe my face on my sleeve. "It's. It's just being here, it's…"

"I know." She drapes what must be Lauren's dress wrapped in polythene on the counter. "It's awful. I've met her twice now. She was so excited to be getting married. And so much loved you and your little girl."

That doesn't make me feel any better. I don't think anything could right now. I try to change the subject. "Thanks for digging that CCTV out for my colleague." I stand and walk towards the counter, trying to be more professional and business-like. "He matches a description of the man in two other locations where Lauren felt as though she was being watched. We're definitely onto something."

"I hope you get him. Poor Lauren."

I tug my wallet out. "What do we owe you for this." *We*. I won't have many more chances to say this.

"Lauren had paid for more than half of it." The woman tucks her hair behind her ear. "We wouldn't hear of taking anything else from you. Please have the dress with our condolences. I've cleared it with my supervisor."

"That's really kind." Fresh tears spring to my eyes. As I leave the shop, I'm filled with raw emotion for the kindness I've been shown in the last few days; text messages, cards, Facebook posts and just the way people treat me.

I drop the dress off with some white underwear and Lauren's white Converse trainers. I don't know what she was planning to wear on her feet for the wedding, but if it could have been Converse, it would have been. I ask them to plait her hair and I read through the newspaper announcement that's due to go in the local paper.

The life of Lauren Frances Holmes, aged 32, was tragically cut short on Sunday January 26th 2020. Beloved wife-to-be of Mark and mother of Alysha. Cherished daughter of Brenda and the late Roy, sister-in-law of William, Eva and Claire and auntie of Heidi. Funeral arrangements to be confirmed, and the family requests a splash of colour is worn. Family flowers only please but donations can be made to CRUSE, Bereavement Counselling Service. Lauren will be forever missed.

CHAPTER THIRTY THREE

I return to the car and decide to check with Eva how the reconstruction has gone, but just as I'm pulling up her number, the station rings.

"Mark. DI Jones here. Denise, the other woman attacked at the stream, has regained consciousness. Earlier this morning."

Like I need reminding who Denise is. "That's good news." I hope I don't sound too half-hearted. I genuinely am relieved, just bitter that Lauren didn't get the same outcome.

"She's up to talking. Just for a short time. I'm going to visit her. See what she remembers."

"I'll meet you there."

"That's not why I was ringing. Honestly, Mark. I was just letting you know. There's no need for you to come along. It could be really hard for you."

"Nothing could be any harder for me than what's already happened. I want to see her. If that's alright?"

"It might be upsetting for her, too. You know, meeting the nearly-husband of a woman who's not been as fortunate as she has."

"Fair point. How about if, for now, I just introduce my name and rank and don't tell her anything about who I am. It's been fine so far with the families I've met when I've been out with Sergeant Hutton and PC Canvey."

"If that's OK? Apparently she's still very weak, and I could do with having another officer with me. There's no one else around at the moment. But let me do the talking Mark."

After parking in the police section of the hospital car park, I meet DI Jones in the foyer. The last time I was here was to identify Lauren's body. I feel cold, despite the heat that's being generated from so many people huddled together in the waiting area.

"They've moved her into the high dependency unit." DI Jones says as we walk down the blue shiny corridor past a little courtyard where several people are sat vaping, in dressing gowns and slippers. "She's out of the woods now and they needed her intensive care bed."

"Is she expecting us?"

"Yes. The doctor has said we can have no more than five minutes. She's very tired. Her husband will be there too."

We report to the nurse's station and are shown to Denise's bay, nodding to the two constables on watch duty. She's hooked up to an array of machines, all bleeping intermittently.

"Denise," the nurse says. "Here are the two officers I mentioned. Are you definitely up to answering questions?"

"I'll do my best," she croaks. She points to her neck. "As you can hear, and see, he had a good go at flattening my windpipe." My gaze flickers to her neck, swollen and purple.

"DI Jones and Sergeant Potts," DI Jones announces. "Thanks for seeing us Denise. We won't keep you long." He offers his hand to the man sat beside Denise's bed.

"I'm Jack," he announces. "Denise's husband. I hope you're going to catch this bastard."

I shake his hand as well. His face wears the tiredness and relief of the last two days he has lived through. *You don't know how lucky you are,* I want to tell him. *I'd give anything to have my wife-to-be here.* But for these few minutes, I have to be professionalism personified.

Denise has a drain from her head, due to having been hit on the back of it with a rock, as the attacker had with Lauren, causing internal bleeding.

"I know you won't feel like it," I say. "But you've had an extremely lucky escape."

"I know. If it wasn't for the man walking his dog."

"We still don't know if there'll be any lasting effects from the head injury." Jack touches Denise's hand. "Not to mention the psychological scars. She'll have to take it easy for a while."

"I just want him caught." Denise croaks, looking from me to DI Jones. "I don't think I'll dare leave my house again until you have him locked up."

A minute's gone already. We need to get asking questions. Without waiting for DI Jones, I decide to wade in. "Have you any idea why anyone might have done this to you?" I stare at the terrible bruising on her arm as she raises her hand to rub the side of her head.

"None whatsoever. I was minding my own business." Her voice is raspy. "On my bike, on my way to work."

DI Jones frowns at me and I know that's my cue to butt out and let him do the talking.

"What time did you leave for work?"

"About half ten. In the morning."

He pulls his chair slightly closer to the bed. "You live fairly close to the cycle path, don't you?"

"Yes."

"And he pushed you from your bike, presumably. Can you remember which direction he came at you from?"

"It's all hazy." She's rubbing her throat now as she looks at her husband. "I've been trying to remember as much as I can, but thinking makes my head hurt more." She coughs. "Sorry, it hurts to talk. I think he jumped out at me."

"I bet it does." I notice her husband's concerned face and feel the urge to weep. I would give absolutely anything to be at Lauren's bedside right now. Instead, in another part of the hospital, she'll be getting collected any time soon, and taken to the funeral home. It's so cruel.

"He seemed to jump out of absolutely nowhere."

"Did you get a look at him?"

"Not really. He hit me over the head before I realised what was going on. It all happened so quickly."

"Can you remember anything at all about what he was wearing?

I don't mind keeping quiet. DI Jones is asking all the right questions. I'm glad to be here though, hearing it all first-hand. I feel as though I'm helping Lauren by being here.

"A hoodie," Denise replies. "And he was quite a lot taller than me. When he had his arm around my throat, I wasn't even up to his shoulders."

"What about his build?"

"Average build, I guess. Like I said, it's hazy, and it all happened so fast. I can't remember getting away from him."

"Do you recall anything about his hair or the colour of his eyes?"

Denise shakes her head.

"It was a dog walker who rescued you and raised the alarm. Do you remember him?"

"No, it's all a blank after I was hit over the head. Though I do now remember having my face under the water and thinking I was going to die. I recall feeling the stones at the bottom of the stream cutting into my face." She raises one hand to touch the extensive lacerations.

"You must have been terrified." Jack squeezes her other hand. "I'm never letting you out of my sight again."

She squeezes his hand back. "You know me. I'll be back on my feet in no time. He's not ruining the rest of my life."

I swallow, wishing more than anything on earth that Lauren could talk about the rest of her life. I hate this bastard more than ever. I'm keeping calm and quiet but I will get him and I *will* get access to him after we've brought him in. He'll wish he had never been born.

DI Jones pulls the CCTV image and the e-fit impression from his folder. "Do these pictures jog your memory at all?" Denise is laid nearly flat, so he places the images on his folder then angles them towards her.

She tries to sit up and looks from one to the other, then back to DI Jones. "I'm trying, but no – it could be anyone really. Apart from the hoodie. I do remember he was wearing a hoodie. That's all I can be definite about."

"Did he say anything?" I ask.

"Not properly," she replies. "He was kind of snarling. It's the most terrifying thing I've ever gone through." She leans back into her pillows. "I can't believe I'm still here to be honest. I honestly thought he was going to kill me. I'm shocked that I survived it." Tears are spilling from her eyes down the sides of her head. "I don't know why he came after *me.*"

"I think that's enough for today," Jack says, letting go of her hand and looking at us. "Can you come back another day if you've got any more questions?"

"Yes, if you don't mind," Denise croakily agrees. "I'm feeling a bit sickly."

I don't go back to the station. After visiting Denise, I drop the dress off at the funeral home. There's a private ambulance parked at the side entrance, and I wonder if it's transferring Lauren. The reconstruction will be underway now. I give Chris a call and discover he and Hutton have made appointments to meet with two more of the families today. At first I'm annoyed that they haven't kept me informed of their plans. Until Hutton explains he was told I was visiting Denise.

Because I'm finding that I'm totally unable to stop, I arrange to meet them at the first appointment they've made. If I allow it to, my misery might just devour me. With every day that passes, I'm sinking a little bit further, I have to keep fighting to stay afloat.

CHAPTER THIRTY FOUR

Veronica's Family

Chris digs his hands into his pockets. "This feels like a waste of time. It's not as if anybody is telling us anything we don't already know."

"I disagree." Hutton looks at him as we stride towards the gate. "We owe it to these families to show we're taking their loss seriously. And I know it would sound cynical if anyone knew, but it might also make the difference between receiving official complaints, or not."

"And more importantly, even if the tiniest bit of new information comes to light," I add. "It might lead us to the scumbag quicker."

"Before he kills any more women."

"Yeah, you're right. Sorry." Chris leads us up some steps to the door. "What do I know? You two have been at this a lot longer than I have."

As I look from the porch towards the bay window, nothing seems to have moved from when I was here two months ago, apart from the Christmas tree. I imagine that got ripped down straightaway. Personally, I can't imagine celebrating anything anymore.

"Hi." Tricia opens the door. She's different to how I remember. Thinner. Older. Much more serious. This is what grief does; it etches itself into every line on your face. "Come in."

We file past her, me first. I know where we're going from last time. Out of the latest victims, Veronica's family was the last one I was allowed to have any involvement with before Ingham made me take a back seat when Lauren had started digging.

God, what I'd give to turn the clock back. December. I had everything to live for then.

The room looks much bigger without the imposing tree. Tricia must notice me looking around.

"I can't bear to change anything in here." She wipes a tear away. "I know I'm going to have to get the house on the market soon and I'll have to pack Mum's stuff up at some point. I just can't face it yet." She pulls a tissue from the box. "I'm sorry. I didn't expect to cry. It's just – seeing police again, it kind of brings it all back."

"It must be very difficult." Hutton points at an armchair. "Do you mind if we have a seat?"

"Of course not." She gestures towards the sofa for me and Chris, then sits on the other armchair and blows her nose. "So what did you want to see me about?"

I pull out my notebook which, so far, isn't doing too well at recording anything additional.

"We just want to go over the evening of your mother's death again. Now that it's become a suspected murder investigation, we're going back over all the evidence, checking that we haven't missed anything."

Tricia nods, looking deep in thought. "It's horrendous. One day, I'm thinking Mum's fallen in under the influence. Then people are suggesting she'd jumped in because she was missing Dad, which is rubbish by the way. She would never have done that. And now…" her voice trails off and she dabs at her eyes.

"I know," Hutton says. "We hate to make you go back over it, but if there's the tiniest bit of something that we've missed. We just need to catch this person."

"I gave you a full account back then." She sighs and blows her nose again. "Sorry for getting so upset. I think it has brought Dad's passing back to me too. We'd gone out to cheer Mum up. She hadn't had a night out since he died. But we hadn't eaten, and she'd been drinking gin. It's all my fault. I should have insisted that we ate earlier. We got carried away."

"It happens to the best of us," Chris smiles. "Drinking on an empty stomach. It's not your fault at all."

"Mum only went to the loo. Suddenly I realised she'd been gone for a while and had an inkling maybe she wasn't well. She didn't drink a lot, usually."

"What time was this?"

"I don't know. Possibly around midnight. We were about to go to the Jewel of India for some food."

"It's open all hours, that place," Chris says.

I frown at him. The middle of a murder investigation is not the time to discuss the opening hours of Indian restaurants. He's alright is Chris, I like him, but he's got a lot to learn as a constable.

"Thinking she was still in the loos. I went to check on her," Tricia leans forwards in her chair, briefly hugging her knees as though trying to comfort herself. "I was shouting *mum, mum* and banging on the doors. I thought she must have fallen asleep. I wasted time waiting for people to come out of each loo. If I'd gone out sooner, I might have been able to stop whatever happened from happening."

"How long were you in the toilets for?"

"Easily five minutes. Maybe even ten."

I look at the smiling photos all around the room. This is what family boils down to. Eventually, this is all that's left. Photographs and memories. It's agony, this grief business. I'd rather have my leg sawn off with a blunt blade. "Then what."

"I went back down into the pub, thinking she must have somehow slipped passed me, but my friend, Hazel, hadn't seen her either. I ran around the pub for a bit, asking people. The man behind the bar thought he'd seen a woman, possibly Mum, leave with a man but, that must have been someone else. Mum wouldn't have left the pub with a man. As soon as he said that though, I ran outside."

I make a note of the woman leaving with a man bit. "Did your friend go outside with you?"

"After a couple of minutes. We tried ringing Mum, but really, I knew there was no way she'd have just gone. Hazel and I were due to sleep here, at her house that night, and even if we weren't, she'd have let us know what she was doing."

"We received the three nines call from you at 12:34 am. Can you recall seeing anything untoward outside the Yorkshire Arms whilst you were waiting for us to get there?"

"Nothing." Tricia runs her hands up and down her arms. "I can't believe that just yards away, my mother was underwater."

"Has anything else come to mind since?" Hutton has a sip of water from the bottle he's brought in with him. It's a very warm house. "Did anyone unexpected attend her funeral?"

"No. I knew everyone there. And Mum didn't have an enemy in the world. I can't imagine anyone who'd have wanted to target her."

"We don't think your mum was *chosen* by someone who knew her personally. We think we're looking for someone who's targeting women who look a particular way, and on their own after drinking."

"Mum was in her fifties." Tricia glances at a photograph of her. "How can she be compared with some of the others? In terms of looking a particular way. One was in her early twenties."

Hutton follows her gaze to the photograph. "It's the dark hair worn long, and the green eyes. She had green eyes, didn't she?"

"Yes. Like me." Tricia's eyes fill with more tears. "I can't seem to get myself together. I haven't since she died. I wish I could remember something to help you. But she was a normal, lovely mum, grieving for her husband. She didn't deserve to die. Please catch him."

Chapter Thirty Five

Jennifer's Family

It sounds like some kids are having a fight as we walk up the path. "Get off me!" Then there's a thud against the window.

"I'm telling!"

A male voice shouts from inside the house. We look at each other as we ring the doorbell. A woman answers. I haven't met her before, but she resembles the photographs I've seen of Jennifer.

"Sergeant Robert Hutton, Sergeant Mark Potts and PC Chris Canvey." Hutton gestures to each of us. By now, a man has emerged behind her in the doorway.

"Alan Fairburn." He extends a hand past her. "It was me you spoke to on the phone. Jenny's husband."

"I'm Natalie Farley," says the woman, holding out her hand too. "Jenny's sister. Stop it you two!" She turns towards the stairs. "I'm just going to read them the riot act. Then we might be able to hear each other speak."

"Can I get you a drink?" Alan asks as we follow him into the kitchen. "I was just making one for us." He gestures towards the large kitchen table for us to sit.

"If it's no trouble," I reply before Hutton can refuse. I know he likes to keep these visits brief, but I'm sleeping so erratically that I need all the caffeine on offer to keep me going.

"As you know, Jenny and I had parted company before she died." Alan fills a teapot and a cafetière with boiling water. "But I'm living back here now to look after my kids." He brings the pots to the table and gives us all a cup.

I nod and fill a cup from the cafetière. "Thanks. Much appreciated."

Natalie returns and pulls a chair up at the end of the kitchen table. The late afternoon sunshine and the crocuses coming up in the garden are completely at odds with the discussion we're about to have and the darkness I'm feeling. "So," she says. "You're definitely looking for someone who *killed* my sister? She didn't just fall into the river?"

"I'm afraid it would appear so." Hutton fills his mug with tea. "And in light of that, we are here to see if you can remember anything since we last saw you that might help us with the investigation."

"They should bring back hanging." Alan adds milk to his cup. "Men like him shouldn't be allowed to breathe fresh air. He robbed my kids of their mother."

"It might not be a man." Natalie looks across the table at him, squinting in the sunshine.

"We're fairly certain it is." Hutton's gaze flicks towards Alan, who is tilting one of the window blinds to alleviate the sun in Natalie's eyes.

"Well, there's nothing much I can tell you," Alan says. "I didn't know anything had happened until the next day, when Natalie rang me."

"Did you have any contact with her the day she died?" I ask with my pen poised over my notebook. Hutton seems reasonably OK now with me occasionally speaking at these meetings. I think he knows I'm not going to break down or take over the conversations by mentioning Lauren. My grief can wait until we have the maniac behind bars.

"No. I'd moved out a few months before," Alan replies. "I'd been living with someone else. Before I came back here to look after the kids, I mean."

"Has your new partner come with you? Here, I mean?" Chris speaks now.

"No. The kids get on her nerves. Well, you can hear them, can't you? Little sods." At that he jumps up and heads for the door of the kitchen. "Keep it down," he calls up the stairs. "Auntie Nat and I are trying to talk to the police about your mum." After that there is deathly silence.

"Did Jenny and your new partner have many dealings with one another?"

"Nah." He laughs a little. "Are you suggesting that Kirsty might have had something to do with it? No. She wasn't keen on Jenny but wouldn't have wanted her dead!"

"*I've* remembered something that I haven't mentioned before." Natalie chews her lip. "It's come up in my head a couple of times since my sister's funeral."

"Go on," Hutton says, looking at me.

"It's probably nothing." She frowns as she takes a sip from her cup. "But when Jennifer left the Yorkshire Arms that night, a man left at the same time. She held the door open for him if I'm remembering correctly. I didn't treat it with any importance at the time because she turned left from the exit towards the road and he turned right towards the riverbank path."

"Can you remember what he looked like?"

"To be honest, I only saw him from the back. He was casual. But like I say, he went in the opposite direction."

Chris wraps his hands around his cup. "Did you continue watching after that?"

"Erm, no. I don't think so. After all, Jen was getting a taxi to get home to them two upstairs. They were throwing up, and the babysitter had rung. Jen hadn't wanted me to go with her, so I just carried on with my evening. And it was chucking it down so I didn't go out and wait with her. She was supposed to text me from the taxi."

There's a thundering of footsteps down the stairs and a door bangs. "Obviously she didn't. " Alan glances out of the window as one of his kids, and one that must be Jennifer's, walks towards the garden shed. I think of Alysha and wonder what she'll look like in a few years' time. She might be like this girl I'm watching now, growing up without her mum. I take a deep breath to avert the sorrow that threatens to engulf me and turn back to Natalie. She's very matter-of-fact and cool for someone whose sister has died in this way.

"To be honest, it slipped my mind to get in touch with her. It's only when I got a message from her babysitter through Facebook an hour later that I realised something was up. And then I called you."

"You've been really helpful," Hutton says, draining his cup. "The brief description you've given of the man ties in with the investigation."

"We'll keep you posted." I stand. I've had enough for one day and decide to go for a walk before going home. I need to be alone with my thoughts. "Thanks for your time."

CHAPTER THIRTY SIX

I poke my head into the lounge where Brenda and Claire are staring at the TV.

"Drink anyone?" I say. "I'm having a brandy."

They both nod. None of us ever really drink like this, but over the last few days, it's been deemed acceptable. I will be an alcoholic if I'm not careful. It's the only thing, apart from sleep, that can numb the pain. Sometimes the grief is overwhelming and nearly knocks me over. It ebbs and flows, but it's more manageable when I'm occupied, like at work, or when I have a brandy in my hand. I stride into the kitchen and pull out three glass tumblers from the cupboard.

"Daddy," Alysha calls into the hallway. "I'm back."

I step into the hallway and spot my sister-in-law behind her. Alysha thrusts a picture into my hand. "It's Mummy," she says, pointing at the smiling stick figure with blue legs, a big red smile and two long brown plaits, one sticking out from either side of her head.

"Grandma and Auntie Claire are in the lounge." Tears fill my eyes as I point at the door. "Why don't you go and say hello?"

As she pushes the door open, I turn to Eva. "Thanks Eva. You've been incredible this week."

"Don't be daft. I've just helped out with my niece – it's what anyone would do. How are you doing?"

She follows me into the kitchen. I take the brandy down from the top of the fridge and fill the three tumblers.

She refuses when I offer her one. "I'm driving."

"It might settle me down," I reply. "I feel sick all the time. I keep expecting her to walk through the door. It's shit Eva, it's just shit." I don't swear often. I made a point not to after Alysha was born.

"Will and I are thinking of you all the time. Come here." I step towards her and put my head against her shoulder. She wraps her arms around me and we stay there for a moment. It's unheard of, me and my sister-in-law hugging, but these are exceptional circumstances. I think the last time we hugged was when Lauren and I got engaged. But I need all the hugs on offer right now. However, I don't quite believe that Will is thinking of me.

"I'm going to get back so Will can get off," she says. "I still feel shaky after the reconstruction. Will tried to stop me from doing it, but I wouldn't have it. I wanted to help."

"Did he?"

"Yeah. He reckoned he knew it would have this sort of effect on me."

"I really appreciate what you've done, you know."

"I know. I did it for Lauren and I don't care what Will thinks."

"Why do you have to get back? Where's he going?"

"He's taken an extra shift. He reckons we need to get away more than ever now and is on about inviting Alysha as well - he thinks it might give her something to look forward to."

"I'm hungry." Alysha appears in the kitchen doorway before I can reply.

"I'll give you a call later." I reach for the biscuit tin on top of the fridge. "When I've got this one settled and watched the reconstruction."

"You shouldn't be hungry." Eva ruffles Alysha's hair. "After the huge tea Uncle Will cooked for you and Heidi. I'll just say hello to Claire and Brenda before I set off."

I do my best to listen and engage with Alysha whilst she pushes her toys around in the bath, but like lots of parents, I've become well practised in saying 'um' and 'yeah' in the right places and looking like I'm listening when in fact, I'm stuck in my own foggy world, one that's dark and closing in on me.

"I miss Mummy," she says. "I want her to come home. Can we pick her up from heaven Daddy?"

"God, I wish we could, sweetie." I reach for the towel on the radiator and wrap it around her whilst lifting her from the bath.

"I feel really sad Daddy. It's like a funny feeling in my tummy that won't go away."

I rub at her hair with the towel. Hair that's the same as Lauren's. It makes me ache to look at Alysha. She's the image of her mother. "I know. I've got the same feeling in my tummy too. I think we'll both have it for a long time."

"Why can't she come home? Why is she dead? Why didn't she take us with her?"

Questions I wish I could answer. Questions I want answering too. Poor Alysha. And I don't know how I will look after her on my own.

My voice wobbles as I read her a story. This is why I've avoided her all week. I don't know what to say. I can't hold it together. Normally, when it's been my turn to read to her at bedtime, I send Lauren up after I've finished to tuck her in. She's silent when I give her a hug, and I see the pain in her eyes as I pull back. "I'll send Grandma and Auntie Claire up to see you." Then with a squeeze of her arm, I'm out of there before she sees the tears slide down my face. She would have been beside herself with excitement at the prospect of a new brother or sister. She's not mentioned anything about her flower girl role yet either. It's a nightmare.

I open our bedroom door and go straight over to Lauren's wardrobe. I bury my face in the dress she wore the last time we were out for the evening. There's a trace of the Valentino perfume I bought her for Christmas. Breathing in her scent brings forth sobs so violent, I worry Alysha will hear. Then I feel hands on each of my shoulders. Turning me around and into Lauren's mother. "Come here you," she says, and I feel the wetness of her cheeks too. "You let it all out. It's about time."

"I can't cope without her. I can't do this." The voice that's coming from me sounds alien. I don't know how long we stand there, but eventually I pull back. I hear Claire's voice in Alysha's room and feel calmer. "I'm OK," I say to Brenda. "Thanks for the hug. I needed it."

"The reconstruction is on soon," she replies. "Let's watch it. Sometimes they get people calling in straight away."

"I went to see the woman who survived, did I tell you?" I walk behind her on the stairs. "She was in a right state. We need to catch the bastard. Sorry for swearing Brenda. We're revisiting all the other families, in the hope that they remember something now that it's become a murder hunt."

"Is that a good idea?" She turns to me as we reach the bottom. "You being involved, I mean?"

"Yes. I want to do everything I can to help catch him. The police investigation has been a mess. Don't repeat that though – keep it between me and you." I follow her into the lounge.

"Lauren had written about it, hadn't she?" Brenda tilts the blinds. "I begged her to be careful. It's possibly why she was killed, isn't it?"

"The original Detective Chief Inspector has come off the case. I don't know if he offered to or was asked to." I point the remote at the TV. "He's been going through a split with his wife and his mind has not been on the job. There's a DI on it now who's really thorough. DI Jones, he's the one who collected you after... anyway, he's being overseen by another DCI. We'll get him, don't worry."

"I bloody hope so." Brenda sinks to the sofa beside Claire. "And then they should leave me on my own with him. That would be the best punishment he could possibly receive. After what he did to my daughter."

My stomach churns as the opening music begins. Claire used to be scared to death of this programme when we were kids. We would always watch it, and then she'd be really worried for days afterwards. I suppose it does have the effect of making people think the world is full of crime.

"We start tonight with a dreadful case involving a series of drownings in Alderton in Yorkshire," the host begins. "Since September last year, a total of seven women have lost their lives in the River Alder and there have been two further attacks - one fatal, at a nearby stream that runs into the river." He goes on to flash up their pictures, one by one, then stops when he gets to Lauren's. I stare into the smiling face of the only woman I have ever properly loved. She looks so full of vitality and happiness. Claire and Brenda reach for each other's hands and I sit forwards in my seat.

Denise, it is said, can't yet be named for legal reasons, but Lauren is described. They talk about her being in the early stages of pregnancy and progressing well in her career.

My breath catches in my throat when the reenactment starts and the camera follows Eva up the familiar cycle path. It was similar weather this morning to what it was like on the day she died. It really could be Lauren on that bike as Eva's brown hair billows out behind her. I can understand why Will didn't want her to do it, but I'm proud of her for going ahead anyway.

But I know what's coming. My flesh creeps as a hooded figure emerges from the overgrown grass and bushes bordering the cycle path, blocking Eva's path, before grabbing hold of the front and back of the bike, and shaking her balance. She is thrown off, and tries to run, but the assailant gives chase and quickly catches her.

I know he's an actor, but watching this is making me shake with terror, misery and a guilt I can't explain. Why couldn't I have protected my fiancée? Why did I have to go to the stupid fire station that morning?

Eva is yelling and wriggling whilst the man wrestles her to the ground. Eva stops yelling when he imitates bashing her on the back of the head with a rock. He then drags her supposedly limp body towards the stream. The camera doesn't zoom in on his face, after all, we haven't had a decent shot of him, but he's the same darkly dressed, hooded tall figure, as in the CCTV stills. And he's a bloody good actor.

The focus switches back to the studio where the host completes the story about Lauren being drowned in the stream and abandoned there with her attacker making no attempt to conceal her body. Information is given around the suspicion of her being watched in four different locations, before she was pursued in a final attack. The picture of Lauren is shown again, followed by the photographs of the other seven women on two separate screens. The helpline number is continuously rolling across the bottom.

"Why did it have to happen," Brenda sobs as the programme moves onto the next item. "I can't believe she's never coming back."

"I knew she was going too far - and sticking her neck out at the probability of foul play as opposed to the drownings being accidents. We suspect this spooked whoever was preying on women by the river." I'm in police mode again. "In my mind, the crucial link is her being watched in four different locations - always by someone in a hood, three of which have CCTV to evidence it. One of those occasions being at the river."

"I told her to be careful. She seemed to think she was invincible."

I think now of Denise, who is recovering. "The woman who survived a similar assault, at the same place as Lauren, was attacked by a hooded figure as well."

Brenda doesn't look convinced. "Lots of people wear hooded tops. You do."

"There's also the fact *drowning* was the cause of *all* the deaths. And, where Lauren was found in the stream, it's only a hare's whisker from the river." I lean over the side of my armchair to pick up my phone. Anyway, I'm going to give Eva a call. She was a bit shaken when she was here before."

"I'll have a word with her too." Claire tucks her legs under her.

She picks up straightaway. "Did you watch it?"

"We all did. I really appreciate it Eva. It must have been tough for you."

"Yes, it was. But I didn't want anyone else playing her. She was my sister-in-law."

"Well I just wanted to say you did really well. And to say thank you."

"Let's just hope it leads to the man being locked up for a very long time. I certainly won't be walking anywhere on my own until he's caught. And please tell me if anything comes in as a result of it."

"Of course. I'll be going into the station tomorrow. What time's Will back?"

"He's doing a full night shift now – he was only supposed to be going in for a few hours. It's like he doesn't want to be here."

"It's not that Eva. He's always been the same. When it comes to anything traumatic or emotional, he's off. He can't handle it."

"You're so different, you and him," she sniffs. "He's about as sensitive as a house brick. He forgot to ask if I'm OK after the reconstruction. Oh, I know what I meant to ask – has your mother been in touch?"

"Only by text. She's as useless as Will, to be honest."

"I don't know if useless is the word I'd use Mark. For either of them right now. I can think of other words."

So could I, but we're best not going there. As we hang up, I make a mental note to speak to him. He doesn't know how lucky he is having the home life he's got. He needs to sort his act out. There are more important things in life than overtime. Eva and Heidi need him around more than they need to go to bloody Florida.

CHAPTER THIRTY SEVEN

I'm rostered on for a long shift today, but I've been told, and it's continually reiterated, that I can work as much or as little as I want. I get to the station early though. I was up before anyone else had stirred in our house. I want to know if the reconstruction has yielded any results. Apparently their operators pass information straight onto us.

There's a message scrawled on the whiteboard in the staffroom. *Meeting 9am sharp – incident room. Bring all findings re: river/stream inquiry.*

"How long's Ingham off for?" I ask Tina as we head to the incident room. As our admin, she knows everything.

"I don't know. Indefinitely as far as I can see."

"Does he have a doctor's note?"

"Mark. You know I can't give details like that out. Why do you ask?"

"It's just - if he's sitting on any information. You know, he must have done some work on this before he went off sick. If he knows anything that can help."

"Why don't you mention it to DI Jones?" She clutches her notebook to her chest. "He's probably in touch with DCI Ingham and should have access to his files. I'm only asked to these meetings to take the minutes."

The room is packed. Everyone wants this nutter caught. I've noticed that my colleagues either avoid my gaze or stare at me sympathetically. No one seems to know what to say to me. A few of them, like Hutton and Chris, are being fairly normal and I prefer that, really. Being at work is as close to normal as I can get.

"We had a significant response to the TV appeal last night." The room falls quiet as DI Jones stands. "We've had several eyewitnesses come forward that believe they saw our man both before and after he killed Lauren Holmes, in the vicinity of the attack." Hearing her name out loud is still a knife in my chest. "So we'll be talking to those people today and viewing any CCTV footage we can for the locations they've put forward."

DI Jones looks down at his notepad before continuing. "We've also had three reports of other women who worry they've been followed or watched, whilst entering or leaving the Yorkshire Arms in recent weeks. We'll get statements from them today as well. I'll give out roles and responsibilities before we get cracking. Everyone needs to be doing their bit, and some. Today could be the day we get him."

"There are also a number of people who claim they know who the man is. A particular person of interest is saying that their partner has been coming in at all hours and has been acting strangely. We need to investigate these claims carefully. They could well prove to be cranks." He glances at the board with all the photographs displayed. "Awareness has certainly been raised amongst local women to keep themselves safe whilst he's at large, so that's a positive thing. Mark, are you OK with me discussing Lauren's results whilst you're in the room?" DI Jones looks at me.

I swallow. "Yes. It's OK." It's not, but I have to be here. I'm not missing anything.

DI Jones repeats what he told me the other day about the results at Lauren's post-mortem, including the bit about the baby. All eyes are suddenly on me.

"God Mark, I'm so sorry." Tina drops her pen from taking minutes and grabs my arm. I can literally feel the wave of sympathy.

"Carry on." I nod towards DI Jones.

"You OK mate?" Chris calls out.

"Honestly, everyone, save your sympathy until we've caught him. Then, I'll be needing it." I bow my head so my colleagues don't notice my welling tears.

DI Jones goes on to add details about the forensics report, which I haven't heard yet. "They found dark fibres on Lauren's clothing…"

"But that's only going to do us some good if we've got a suspect whose clothes we can take as evidence." I feel like banging my head against a wall. It feels as though we're getting nowhere. "Is there no DNA?"

DI Jones shakes his head. "Unfortunately not Mark. He's been very lucky or very careful."

"How are we getting on with the house to house inquiries Sir?" One of the constables, Ben Roberts, speaks now. He's been tasked with social media so far.

"Slow," DI Jones says. "The officers involved reported back to me yesterday. In this day and age, I'd expect more houses to have their own CCTV and more cars to possess dash cams. The public are sympathetic, but no one has seen anything."

"People just aren't nosy anymore," Chris says. "My parent's generation were right curtain twitchers."

"I think one of the issues is CCTV is often wiped automatically after a set time. It's usually not so long after being recorded if nothing has happened."

"I haven't really got anywhere with my searching of social media either," Ben adds.

"We've spoken with the families of four of the drowning victims," Hutton speaks next. "And haven't turned much up, apart from a mention that the fourth victim divulged in a telephone conversation that a man wearing a hood was staring at her in the Yorkshire Arms before she left."

"And someone at the same time as one of the victims, it was said, left with a tall, stocky man, casually dressed."

"That's interesting," DI Jones writes something down. "It ties in with the CCTV we've got. But don't get too hung up on the hoodie. After all, that could just be what he or she wears when planning an attack. And it is a garment that's fairly commonplace."

"There was no mention of one woman being stared at, or another leaving with someone in either original statement. I've yet to get someone onto the pub CCTV for those particular days. Hopefully, we still have that footage." Hutton continues speaking. "The family of one of the other victims also mentioned the possibility of the woman being followed out of the pub by a man."

"This hooded or casually dressed male seems to be the only lead we've got." DI Jones glances towards the pictures of the women as he speaks. "So far, there's been no DNA or forensics available nor evidence to suggest that it was anything other than a combination of alcohol and a muddy riverbank causing the women to fall into the water."

"We'll find the evidence," I say through gritted teeth. "We've another three families to visit yet. And still some CCTV to look at and witnesses to interview from the reconstruction responses." All eyes are on me. "Look I know the figures; fifty percent of drownings are alcohol related. But I know, I just know, Lauren was targeted because she was onto something that was going to discredit the accident theory."

"I think I agree with you Mark." DI Jones's tone is cautious. "But I think we need to keep an open mind. The lack of forensic evidence with the drownings is a problem."

"If CCTV had been properly installed when it was needed, we would have all the evidence we needed now." My fists ball with frustration. "And if the additional patrols had been organised straight away, we might have caught the man responsible. There is more evidence. And I'm going to find it."

As we all file out of the room at the end of the meeting, my phone beeps with a text from Claire. *The funeral home has rung. We can go and see Lauren if we want to.*

I catch Hutton's elbow in the corridor. "Do you mind if I get off for the day?"

"Not at all. You OK? Sorry Mark – daft question. Again."

"We've had a call from the funeral home. I'm off to see Lauren."

"God, I can't imagine what you're going through." He squeezes my shoulder.

"Don't even try to." Several people pass us. "Listen. Do you mind leaving the rest of the family meetings until tomorrow? I really want to be there, but this, it feels like something I've got to do today." My voice is wobbling and I know that I need to get out of here.

"As none of the other families have given us anything much new, I'm sure it can wait till then, Chris and I can get on with checking the CCTV today. I'm thinking if there is a killer, he knows what he's doing. If we turn anything up, I'll get a message to you."

"Thanks."

"Have you got someone to go with you?" He calls after me.

I turn around. "Yes. My sister."

"I *will* come into the room with you Mark." Claire shuffles from foot to foot in front of the undertaker's desk. "To see Lauren, I mean. I've changed my mind. It might help me accept that she's gone. I still keep expecting her to burst into the house, large as life."

"I know what you mean. But are you sure? I won't think any less of you if you don't. Even Brenda decided she couldn't see her."

"I reckon she'll change her mind before the funeral. I'm just scared. I've never seen anyone who's died before. If you remember, I couldn't even see Dean when..."

"I know. If it gets too much, just come back out here again."

"I can't believe we're having to do this." She plucks a tissue from the box on the desk. "I really can't."

"We can offer you a date for the funeral now." The undertaker flicks open a diary. "Now that Lauren's here with us. Is a week tomorrow any good? 11:40 am?"

I want to say, *how can anything be any good? My fiancée is dead.* Instead, I mumble *OK* and stare at the press announcement in front of me, the words jumbling in front of my stinging eyes. We can publish it now that we have the funeral details. I'm absolutely sick of crying. I am supposed to be checking it, but I can't focus.

She writes the date and time on a card and slides it towards Claire as though it's a dental appointment. "Just so you've got it written down," she says. "I know it can be difficult to remember things when everything is upside down. Did you decide on any readings you would like, and music? There's the flowers to choose as well?"

I haven't got a clue. I don't admit that I've not even thought about stuff like that. "Erm, no. I'll come back with Lauren's mum to discuss them. She should be part of it."

"Very wise." she snaps her diary shut and smiles.

What is there to smile about? Now I'm feeling like I want to shout at her. But I swallow my anger and say, "when we go in," then hesitate. "Is she in, like, the coffin?" I've seen people dead in the course of my work, but someone laid, funeral-ready is another matter. This is the second time it's been someone I loved. I was only fourteen when Dean got mown down by a drunk driver. Although there was a sizeable age gap between us – it was horrendous. I admit it was far worse for Will though, having being hit by the car as well. It's why I make allowances for how detached he is – Dean's death made it hard for him to get close to people. Even his wife and daughter, at times. It's also made him vehement at work in the traffic division. It has given him a mission.

"Yes. She's ready for her final journey - wearing her wedding dress. She looks absolutely beautiful."

Claire sounds as though she is choking on a sob. "I can't believe it. I just can't believe it. It's like a bad dream."

"I'll check she's ready for you." The undertaker rises from her chair and walks silently across the carpet. I'm baffled when she knocks on the door saying room two, and walks in. I hear her speaking inside the room. Claire and I look at each other, clearly the same thought is whizzing through her head as mine.

"Is someone already in with Lauren?" I ask as she re-emerges.

"No, that was just me talking," she replies. "I was letting her know you're here."

"Why did you knock on the door?" Claire has the same baffled expression I probably have.

"It's just a mark of respect."

"Oh."

"If you'd like to follow me. I'll take you in."

Claire firstly grips my arm then hangs back behind me. It's like when we were kids and going into the local woods on the edge of town.

I walk in behind the undertaker, gobsmacked at the sight in front of me. Framed in a white coffin, wearing a dress that was meant for the Maldives sunshine, is the love of my life. They've plaited her hair as we asked, and it looks as though they've put a hint of make-up on her.

When I saw Lauren in the hospital mortuary, her eyes were open a fraction, but they've now been sealed. Her mouth looks odd – I think they've sealed that as well. Her hands are clasped across her chest, nails still painted with the pink varnish she'd put on a day or two before she died. I remember moaning at her about how strong the nail varnish smelt.

"Oh my God." Claire gasps, her hand flitting to her mouth.

"I'll leave you to spend some time with her," says the undertaker. "Take as long as you want and I'm just out here if you need anything."

I notice a long-stemmed red rose at the side of Lauren in the coffin. I'm just about to ask if anyone else has been in to see her, but the door has already closed.

"Oh Mark." Claire clasps my arm. "Poor Lauren. She looks so…"

"Dead?"

"Yes, but she looks peaceful too."

"Considering what she's been through. At least we can't see the injury at the back of her head now."

I can't take my eyes off her. My guts feel tightly twisted, perhaps it's the swell of love I suddenly feel. "Look at her dress," I say to Claire. "It's stunning."

"Just like she was." Claire turns and looks at the coffin lid. I follow her gaze. *Lauren Frances Holmes. Born 2nd July 1988. Died 26th January 2020.*

I shudder as I imagine the all-too-near a time when that coffin lid is put over her for the last time and I never get to see her face again.

"I've heard people are supposed to look like they're sleeping when they've died." Claire whispers in the silence of the room.

"Lauren doesn't. She looks like she's gone. It's as though just the shell of her is left." I reach and touch her hand. It's freezing cold, with a waxy texture. "I just hope wherever she is, she's at peace." My voice cracks as I gaze at her. "Can you give me a few minutes with her sis?"

"Will you be OK?"

"Course I will."

"I'll just be out there."

I take a step closer to the coffin, this time touching her cheek. "I miss you so much sweetheart." My voice sounds alien in the silent room. "I hope you don't mind me deciding on your wedding dress for you to wear. It's gorgeous – just like you. I would have given anything to have seen you in it on our wedding day. For you to have walked down the aisle and been my wife." Tears are running down my cheeks. This is awful. Bloody awful. "You made my life complete Lauren. I hope I did for you too. You gave me a wonderful daughter and I'll take the best possible care of her."

Then I remember. "We should have been having baby number two." I stroke the finger where she's still wearing her engagement ring. I've asked for it back before she's cremated so I can give it to Alysha when she's older. "We'd have been so happy. I can't believe you're gone." I feel slightly daft talking to someone who's never going to answer me but it's helping so I carry on. "Can you hear me Lauren? If you can, somehow, give me a sign. God, why did you have to die?"

I'm quiet for a few moments as I wonder what to say next. "I'm going to get who did this to you. I promise. I'll make sure he doesn't do it to anyone else. I'm just so sorry." My chest aches with emotion. "I should have looked after you. I shouldn't have let this happen. I'm sorry. I'm so sorry." The sobs threaten to engulf me.

I manage to pull myself together and wonder if they can hear me outside, so I lower my voice. "Wherever you are, lovely lady, wait for me. When I'm older and I've brought Alysha up, I'll come and find you. You just make sure you're looking out for me."

I stand, continuing to stare at her, drinking in every aspect of what I can see. This image will always be imprinted on my memory, but it will never detract from the other images I have of her.

When I return to Claire and fall into her hug, I'm utterly wrung out. It's been the worst ten days of my life. But now I've seen she's at peace, I've taken another step towards accepting it.

Claire and I make the drive home in near-silence.

"Are you not going to pick Alysha up?" she asks as I drive past the bottom of Will and Eva's estate without turning in.

"No. I'm going to ring and ask if they'll keep her for tonight." I try not to feel guilty, especially after the promise I made to Lauren. "I left some more clothes there this morning on my way to work."

"Mark, you can't keep on like this. She needs you."

"She's being well looked after. She's got Heidi to play with and both Eva and Will are fine with it. Cut me some slack Claire. It's only been a few days."

"So what are you going to do for the rest of the day?"

I pause for a moment. Nothing means anything anymore. "I don't know. Maybe a brew. Or a brandy. A shower. A chat with Brenda." We pull up on the driveway. "The first thing I want to do though is to give the station a ring and find out the latest with the TV appeal."

CHAPTER THIRTY EIGHT

Olivia's Family

We hurry up the garden path of Petra Yates, Olivia's Mother. "It's starting to feel like groundhog day." I say to Chris and Hutton. It's pelting with rain and I feel as desolate as the grey sky.

"I don't think we'll get any additional information from this visit." Hutton reaches for the doorbell. "It's more about touching base with her now that the inquiry has changed direction."

"*Changed direction* is putting it mildly." Chris straightens himself out as the door swings open. "Mrs Yates, I'm PC Chris Canvey. We spoke on the phone yesterday."

"Come in," she says, stiffly. "Though I don't think I can tell you anything new."

We follow her into her kitchen where she moves papers and books from the chairs so we can sit down. She straightens up and looks at us with an air of suspicion.

"I'm Sergeant Robert Hutton, and this is my colleague Sergeant Mark Potts."

A strained smile appears on her face as she takes a seat at the fourth side of the table. "Well, I'd like to say, *it's nice to meet you* but obviously, given the current circumstances, that wouldn't be true."

"It must be extremely difficult for you, Mrs Yates," Chris says.

"Call me Petra," she replies. "It is more difficult now. An accidental death is hard enough to bear, but to know some brute did this, just snatched her life away, is dreadful. Are you any closer to catching him?"

"We're following up on leads from these second meetings with all the victim's families, and those we've received through the TV appeal."

"I saw that." She looks straight at me and I wonder for a moment if she knows who I am. "That poor girl. There's a crumb of comfort in believing that Olivia's death will have been relatively quick. What that Lauren Holmes must have…"

Hutton glances at me and then quickly cuts in. "Which is why it's imperative we catch whoever is behind these killings. The reason we're visiting you, in light of the recent turn of events, is to check there's no new information you can think of that might add something to the inquiry."

"Like what? I wasn't with her that night." The rain is slashing against the window pane, and I think of Lauren, laid in that coffin with the same rain drumming overhead. Rain she can't hear anymore. "The man who was with her. He was cleared wasn't he?"

"Yes. We investigated him along with checking the CCTV from the Yorkshire Arms. He was clearly visible, sat at the bar at the time when Olivia left the premises, and for about an hour afterwards." Hutton clasps his hands in front of him on the table. "He didn't move from there - he just ordered more drinks."

"How can you be so certain that he didn't do anything after that?"

"We've also checked with the taxi company's log. He was picked up immediately after being accounted for on the CCTV."

Chris speaks now. "Haven't you already been told all this by DCI Ingham?"

"Him." She snorts. "He was supposed to visit, then he didn't turn up. He was supposed to ring me back, but he never did. He was useless. To be honest, I've been thinking about making an official complaint. The way this whole thing has been handled isn't good enough."

"Another two senior officers have taken over the case." I try to keep the bitterness out of my voice. "Which is partly why we're going over all the facts again. Just to make sure there isn't anything that has been missed."

"We're obviously at more of a disadvantage," Hutton adds. "As things are forgotten over time. But, things are sometimes remembered."

"I'm sorry there's nothing I can add." Petra sniffs. "I wish there was. I didn't even speak or text her that night. She'd shut herself off. And me." She looks towards the window. "Gosh, it's coming down a bit out there. I was leaving Olivia to it. I knew she was licking her wounds after her break-up with Ben."

"Do you know of anyone who may have been out to hurt her? An ex, for example? I'm sorry we have to ask, but we need to cover everything."

"No. She'd recently split with Ben, who I didn't particularly care for. He was a lot of things, but certainly not violent or psychopathic. Their relationship, from what I can gather, had just blown itself out."

"It wasn't you who reported her missing, was it?"

"No. Like I mentioned, we hadn't had a great deal of contact in her last few months." Her voice wobbles. "Something I really regret now. It was the man she was with in the Yorkshire Arms who made enquiries, when a body was recovered later the next day.

He said Olivia had been drunk and had suddenly disappeared from the pub."

"Yes. We've got a statement from him to that effect."

"I feel sorry for the poor woman who found her." Petra's eyes fill with tears that she tries to blink away. "I didn't find out until the day after, when I got the dreaded knock at the door from your friend DCI Ingham."

CHAPTER THIRTY NINE

Charlotte's Family

Charlotte's mum only lives a few streets away from where we've spoken to Olivia's mum. As we pull up, so does another car. A woman around the same age as Lauren gets out.

The front door is thrown open before we get to it.

"Mrs Knowles?" Hutton says.

"Yes. Hi Sofie. This is Charlotte's friend and flatmate. She was with her that night."

I step aside and Mrs Knowles embraces Sofie when she reaches her.

"It's good to see you Jan." After a moment or two, she pulls back.

"I'm Sergeant Robert Hutton, and these are my colleagues PC Chris Canvey and Sergeant Mark Potts."

I've found the public never really seems to take note of our names. They're always more interested in our rank.

"Would you like to come in?" Mrs Knowles and Sofie, now in front of us, step into the hallway with the three of us following. "It's this way to the lounge. Charlotte's Dad has taken the afternoon off work."

"Thank you."

We click along the tiled floor, obediently following to where she pushes a door open.

"Hello again Mr Knowles," Hutton shakes hands with Charlotte's dad who rises from his armchair as we walk in. It's a huge lounge and Sofie makes for the window seat. She's clearly used to coming here.

"PC Chris Canvey, we haven't met before." Chris also shakes hands with him. "And this is my colleague, Sergeant Mark Potts."

Mr Knowles and I nod at each other.

"Take a seat." He sinks back into his chair.

Mrs Knowles sits in the chair beside him. Hutton and Chris sit facing them, leaving me no option but to join Sofie in the window seat. I take out my pocket book. There was nothing much to note from Olivia's mum. But something, anything may emerge from revisiting these families and if it gives us the breakthrough we need, then it's worth it. Besides, a personal visit in light of the perceived police failings and the new slant on the investigation isn't a bad thing.

"How are you all doing?" Hutton begins. There's a collective shrugging of shoulders.

Mrs Knowles eventually replies. "You know. Bad days, worse days, and not quite so bad days. It's only been two months."

"How do you think we're all doing?" Mr Knowles's voice drips with sarcasm. "Our daughter is dead."

"She'd have been showing by now," Sofie says. "I can't believe she didn't know she was pregnant. If she had, she wouldn't have been drinking and might not have had to go outside to be sick."

"Did you know she felt sick?" Hutton twists his neck to address her in the window seat.

"She had felt sick earlier, however she had drunk a bit whilst we were out, so I thought she was OK. I was going to the bar, and she was asking for water, but I just laughed at her. For asking for water, I mean."

"I know we've been through this before Sofie, but did you actually see her leave the pub?"

She looks down at the floor. "No, I was busy talking to someone."

"She could have been followed out then? Or even have been persuaded to leave?"

"I don't know. I doubt it."

"You should have stayed together," snaps Mr Knowles.

Chris jumps in quickly with another question. "How long was she on her own?"

"Just a few minutes."

The tension in the room is palpable.

"What about the baby's father?"

"Luke?" Mr Knowles's voice is sharp. "We haven't heard from that one since the funeral."

"We haven't been able to understand it," Mrs Knowles adds.

"They weren't all that serious." Sofie's voice sounds loud beside me.

"Did Luke know she was pregnant?" Chris asks. "Before she died, I mean?"

"No," Sofie replies. "I don't think he'd have been interested. He's a bit of a player if you ask me."

"A player?" Mrs Knowles looks at her. "What do you mean?"

"Someone who likes to play the field." Chris offers an explanation. I frown at him.

"Was he in touch with Charlotte that night?" I ask, once again forgetting that I'm supposed to be keeping quiet and leaving the questions to Hutton and Chris. I always kept in touch with Lauren when one of us was out. We couldn't let a whole evening go without a text, even if it was one just to blow a kiss with an emoji.

"No. I think she was feeling down about it. Some lads there were giving us some attention, but she didn't want to know. She only had eyes for Luke."

"You've already checked the CCTV to make sure no one followed her out, haven't you?" Mr Knowles takes a sip from a mug beside him.

"We've seen the CCTV both inside and outside the pub, but there was none on the entrance itself. As you know the cameras outside didn't offer much coverage either."

"Heads should roll for the lack of surveillance that's installed around there." Mr Knowles is looking at me as he speaks. "One, even two deaths are too many, but *seven?* Why wasn't something done earlier?"

"It is being done now." I hope my calm tone will placate his anger. "It's too late, I know, but we honestly felt, at least in the beginning, that the drownings were tragic accidents." As I speak, my eyes rest on a large graduation photograph of Charlotte. She reminds me of Kate Middleton.

"The investigation is now being headed by DI Jones." Chris seems to follow my gaze to the photograph. "He's very thorough and will follow every line of inquiry."

"Why wasn't that the case in the first place? I just don't get it."

"I can assure you sir," Hutton says. "That everything is being examined."

"How long," asks Chris, "was it before you noticed Charlotte hadn't come back into the pub?"

"To be fair…" Sofie's eyes are still fixed on the floor. "I didn't notice she'd gone. I think I just assumed she was in the loo or something. After all, she had complained of feeling unwell earlier."

"Did you not think to check on her?" Mr Knowle's voice is sharp again.

Sofie stretches her legs in front of her and raises her gaze to meet his. "I know. I feel terrible. I was talking to someone. I'll never forgive myself."

"I think we can establish," says Hutton. "That all these women have been alone, some slipping out totally unnoticed."

"Whilst others," adds Chris, "have left the pub with people knowing they were leaving, but their safe arrival home has not been followed up on."

"With all respect," Mr Knowles sits forwards as though he's going to stand up. "I'm not interested in these other women. I want to know what happened to my daughter."

"Stay sat down love." Mrs Knowles tugs at his arm. "But you're definitely now saying, my Charlotte's death was no drunken accident. Someone had definitely planned to hurt her?"

Mr Knowles drops back into his seat. "Look – I know I'm being abrupt, but I can't believe that so many women have died before this line of investigation is being taken."

"That's why we're here," Hutton says gently. "My colleague DI Jones is examining every shred of evidence and we're going to keep you informed each step of the way."

"One thing I've noticed," Sofie says. "There was something in the paper recently. When around seven women had died. I thought all of their faces looked really similar. Even with the age differences. They all had long dark hair too."

The mention of the paper makes me sag inside. She's probably referring to an article Lauren wrote. But I recall Lauren also saying something about appearances. In fact, it was on the list she wrote. Something, again, overlooked by the police in the beginning.

"It sounds to me." Mrs Knowles sits forwards in her seat. "As though no woman or girl is safe being out and about in the city centre right now. Not until he's caught."

"So you lot…" Mr Knowles looks at us like we're insects. "Should be out there, trying to catch this man rather than coming around here with pointless questions that you've already asked us." He stands this time. It's our cue to leave.

CHAPTER FORTY

Gemma's Family

I look into the agonised eyes of Darren Hopkinson who lost his wife only hours before I lost Lauren. We're both having to survive without the women we love. I wonder if he can see the same pain in my face as I see in his.

"Can we come in?" I step forward.

"Have you got him?" His eyes harden like marbles as he opens the door wider. "You'd better be here to say you've got him."

"I wish we had. But we've got new leads that we're following up on." Chris's voice sounds from behind me.

"And that's it? It's been a week since she was thrown into that river. You should be out there finding him, not here, bothering me."

"We've just got one or two questions to ask you." Hutton says. "Then we'll be out of your hair."

"Come through," he says, his anger seemingly subsiding somewhat. "Sorry for the mess. I'm not coping very well." He sinks onto a chair at his kitchen table and drops his head into his hands. I hope he's got a sister like mine looking after him. But with pots everywhere and an empty whiskey bottle in the middle of the table, I suspect not.

Hutton comes up behind him and rests a hand on his shoulder. "We're doing absolutely everything we can. I promise we'll catch whoever is responsible."

"So what are you doing *here*?" He shakes Hutton's hand off and looks at us in turn. "You should be making sure that this isn't happening to someone else's wife. It's a fucking disgrace that so many women have died in that river without you catching whoever's behind it."

"The entire team is on it," I say. "There's a lot of us. Our role," I point at Hutton and Chris, "is to visit families of all the victims. We're looking for commonality between them or any information you might have remembered since my colleague took a statement from you last Monday."

"Commonality? They were all pissed, weren't they? And all on their bloody own – easy pickings for some maniac." His eyes are red raw. I wonder whether he has any support at all and realise again how lucky I am.

"He's robbed my whole life from me, and you're sitting here like it's some sort of social call. You should be out there catching the bastard who did this to my wife. I bet you'd have him by now if it was one of *your* wives he'd chucked into the river like a piece of old rubbish."

I open my mouth to retort, but Hutton puts his hand on my arm and says, "you've every right to hit out. This is just a brief visit, so you're being kept in the loop and to give you the chance to let us know if there's anything you've remembered that could help catch this killer."

"There's nothing more I can tell you." Darren lowers his gaze to the table. "Only that I'm an absolutely shit husband. I should have been picking her up, instead I had a few beers here. What the hell was I playing at? She asked me to pick her up as well. And I knew about the nutter that had been hanging around the river at weekends. I can't believe I made such a terrible decision. I couldn't have driven after the beer, but I could have gone in a taxi to pick her up. I'll never forgive myself."

This has been a common theme with all the families we have visited. Beating themselves up over what they could have done differently. I've done it myself. Berated myself for not insisting Lauren came with me and Alysha that morning. Telling myself I should have left her the car. I only hope she knew how much I loved her.

I take a deep breath. "I know exactly what you're going through." My words break the silence. Chris and Hutton look at me. This is our last family visit. Darren looks to have very little support. It might help him to know he's not on his own.

"How could you?" He spits the words out. "It's not *your* wife that's laid on a mortuary slab."

"No, but my fiancé is laying in a coffin in the funeral home right now. Lauren Holmes?"

He slowly raises his eyes up to mine. We're part of a club no one would ever want to be part of. "The newspaper reporter? Oh mate, I'm sorry. But… you're *working*. There's no way I could work. My head's wrecked. Full respect to you for that."

"There'll be time for me to grieve soon enough. Once we've got the killer. From now on, I will personally keep you informed, I promise."

As we leave the house, I wait for my bollocking from Hutton for being unprofessional. Instead, he asks me if I'm OK.

"Far from it," I reply. "The only thing keeping me going at the moment is the compulsion to get this nutter locked up. After that, I don't know."

CHAPTER FORTY ONE

Claire stands from the sofa. "I'm going to nip home." She stretches her arms above her head. "I could do with getting some clean clothes and having an hour to myself."

"Yeah, course. Would it help you to spend the night at home sis? You've done a lot for us lately."

"No. I'd rather be with you. I just need to clear my head."

"Do you want to take the car? I don't need it. I might have a beer or a brandy anyway."

"Well, save me one." She smiles for the first time since I got back. "And no, it's not far. I'll walk. It'll do me good. Blow the cobwebs away."

Brenda is knee-deep in ironing. The smell reminds me of Lauren. She hated cooking but loved ironing. I used to laugh at her. She even ironed tea towels and pillow cases. "Thought I'd make myself useful. Earn my keep."

"You don't need to earn your keep or make yourself useful. I'm glad you're here. But I think this is the first time I've ever seen you behind an ironing board." For a moment, I forget my misery and smile at her. "Brenda, you must be turning into your daughter!"

"I've been moping about too much. Keeping busy is a better idea. It's worked for you, hasn't it?"

Her tone is slightly 'off.' I'm not sure if she's getting at me for leaving Alysha with Eva. Or for continuing to work. "We all have our own way of handling things," I say. "And there's nothing wrong with moping, as you put it. It's a wonder we're still standing after what we're coping with."

"I've had moments of wishing I could've gone with her and even more moments of wanting to have gone *instead* of her." She places an ironed jumper onto the pile. "It's the way she's died that's haunting me."

"I know. And I'm aware that I've wrapped myself up in finding her killer." She's ironed some of Lauren's clothes and I stop myself from commenting. "Somehow, we're all going to help each other get through this."

"Can you ever get through something like this? I've lost my only daughter, Alysha's lost her mummy and you, well – it's just horrendous." She slams the iron onto its holder. "It's not the normal order of things is it? It should have been me who went first, not her."

I walk towards her. "Come here. You need a hug."

She leans into me for a few moments, I feel the wetness of her tears on my shoulder. This always used to be a cheerful house. Now it's full of misery, and it's hard to imagine happiness again.

"Anyway, how did it go yesterday? Seeing Lauren, I mean? At the funeral home. You never mentioned it."

"You were pretty certain you didn't want to see her, so I didn't think you'd want me to talk about it. It was like you'd expect really - awful, but I needed to do it."

"See you in a little while," Claire calls from the hallway.

"OK love," Brenda calls back. "Did she look peaceful?" She folds one of my shirts and starts on another skirt belonging to Lauren.

I think for a moment. I don't think the image of Lauren laid in that coffin will ever leave me. Because they had sealed her mouth, she didn't look quite like herself anymore. But I'm not going to tell Brenda that. "Yes, she did," I reply eventually. "Although, you could tell she had gone. That it was just the shell of her left behind."

"I wish I knew where she'd gone." Brenda sniffs. "If I knew she was alright. Wherever she is. I hate to think she's just, *dead*, but if I knew she was going on somewhere else…"

"We just can't know." I feel an extra heaviness within myself. I know what she means, though. I'm not sure what I believe about the afterlife, but I worry that Lauren has taken her violent death with her somehow. I know I'm going to need counselling once I get through this initial shock. "I think a beer's in order." I walk towards the door. "Can I tempt you Brenda?"

"Go on then. Can't have you drinking on your own." She wipes her face with her hands. The tears are never far away for either of us.

Brenda abandons her ironing and we sit with our drinks on the sofa, looking at a photograph album Lauren put together. It's probably not going to do me any favours looking at this so soon, but once I start, I can't stop. I realise for the millionth time how wonderful she was, capturing our most precious moments in a book like this. As a bloke, I could never have been bothered. We look youthful and deliriously happy when we first met, and a tiny bit drunk in our engagement photos. My breath catches when the page falls on two of her when she was heavily pregnant with Alysha.

"It breaks my heart that I should have been a grandma again." Brenda stares at the page. "Do you think she knew she was expecting?"

I shake my head. "She categorically didn't want to try again until after the wedding. So I'm sure it would have come as a shock to her. And I'm certain she'd have said something to me if she suspected. They said she was only in the early stages."

"It's so unfair." Her fingers brush the surface of the photograph. "So bloody unfair. What that monster has robbed from us."

"I know." I put my arm around her shoulders. "And I couldn't have got through this week without you. I know its early days, but you, Claire and Eva, have been absolute rocks. We just have to stick together and look after each other." I haven't mentioned Will. We've barely had any contact apart from when he came with me to identify Lauren. If this had happened to him, I wouldn't have left his side.

"I'll nip home tomorrow and bring the albums of Lauren from when she was younger. I've not subjected you to them since she first brought you round to meet me."

I laugh then. The sound is alien. "Lauren was mortified. Especially over the one of her in the bath. No doubt we'll do this with Alysha when she's older." It dawns on me again that there will be no we, only I. And I'm going to have to be both father and mother to Alysha.

We continue flicking through the photos and open a second beer, looking at Alysha's birth, her Christening, our family holidays, Christmases. Smile after smile after smile. We were so lucky. Too lucky perhaps. And now it's all been snatched away.

"Shouldn't Claire be back by now?" Brenda has put the ironing away and we've packed the photos back into their cupboard. We've watched the news where I'm pleased to hear it officially confirmed that several solid leads from the TV appeal are being investigated. I'll get back on it tomorrow.

It's starting to get dark. My stomach growls and I realise I haven't eaten since I forced some toast down this morning. "We should eat." I grab an apple to keep me going. "I'll give Claire a ring, then get started on making us something." The beer has relaxed me slightly. I take a bite of my apple whilst pressing the call button on my phone. Hers is switched off.

"She's been gone for over three hours," Brenda says. "And she always has her phone. Lauren used to joke about how attached she is to it. Mind you, she was the same."

"Claire needed a walk to clear her head. It really got to her yesterday. You know, the funeral home. She's nipping in at her house too."

"Needed a walk? If I'd have known I'd have stopped her." Brenda walks to the window and separates the blind with her fingers to look out. "She should *not* be going for a walk. Not until that man is caught. Why didn't she take your car?"

A chill creeps up my back. "I never thought. I'm sure she'll have just got comfy at home or something. I'll have a drive round. I've only taken the top of this second beer."

"I'll come with you. I need to get out of this house." Brenda walks towards me. "Has Claire got a key? If she gets back before us?"

"Yes. You and her have always had one."

We jump into the car and make the brief journey around to Claire's house. "Check round the back," I say to Brenda. "It's all locked up. See if there's any clue she's been back and gone again."

"Like what?"

"I don't know. Post not on the doormat, or something."

"Where else might she have gone?" Brenda's face is filled with panic.

"Will's house? Or to one of her friends?" I think for a moment, trying to keep calm. She will turn up. There'll be a rational explanation. "I'm not sure how to get hold of her friends though. I could put a post on Facebook, but that might worry everyone. I'll give Will a try first."

"You've not heard from Claire, have you?" I say as we're connected. "She's disappeared into thin air."

"No. When did you last see her?"

"Over three hours ago. She was calling home for more clothes."

"Three hours. Is that all? She's a grown woman Mark. You worry too much."

"You would if you were going through what I am. It's just, she said she'd only be an hour, and she's walked. With that man still not having been caught…"

"Sorry. No idea. But if we hear from her, I'll tell her to ring you. She'll be fine."

I'm not reassured. "How's Alysha? Is it OK if she stops with you another night?"

"Yeah, no problem, she's upstairs, playing with Heidi. They're fine. Eva's been asking whether you're planning to send Alysha back to school next week? Heidi could do with getting back."

"Yes. They could both do with getting back into a routine."

"Mark." Brenda tugs at my elbow. "It's nearly dark. We need to find your sister."

"I'm going to get off the phone Will. I'm off to find Claire."

"I'll get her to call you if she turns up here."

"Cheers. I'll go back and check our house again, then have a drive round."

Ten minutes later, we're back at the house and there's still no sign. "Brenda. You wait here in case she comes back. I'm going to look for her."

"Shouldn't you be calling the police?"

"She's thirty-three years old. And she's only been gone for three hours. They won't do anything yet." Will was right in that respect.

"They'd keep an eye out for her. Especially with that lunatic hanging about."

"True." The prickling returns to the back of my neck. "I tell you what. I'll have a drive around and if I don't find her, I'll ring the station. I can think of a few places she might be. You keep trying her phone."

I can't shake the feeling of dread as I set off again. Brenda's right. Claire is never parted from her phone. Although it's conceivable her battery has died. It's nearly dark, but the sky is well lit by a nearly full moon.

I take a different route between my house and hers, then check the mini-market coffee shop. It stays open until eight and I know she occasionally goes in there. No sign. They've closed up already. I don't think she'd have gone to a pub on her own. Whenever Lauren and I have arranged to meet her at a pub, we've had to wait outside for her.

I look on Facebook to see if any of her friends show up as places she might go. The only posts are about what's happened to Lauren. I decide there's nothing else for it and type out a post on her page.

This is Claire's brother, Mark. Has anyone seen her in the last few hours? No need to panic but her mobile is off and we're not sure where she is. Hopefully that will turn something up.

I'm not far now from trying to pull in some police units to look for her. I hope, given the circumstances, they'll relax the usual stance of not looking for a missing adult within the first twenty-four hours, unless they're vulnerable.

I drive through the city centre, shivering as I pass over the river bridge. In the now brightly lit security lights, I can see flowers carpeting the ground and there's wanted posters of the man's e-fit. They've sorted the CCTV out now too. At least this would have pleased Lauren.

As soon as I'm away from the restricted city centre zone, I park up. I could do with some fresh air as I'm feeling light-headed. Claire likes to walk in the nearby park to clear her head. However, I'll go mad with her if I find her there – she's always had a peculiar sense of danger and seems to think she's invincible. I realise that I've been so preoccupied with finding Claire, I've pushed my misery about Lauren out of my mind. I don't know if that makes me feel better or worse.

As I reach the park's entrance, I hear a sound. It's like a muffled scream, but it's enough to make my heart feel as though it's stopped. It's coming from the cycle path which runs adjacent to the park. Where Lauren was found, and Denise was attacked. I tug my phone from my pocket as I begin to walk faster. Then I hear a sort of deep growl, which could be a man. It could be a couple having an argument, but I pick up my pace. As I approach the far entrance onto the path, I've pressed nine, three times with shaking fingers and say *police please.*

There's definitely someone there. I see movement in the bushes and can make out a shape in the moonlight. I sprint towards it. "This is Sergeant Mark Potts," I try to steady my voice as I'm connected. "Get some units to both sides of the cycle path by Alder Park. I think we've got another attack taking place."

Chapter Forty Two

"Stop!" I bellow. There's a cry, a thud, then a figure comes hurtling through the darkness towards me. I crouch, ready for him as the gap between us closes. I stick my leg out and bring him crashing to the ground. With a grunt, he lands heavily. As he tries to spring back up, I leap on him. We wrestle for a few moments, him trying to get away, me knowing I'll be keeping him here. But he's strong. My arms shake with the force of pinning him down as he writhes beneath me but adrenaline courses through me. I've got the bastard – I just need to keep hold of him until backup gets here.

I momentarily pause in my struggle as I realise I'm looking into the moonlit face of Detective Chief Inspector Jonathan Ingham.

"You." I gasp. "It was you."

As I fight to contain my shock, I'm thrown off balance as he rolls from under me. Then stunned by a solid blow to my head. He's going to knock me out if I don't get my wits about me. As blood seeps into my mouth, I use every ounce of fight to wrestle the rock from him then deliver the same blow back to him, that he gave to me, and two more. My anger is unleashed with every blow

I deliver to his face and head. I want to reduce him to pulp, I want to kill him, just like he killed Lauren. Thankfully, I realise he's unconscious and return to my senses. It's the first time I've ever unleashed such violence.

Still trembling with anger, I climb off him and stagger over to where he emerged from the bushes. Looking back at him lying unconscious, I realise I don't want him to die – I want him to pay. I want him to answer to what he's done in front of a court. I want him in prison, known as both a Detective Chief Inspector and serial woman-killer amongst his fellow inmates. He won't last five minutes in there.

"Over here," a female voice gasps. "Please help me." It's so weak I don't recognise it at first, but as I get closer, I realise it's the voice of my sister.

"It's me, Claire." I tug off my coat and wrap it around her shaking form. I cradle her head, then realise that like mine, it's oozing blood.

"He was dragging me to the stream," she whimpers. "He had his hands around my neck. He was going to drown me, just like he did with Lauren."

"It's alright. You're safe. I'm here." Thank God I got here when I did.

"I'm not going to die, am I? I feel really strange." She slumps within my arms and I see her eyes fall closed in the faint light.

"Claire, stay with me. Do you hear me? Claire! C'mon, c'mon." I feel for her pulse. It's faint. I call 999 again. It takes longer to be connected this time. "This is Sergeant Mark Potts," I gabble into the phone a few seconds later. "Where's the police backup I requested?"

"It's on its way Sir. Why haven't you used your radio for assistance?"

"I'm off duty and haven't got my radio. We need two ambulances as well. Please hurry. It's my sister. She's been attacked. Badly."

"Why do you need two ambulances sir?"

"Because I've got hold of the man responsible. He's unconscious a few feet away." I can hear the sirens. I keep my finger on Claire's pulse. "Don't you dare leave me sis." I've lost Lauren. I can't lose my sister too. "They're here. Can you hear them?" I cradle her head in my lap. I daren't move.

I flick the torch on my phone and shine it into the air. "Over here," I shout as police van doors bang. "Help us."

As they're running towards us through the undergrowth, torches ablaze, the ambulances I've requested screech up and two paramedics jump from each.

"Chris," I say. "You've got to help us. He attacked us both. But Claire, my sister, she's in a bad way."

Momentarily Chris stands there, as though rooted to the spot, but then swings into action. "Where is he?"

I point in the direction I left him. He and Paula head that way and the paramedics gently slide Claire from under me, lighting the space with their torches.

I stand, going dizzy with the movement as I lurch towards where Paula and Chris stand, flashing their torches all around. "Where is he Mark?" Chris says. "Did you get a look at him?"

"Ingham." I forget the pain and dizziness as I get to them. "He's done this to my sister, my fiancée, and all those other women."

Paula gasps. "You've got to be joking. D-C-I-Ingham?"

A few feet away, I can see the paramedics working on Claire. There's no resuscitation going on which reassures me – they'll be assessing her so they can move her to the stretcher.

"Ingham," Chris echoes. "So where is he?"

"I'm sure it was here." I turn a circle, taking the beam of my phone's torchlight with me, the motion making me dizzy again. There are more police and paramedics running towards us.

"Sergeant Donaldson, Murton Division," one of them announces. He looks to where the paramedics are with Claire. "Who are we looking for in relation to this?"

"DCI Ingham," Chris replies with a shake in his voice.

"DCI Ingham. There must be some mis…"

"I can assure you there isn't," I say. "He was here. He beat me around the head with a rock. I managed to get the better of him though. He was out of it. Right here. I can't understand how he's managed to get up again."

"We're really hampered with the darkness," Paula says, flashing her torchlight around. "Looking for anybody."

"We're not looking for anybody. We're looking for DCI Ingham. He can't have got far. Is she OK?" I call over. "My sister?" I walk towards them.

"She's stable," calls back one of the paramedics. "Her blood pressure's very low, though, and we need to get her to hospital as soon as we can.

I scan the darkened horizon for a figure trying to slip away in the moonlight. "We need to find Ingham. He was unconscious. He can't just have got up and walked off."

"Are you absolutely sure it was him? It's very dark here," says Sergeant Donaldson, tugging his radio towards him.

"Definitely. I'm certain. Do you think I'd make something like that up?"

"Sergeant Donaldson." He speaks into his radio. "We need as many units as possible and the dog handlers. We've had another serious attack on the cycle path, South West of Alder Park."

"What's the condition of the victim?"

"Not sure. She's with the paramedics and is about to be taken to hospital. I've got her brother with me now, Sergeant Mark Potts. He's also been assaulted and injured."

"What information do we have on the perpetrator, sir?"

"DCI Ingham. North Yorkshire Police. We believe he is responsible for these attacks."

"And the others." I hold my hand out for the radio. "Can I speak to them?"

"Sergeant Mark Potts," I say into it. "My sister's been badly attacked by DCI Ingham and I have every reason to believe that he's responsible for the murder of my fiancée a week ago, and all the river deaths."

"Do you have evidence for this Sergeant? Did you see…?"

"Of course I did."

"Are you off duty, Sir?"

"Yes. But I want to stay here and find him."

"A patrol car's been sent and we'll get to his house once the search is coordinated here. If he's there, we'll bring him in."

"I can't imagine he's got very far. I did the same to him as he did to me with a rock. He was unconscious."

Sergeant Donaldson takes his radio back. "I think you need to get that head of yours looked at Mark."

"I will."

There are vans and flashlights all over the place now as word is spreading about what, or rather who we are looking for.

"Where are those bloody dog units?" Sergeant Donaldson yells.

"At a suspected hit and run by a drunk driver," comes the reply from someone in the darkness.

"Bloody hell."

The scene is swimming around me. Claire's still unconscious as the paramedics pass me. "Are you coming with her in the ambulance Mark? She's stable, but we need to get her to the hospital right now. We're still not happy with her blood pressure."

"I'll be along as soon as I can," I say. "I'm going to ring our brother and he'll meet you there."

"I really think you should be looked at Mark." One of the paramedics with her hands free, shines a light towards my head. "I can see from here that you're going to need stitches. And there's the risk of concussion."

"I'll be fine. I'll be there soon."

"You're a stubborn sod." Chris turns to the paramedic. "Don't worry. I'll keep an eye on him and I'll bring him along myself to be checked out shortly."

The dispatched patrol car is parked outside DCI Ingham's house when we get there. As we come to a halt, one of the officers steps from it.

"Any sign of him?" asks Sergeant Donaldson.

"No, Sir."

"OK. Get the door forced with the battering ram."

"Yes, Sir."

More units arrive as the officers step up to the door. Ingham doesn't stand a chance if he's in. Paula has patched my head up with the first aid kit as we've made our way here. Patrols have been deployed all over town in the search for him and the helicopter is up. Sporadically its beam can be seen from here shining into fields and between trees.

The door splinters off its hinges with the impact and two officers run in shouting "Police!"

As suspected, no one's here. Ingham's home is what I would expect to find of someone having a mental health episode. Pizza boxes and crockery congealed with food litter the surfaces and floor. But there's no sign of him. What really strikes me is the noticeboard above his table, filled with the newspaper clippings of articles detailing all the murders he's perpetrated; many of the articles written by Lauren. I hold my phone up and take a photograph.

"Why would he have done it?" Chris looks shell-shocked. "He's not wired right. How did he ever get to where he is in the force?"

"I don't know." I take a couple more photos then tuck my phone into my back pocket. "And Lauren knew too. We should move out of here. The forensics will be here soon to do their stuff. We don't want to contaminate anything."

We make our way out into the garden and radio through again. Whilst we're waiting for an update, Chris shows me the latest news bulletin on his phone.

Net closes in on corrupt DCI, it says, before telling the story, warning women at the end of the article, not to go out of the house on their own until DCI Ingham is in custody. There's a large photo of him in the centre of the webpage and underneath, the caption. *If you see this man, he may be armed and should not be approached. Instead, call 999 immediately.*

"It won't be long until we've got him." Chris slips his phone back into his jacket. "How are you feeling, mate? Are you still adamant you don't want that head looking at?"

"I will actually," I concede. "I'm feeling sick and dizzy. It could be concussion or it could just be stress. I'll get it checked out. And I need to be with Claire."

"The entire force is looking for Ingham." Chris squeezes my shoulder. "If I have to work overnight and all day tomorrow, I promise we'll get him. But let's get you seen to first."

I lean against Chris as we walk into A&E. I'm not feeling too good at all. The triage nurse helps me onto a trolley, then wheels me into a nursing bay and pulls the curtain around us. "You go," I tell Chris. "My brother should be here somewhere with Claire. I'll be fine."

The nurse looks at me. "Well, if possible, we do need a next of kin to know where you are. Where would your brother be?"

"He'll be with our sister, Claire Potts." I hold my hand in front of the florescent light that's hurting my eyes. "She was brought in an hour ago. She's been attacked on the cycle path. I could do with knowing how she is."

"Right. I'll see what I can find out." The nurse slips back out of the curtain.

"Do you want me to wait until your brother gets here?" Chris sits beside me.

"No, but you could pass me that." I gesture to the cardboard sick bowl.

He passes it to me and scoots away with a quick, "Right, that's my cue to go!"

I wouldn't have thought there would be enough inside me to cause so much puke. I've barely been eating. I literally turn myself inside out and am still retching into the bowl when the nurse reappears.

"Oh dear." She takes it from me and passes me another. "A side effect of concussion, I'm afraid. You did the best thing coming in. We'll probably keep you overnight for observation."

I lean back against the pillows, my head throbbing and my throat burning. But I feel slightly better for throwing up. And I'm not going to argue about being kept in. I feel too ill to go anywhere. "How's my sister? Have you found her?"

"Your sister-in-law will be here in a few minutes," she says. "Can I get you some water?"

"Yes please."

She returns with my water at the same time as Eva arrives. She doesn't say anything at first. She just sits on the stool Chris vacated and stares at me.

"Claire?" I ask. "Please tell me she's OK."

"They're waiting for an intensive care bed." Eva clasps her hands together and leans forward. "She might have to be moved to a different, more specialised hospital. He's crushed her windpipe. They've had to sedate and intubate her."

"Where is she now?"

"Resus still. So she's in the right place."

"Where's Will?"

"He stayed with the girls."

"What's wrong with him? Why didn't he come?"

She looks apologetic. "I told him he should be the one to be here, but all he could say was hospitals give him the heeby-jeebies. I've promised to keep him updated."

"I want to go to Claire but I can't move my head." I feel as useless as I did when I found out what had happened to Lauren.

"You stay where you are Mark. You look awful. Thank God you got to her when you did."

"Cheers." Trying to smile makes me wince. "If they move her to another hospital, I'm going too."

"Have you seen someone yet?" Eva looks knackered. Since Lauren died, she's obviously been coping with her own grief, whilst looking after the girls.

I feel guilty. As soon as I'm out of here, I'll take Alysha back. "I'm just waiting for the consultant. I've been told they'll be keeping me in overnight. Concussion. Anyway, I'm going to be fine – I'm more concerned about Claire."

She squeezes my hand. "You lot – you're fighters. All they've really said is that she might have to have an operation. For airway stenosis or something. But they're taking good care of her."

"Has she spoken at all? Since they put her in the ambulance? She was barely talking when I first got to her."

Eva shakes her head. "They were trying to keep her awake. She was out of it by then though. They're not sure about her head injuries, there's a lot of blood, and she's got a hell of a lot of bruising. Then there's her windpipe. She's sedated and intubated now so can't talk."

I'm struggling to keep my eyes open too.

"Don't close your eyes Mark. Not with concussion." Eva nudges me. "You can't go to sleep."

Her voice sounds faraway. I want to drift off and find Lauren wherever she may be. Die and be with her. Then I remember Alysha and my eyelids snap back open. "Have you heard who they're looking for?" I ask. "I can hardly believe it. I never liked Ingham and suspected him to be unprofessional and inept of late, but I would never have had him down as a killer."

"Yes. I can believe it."

"Does Will know?"

"Yes, he never really said much. I rushed out of the house after Chris rang. I just wanted to get here. I hope they throw away the key." Disdain is written all over her face. "I don't know how your division will hold your heads up after this. I don't mean you personally, Mark."

"We'll get him. It's just a matter of time."

"You won't be getting anyone Mark. You're staying right here."

Eva spends the rest of the evening ricocheting between me and my bed in the observation ward and Claire's in ICU. Mum turns up - having driven for two hours. The sight of her when it is not Christmas, Easter or Mother's Day reiterates how serious things must be. Brenda is hot on her heels, panic etched across her face when she sees me. They take their seats at either side of me.

Mum does nothing but cry to start with. "I can't lose any more of my children," she says over and over. "All this is bringing back what happened with Dean. Even though it was so long ago, something like that never leaves you."

She shuts up long enough to drink the tea that Eva brings her. Then the questions begin. *"Why was she out on her own? What was she doing by the park? Why haven't they caught the man yet?* Then the best one. *How could you have let this happen?*

I feel snappy with her because it's taken the attack on Claire for Mum to show her face. She should have been here earlier, after what happened to Lauren, to support me and Alysha. All I have had from her are text messages, not even a phone call. She's offered to get food delivered and has been checking that I'm not alone but I could have done with her, in person, if she *really* cared. To say she cannot handle this sort of thing after what happened to Dean is not good enough.

I'm thankful that Eva is here to keep Mum and Brenda in some sort of check. Having a weeping, wailing mother *and* mother-in-law alongside concussion is not much fun, even if they have got every reason to weep and wail.

I'm relieved when they all go back home for the night after the nurse persuades them that they'd be better off getting some rest.

Chapter Forty Three

I'm absolutely dog tired, but I keep one eye on the news streaming on the little bedside TV screen. The news bulletins report absolutely nothing to suggest we've found Ingham.

The nurses come in every thirty minutes to flash a light into my eyes.

"How's my sister?" I keep asking them. "Can you find out?"

At 2:00 am, they tell me they've taken her down for surgery. I lay drifting in and out of sleep, willing her to be OK, talking to her inside my head. I remember times together as we were growing up, the fights, the games and the amazing friendship we've always had. I'm not a religious man, but I say a few words to him upstairs. *"You've taken the love of my life,"* I whisper into the shadows. *"Please, please don't take my sister."*

At 4:30 am a nurse appears in the doorway. She pauses, which makes the breath catch in my throat. It's as though she's steeling herself to impart bad news.

"I'm one of the nurses from the theatre team." She steps towards the bed and I try to sit up, wincing with the pain from my head.

"I've been assisting with the procedure your sister underwent – a craniectomy to relieve the pressure on her brain."

"Please tell me she's OK." My voice wobbles. There's nothing I wouldn't give for the nurse not to tell me she's dead. I would go in Claire's place. I know it sounds selfish, but I'd be with Lauren again and Alysha would be OK, no matter what. She's plenty of people to look after her. Will might be a bit of a prat but he would treat Alysha like his own. And there's Brenda too.

"Claire's breathing on her own again," the nurse assures me. "We're weaning her off the sedation now. The only thing we're worried about is potential brain damage. It's always a risk after head trauma. Once we've spoken to her, we'll be better placed to establish that."

"Thank God." I lean back into my pillows. I could weep with relief. I'm exhausted, but at least Claire's alive. Thoughts of Lauren hit me. There was no one around to save her. Which is why she now lies, lifeless in a coffin, wearing her wedding dress.

I squint in the dawn sunshine as a breakfast trolley jangles around the ward.

"Can I get you something sir?"

I must get my strength up if I'm going to feel better, so ask for a cup of tea and a slice of toast. I've barely eaten a thing in the last twenty-four hours. I turn towards my TV screen. Ingham's face is all over it, along with a still of the scene where we rescued Claire last night. It's the BBC national news that I'm watching, I guess that means he'll still get picked up if he gets further afield. I hope they get him soon. Before he attacks someone else.

I never saw the evil in his eyes before. His expression bears the trace of a sneer and chills me right through. I can't believe how much this one man has wrecked my life. I wonder if he's got away with any other killings before the river deaths, whilst masquerading behind his guise as a Detective Chief Inspector. In my mind I echo what Chris said yesterday, *how did he ever get to where he is?*

"What are you watching that for?" I turn to Brenda's voice. "Aren't you suffering enough without seeing his face? I, for one, don't want to see it ever again." She pulls up the chair beside my bed. "Hanging should be brought back, if you ask me."

"In this case Brenda, I agree with you." I turn my head to her, the movement still making me wince. "Where's Mum?"

"We've both been up most of the night. When we got the call to say they were taking Claire down to theatre, she wanted to come back here but they told her to stay where she was."

"I'm surprised she listened."

"She needed a bit of a talking to. We couldn't have done any more good pacing the hospital waiting room than we could have done pacing around at your house."

"Where did she sleep?"

"She didn't. Well she got her head down for a couple of hours on the sofa. Look Mark, I know you and your mother have had your issues, but she does love you, you know."

"It's a shame she doesn't know how to show it."

Brenda reaches for my hand. "I'm so glad you're safe." Tears fill her eyes. "It's tearing me in two that my daughter has been murdered. I'll never be the same. Part of me has gone with her. But if Alysha had lost both of her parents. It doesn't bear thinking about."

"I know. Up until yesterday, part of me wanted to go, and be with her, but the attack last night provoked a fight in me that showed how much I have to go on, for Alysha's sake." I feel guilty for thinking like I was before.

"It's what Lauren would want," Brenda says softly. "You've got to live for the two of you now. He's done you good and proper, hasn't he? Evil bastard." Brenda *never* swears. "Look at the state of you."

"Is my mum coming in again?"

"Now that Claire is stable, she's gone to see Alysha and Will and get a shower. Then she's coming back. So you'll just have to put up with me looking after you."

I don't tell her that suits me fine and I'd rather have her here than my own mother. I'm surprised she came so quickly to be with Claire. She has been on the outskirts of our lives since we lost our brother. She should have gone for counselling. It is as though she's closed herself off to everything and everybody. And she has lost so much from doing so. She could have had the relationship with Alysha that Brenda has.

Brenda sits at my side, either talking about Lauren or lapsing into a comfortable silence for over an hour until the doctors get to me on their ward round. I'm not really up to making much conversation, but I'm happy to have her here. I persuade the doctors I'm good to go, and Brenda assures them that she'll look after me. I promise to return if there's any more sickness or dizziness. The bright blue stitches in my head will dissolve, I'm told. Brenda helps me get out of the hospital pyjamas and into the clothes she's brought for me.

"I can't believe you're having to help me dress," I laugh.

"Let me look after you," she says. "We're family. We always will be."

I'm reassured by that. I might have lost my beloved Lauren, but she's left me the wonderful gift of our daughter, and her mother. In many ways I think more of Brenda than I do my own mother. Many blokes despise their mothers-in-law, but I've been really blessed with mine. My eyes fill with tears at the thought of her being unable to see her daughter wearing the beautiful gown she's currently dressed in.

"Do you think you'll go and see Lauren at the funeral home?" I sink to the bed, exhausted from getting dressed. God, I hope I soon get back to normal.

"No. I definitely just want to remember her as she was. It'll crucify me to see her – gone. Especially in her wedding dress."

Claire's been moved to the high dependency unit. She's not out of the woods yet, after being operated on overnight, but she's stable. Her anaesthetic has worn off, but we've been told not to allow her to speak. Brenda and I sit either side of her. Mum arrives back. The three of us take it in turns holding Claire's hands while she sleeps.

"Is there any news on Ingham yet?"

Mum shakes her head, unable to take her eyes off Claire. "Look what he's done to her. If I could only get my hands on him."

"How do you think I feel?" Brenda's voice is so quiet, I wonder if Mum would have heard her at the other side of the bed.

Mum raises her tear-stained face from Claire to Brenda. "I'm sorry. I didn't mean to sound insensitive. You know, that my girl survived it, whilst yours…"

"Leave it Mum." Mum and Will were definitely cut from the same piece of cloth when it comes to tact.

"If all this has shown me anything," Mum continues. "It is that I want to be here for you all more. I might even move closer."

I don't know how to react to this announcement. I don't know what to think. Right now, I can't think straight anyway.

Claire's eyes widen when she briefly wakes and sees me. I sense she wants to remark on my bruising and blooded head, but I stop her before she tries.

"I don't look as bad as you sis." I stroke the top of her hand. "I'm sorry I couldn't be in here with you last night. I was too busy throwing my guts up. Concussion."

She smiles weakly and nods, the movement clearly hurting her. At least she understands. Hopefully, that negates the chance of major brain damage. She turns her head to the other side and Mum squeezes her hand.

"Your op has gone really well by all accounts." Mum smiles through newly emerging tears. "They've done what they needed to, and it's just a question of getting some rest now. You had a lucky escape."

"I don't know what you were thinking, walking…" I begin.

"Leave it." Brenda frowns at me.

"I'm so glad you're OK." I grab for Claire's hand. Tears fill my eyes now.

Claire's eyes are full of questions.

"Get some rest love." Mum gets to her feet. "We will go for a coffee, then we'll be back."

"We will talk about it all as soon as you're up to it sis. I'll ask the nurse to come in and check you over. We won't be long."

CHAPTER FORTY FOUR

D espite Brenda's protestations, I head to the station the following afternoon. Chris has texted me to let me know they still haven't found Ingham and there's going to be another briefing. I can't just sit here, waiting. I have to help find him.

The search for Ingham is now a full-scale national manhunt. I just pray they get him before he kills someone else and robs another family like he has mine and so many others.

I take a taxi to the station, having decided not to risk driving. My head's still sore, but I no longer feel exhausted, even though I think I slept even worse last night than I have for any night since Lauren died, I'm just tender. I've got to find out what's going on and join in the search, if they'll let me. Claire is going to be in hospital for a few more days, so other than visiting her, she doesn't need me. Chris also said in his text that Denise should be discharged before the end of the week.

I need to get justice. For Denise, and for Lauren and Claire. As well as all his other victims. Alysha's still with Will and Eva, that's if Will is actually there and not at work, and Brenda's got my mother for company. They were both driving me mental when I got home yesterday; from not bothering with us for months, my mother has taken to being critical of me for Alysha not being there, me drinking too much and the state of the house. And that is when she is not crying over what has happened to Claire and Lauren. Then in between time, she goes on about what happened to Dean. She is planning to stay until after the funeral. Then she is going home to put her house on the market. *After the funeral.* The words cut me like glass.

Therefore, work is my preferred place to be. And I reckon this is the day we are going to get Ingham.

"Right." DI Jones stands and looks around the room. "Firstly Mark, you shouldn't be here. I'm beginning to think you're the bionic man." A titter echoes around the room.

"I have to be here Sir, especially now. It'll take more than him to finish me off."

"I understand. But you must take it easy. It goes without saying how much your help is appreciated."

Hear, hear, echoes around the room. I couldn't be more heartened. Chris who's sat next to me, pats me on the shoulder.

"OK." DI Jones glances down at some notes. "This is where we're at. There's been a police patrol at DCI Ingham's house and at his sister's house. We believe that to be the only family he has. His information has been circulated to all ports and airports so he can't get out of the country. His ex-wife's house has been visited, but there's no reply. There's a patrol there as well."

"Can we not force entry Sir?"

"We'll have the warrant through at any moment," DI Jones replies. "The judge mucked up the paperwork so I put another request in first thing. We've checked through all the windows and couldn't see anything."

"Not another cock up." Sergeant Donaldson's loud voice bounces around the incident room. "As if there haven't been enough already.

"To be fair." DI Jones looks at him. "It's highly unlikely we'll turn anything up his ex-wife's house. But we must obviously cover *everything.*"

"Who's going when you get it?"

"At least half a dozen of us."

"You just said it's unlikely that we'll turn anything up there?"

"Just in case. You never know."

"What about his car?" Paula's voice sounds from the back of the room.

"Parked up outside his own house," DI Jones replies. "A team of officers have been checking out CCTV and logs with taxi ranks and car hire companies."

"I can't see him risking being recognised on public transport." The effort of speaking tugs on my stitches. "His face is all over the place."

"How's your sister today?" Hutton asks.

"I haven't seen her yet. She's still being guarded - until we get him, presumably?"

"Yes." DI Jones nods. "There's two constables with her at all times, and with the other lady, Denise."

"They were bloody lucky." Chris looks at DI Jones. "Is that all, Sir? Can we get on with bringing him in?"

"Today's the day." DI Jones thumps the table with the heel of his hand. Which is exactly what I just thought.

Warrant in hand, DI Jones leads the six-strong team to the front door of the non-descript terraced house. I've been ordered to stay in one of the cars, locked in. I watch as he knocks, and others peer in through the windows. I feel utterly useless but would be no match for Ingram if he is in there and sets about me. I feel better than I did, but God knows what damage another blow to the head would do. I'm not going to risk it. I wind the window down to hear what's going on.

DI Jones gives a nod and two of the team begin smashing at the door. It gives after four attempts with the battering ram. "Police!" They all rush in. I can see them through the windows, darting around the house, opening cupboards, kicking doors open. I'm glad I'm here with them, albeit watching from the car. I need to be here, for Lauren and for Claire. I'd have been climbing the walls at the station, waiting for news on my own.

Everything falls silent for a few moments and I can't see anyone. What's going on?

Minutes pass and I wonder what or who they've found. Then, DI Jones emerges from the house. "We've found his wife." His grim-faced expression bears a trace of relief. "In the basement."

"Is she…"

"She's fine. He's been taking food and water to her – well, up until two days ago that is. She's been there for nearly a fortnight. To say she was relieved to hear us shout *police* is an understatement. She burst into tears when we found her."

"That would tie in with him going on the run after I recognised him two nights ago."

"I've rung an ambulance. She needs checking over. I've said we'll visit her - to ask her some questions as soon as she's up to it."

I hear the siren in the distance. As the ambulance pulls up behind us, DCI Ingham's wife is coming out from the house, helped along by Chris and Hutton. She doesn't look too bad to say she's spent all that time locked in a cellar. The paramedics meet her on the path.

"Let's get you inside the ambulance," one of them says. "And have a look at you."

"I just need to let this gentleman know something first." She walks over to DI Jones. "*He*, Jonathan, I mean, overheard me on the phone last Sunday. Arranging to meet a reporter."

"A news reporter?" DI Jones glances at me. A Sunday. A news reporter.

"Yes. We were meeting at the café near the river. I couldn't go to the police because of my ex-husband. I needed to tell someone what I had found out. But he locked me in the basement to go after her."

"And what had you found out?" DI Jones asks.

"I think this will have to wait," says the paramedic. "This lady needs medical attention before answering your questions."

"That he knew who was responsible for the women in the river," she mumbles before the paramedic takes her arm. "But he's been covering."

"So it wasn't…"

"I only found out in the middle of the night on Saturday when he turned up."

"You're not doing this now." The paramedic guides her by the arm. "We need to get you to hospital."

"We'll be along shortly to speak to you."

"I'm fine. Just tired. And in need of a shower and a decent meal. Come and see me in a couple of hours."

DI Jones drops me off at Will's, promising to pick me back up in two hours. I need to see Alysha.

"Daddy, what's wrong with your face? And your head?"

"Daddy's fine. I pull her onto my lap. It happened at work." I listen to Eva, clanking around in the kitchen, making me something to eat. She said Will stormed out half an hour ago. She'd heard him shouting on the phone with someone and had challenged him. He'd had a go at her too, then slammed out of the house. I guess all this must be getting to him more than he lets on.

"Why? Was it a bad man? Have you told the other police Daddy?"

"Yes. Something like that. He's going to get caught now." Though I wonder what DCI Ingham's wife meant when she said he was *covering*. It makes little sense.

"Will he go to prison?" Alysha's half speaking to me and half concentrating on some rubbish on the TV. Heidi is glued to whatever it is. She glanced at me when I walked in, but that was about it. She's always been more for her Auntie Lauren. She adored her.

"Yes. For a very long time."

I bury my face into her hair, inhaling her innocent smell and am beyond grateful she has stayed here. I've been in no state to care for her. I've been too wrapped up in my own grief and vengeance.

"I'm sick of the sight of this place," I say as DI Jones pulls into the police parking bay at the hospital.

"I bet you are. We won't be staying too long. They're keeping Mrs Ingham in for observation. She's dehydrated and had a blow to the head, which has resulted in mild concussion."

"It's probably for the best that she's being kept in. At least she's safe in here. With Ingham still out there somewhere."

"If she's discharged before we catch him, I'll either put a uniform presence there or get her into a safe house."

"I'm sure we'll have him well before we have to think about that."

I nod to the constable standing at the entrance to the ward. We're shown to the side room where Patricia is laid on her own. We walk past a meal trolley and the smell of boiled cabbage turns my stomach.

"Hello again Mrs, erm Patricia. Is it OK for us to call you by your first name?" I can't bear to say the word *Ingham.*

"Call me Pat." She offers her hand.

"You'll hopefully remember us from the house," I begin. "I'm Sergeant Potts and this is DI Jones."

"How are you feeling?" DI Jones briefly grasps her hand in response. "We won't stay long. We were hoping for any more information you have. If you're feeling up to it?"

"Of course. Get yourselves sat down."

DI Jones nods towards me and I gratefully sink into the chair beside Pat. DI Jones plucks a plastic chair from a stacked pile at the side of the sink.

"I just want you to catch him. If he knows I've got out of the basement, he'll come after me. I know he will."

"He won't get anywhere near you. This ward is locked." I point to the officer at the entrance to the ward. "And if he did manage to get anyway near the main door, our colleague who's patrolling knows exactly what he looks like."

"I would imagine he's hiding somewhere by now," DI Jones says, looking thoughtful. "Have you any idea of anyone who might harbour him Pat? Someone, by some fluke, who doesn't know what's going on? An elderly relative perhaps?"

"Absolutely no one," she replies. "He's got a sister, but they haven't spoken for years. He was such a loner. I didn't mind at first. Eventually, the lack of anyone else in his life made him really controlling. Turned me to drinking for a time, it did. Which is why our relationship faltered." She says the last sentence more to herself than us.

"Can you think of anywhere else he might have gone?" I ask. "Some kind of *bolthole* somewhere?"

She shakes her head. "I'm sorry. I really don't know of anywhere." She looks at me closer. "What's happened to you?

Your other half must be having kittens knowing you're still out there working, looking like that. You look like you should swap places with me."

"I was attacked by your ex as well. Both me and my sister had a lucky escape from him two days ago. My fiancée Lauren wasn't so fortunate."

"Lauren? You don't mean the news reporter, do you? Is she your fiancé?" She shrinks back into her pillows and stares at me. "What do you mean, she wasn't so fortunate?"

"He killed her." I close my eyes for a moment.

The silence hangs between us for a few moments and she stares at me, open-mouthed. "I had no idea. Why?"

"That's what we're trying to find out."

"You *have* been locked in your cellar for nearly two weeks," DI Jones says softly. "You're not going to know what's happened during that time."

"I'm fortunate you found me when you did."

I swallow. "It's all part of the service."

"How could I have been with him for so many years and not known how evil he is?"

"I'm surprised he brought you food and drink." DI Jones sounds more as though he's asking a question than making a statement.

"I'm not sure he knew what to do with me. I guess on some level, he felt responsible – we were married for a long time." She rubs her eyes.

"Are you OK?"

"Just tired. There's not much sleep to be had when you're handcuffed to a pipe in a cold cellar."

"What you've been through doesn't bear thinking about and you've still made the effort to speak to us," DI Jones says. "We appreciate it."

"You won't be appreciative when you know the full story. I didn't realise you were Lauren's partner."

"What full story?"

A nurse smiles as she walks in and begins checking Pat's obs. "You won't be telling any stories today Pat. We said five minutes."

I continue. I *must* continue. "When we found you, you said your ex-husband is involved in the river deaths. What do you know Pat?"

"He turned up at my house on Saturday evening. Of course, I didn't let him in. I shouted from the window for him to go away. He could probably hear it in my voice that I'd had more than a couple of glasses of wine. He stood outside ranting again about me being a drunk, then drove off."

"Go on." DI Jones leans forwards.

"He came back a few hours later, in the early hours of Sunday morning. I recognised the sound of his car's engine. He started carrying on again when I wouldn't open the door. Making threats to me about something that happened many years ago. He was on the verge of waking the whole street. So, like an idiot, I opened the door.

Anyway, he told me what he'd done. Said that it was because of women like *me* and women like *his mother* had made him do what he has done. It was our fault, he said. We had driven him to do it. Then he said he was doing the world a favour, covering for him."

"Covering for *who?*"

"To use *his* words – the man who has been getting rid of drunk bitches with no control over themselves."

"What do you mean, *covering?*"

"Apparently someone had been blackmailing him."

"Ingham? Who?"

She looks at me and a strange expression passes over her face. All fight seems to drain from her. "I'm really tired."

"Tell us what you know Pat. Please."

As I watch and wait, I remember what Paula said earlier in the week in the staff room, about Ingham's mother and wife having a drink problem. And his own aversion to alcohol.

DI Jones changes tack. "How long was Jonathan there? At your house?"

"I didn't let him in. Like I said, I opened the door but I had the chain on. Kept him on the doorstep. He said what he had to say, then left. But I didn't sleep after that. I haven't known what to do, to be honest." She swallows and her eyes look watery. "I wanted to ring the police but didn't think I'd be believed. He's a *DCI*, for goodness sake. I was scared you'd think it was sour grapes. And if I'm totally honest," she looks from me to DI Jones, then back again, "I was worried he'd intercept me somehow. I'd no idea when he was on shift, or what information might get passed on to him. Not to mention the repercussions for me after all these years after something I did."

"What do you mean, *repercussions?*" She's talking in riddles. Guilt is written all over her face. About what, I don't know. But we'll get to the bottom of it.

"Why did you arrange to meet Lauren?" It hurts like hell to say her name out loud. I can't help but blame Patricia for involving Lauren. I wrestle with the feeling. Lauren wouldn't have taken much persuasion.

"I'd been reading her articles." Pat closes her eyes and shakes her head.

"What happened next?" DI Jones asks.

"I nipped out for a Sunday paper when I woke up and must have forgotten to lock the front door when I came back in. What an idiot."

"Are you OK Pat?" Another nurse puts her head around the door.

"Yes. I think so. If only I'd have done a simple thing like lock the door – especially after what Jonathan had told me. He will have sneaked in whilst I was on the phone to your Lauren. I was going to tell her everything, and I mean, *everything.* Then, as soon as I put the phone down, he whacked me over the head and got me into the basement. I was out of it for a little while."

"And then he's obviously gone to meet Lauren himself, knowing where she was heading after hearing you on the phone," I say. "She would never have just left it if you hadn't turned up you know. If DCI Ingham hadn't got to her first." I smile slightly, recalling her feistiness. "She'd have come looking for you."

"So we know he was responsible for the attacks at the stream," I begin, "but are you saying that someone else is responsible for the river deaths?"

"Yes. He's been blackmailing Jonathan."

"Who? With what?"

"He had something on him." Her voice rises. "It's all been my fault. I should have said at the time."

"Who had what on *who*?"

Tears are rolling down her face. "I can't tell *you.* I need to speak to someone else. A different officer. You shouldn't be here. I thought I could do this. But I can't. I just can't."

"Pat!" The nurse comes hurrying over. "What's the matter?"

"I can't do this. I can't do it! He shouldn't be here." She's becoming hysterical and is pointing at me. She was OK with me a few minutes ago.

"I'm going to have to ask you to leave," says the ward sister, running in. "She was only admitted a little while ago. Clearly she's not up to this yet."

"We need to finish these questions. I'm sorry. Her husband killed my fiancé."

"I can't talk to you. I need to speak to someone else. Not you."

"Why not? What's the problem here?"

"Perhaps you should wait outside." DI Jones jerks his head in the direction of the door. "I'll talk to her."

"No. No. No. I'm going to be locked up again."

"Can you come back tomorrow? This isn't the time. Pat needs to recover." The ward sister looks at us both whilst the other nurse appears to be trying to calm Pat down.

"Can we take a full statement from you when you're feeling up to it?" My fists ball in frustration inside my pockets.

"I'm so sorry," Pat sobs as we step away from her bedside. "I really am."

CHAPTER FORTY FIVE

I 'm dozing off in the comfy chair next to the heater when DI Jones bursts into the staff room. "They've found him. He's been squatting in a derelict house."

I jump up so fast, I go dizzy and have to sit down again. "Really? Is he being brought in?" Wait till I get my hands round his weaselly, evil neck.

"No. He's made a bloody run for it. There's more units on their way and the helicopter's going up. He won't get far."

I grab my jacket and get back to my feet. "Come on, let's go."

DI Jones pauses. "I think you should wait here Mark. After what…"

"No chance. I can't just sit here."

We run to his car. Within minutes we're heading through the town centre. I can see the police helicopter, already overhead. I can't believe we didn't get the full story out of Pat Ingham, but I've no doubt we will the next time we speak to her. That's if we don't get it out of Ingham first. Catching him is a job only half done. *Who the hell's been blackmailing him? With what? And why?*

The road over the river has been blocked off. We screech up next to the police car blocking the road and hurtle towards the bridge. Blue lights are flashing against the sky darkening to dusk.

"Of all the places to corner him," DI Jones gasps as we see what's happening. *"Here.* I can't believe it."

Ingham has climbed over the railings on the bridge, fifty feet above the river. Whether he has the guts to jump is anyone's guess. Part of me wants him to suffer the same ghastly death he subjected others to, whether directly or indirectly. The other part of me wants him to see nothing but the inside of a prison cell for a very long time.

"Stand back," DI Jones orders the officers. There's a dozen standing just over arm's length from DCI Ingham.

"You bastard." My words are a growl. "You evil fucking bastard. Get down here and face up to what you've done."

DCI Ingham turns his head and smiles, yes smiles, at me. Then he's gone, plunging towards the darkness of the river. Moments later, there's a sickening smack as he hits the water.

"Sir?" Chris looks at DI Jones, panic stricken. "What do you want us to do?"

"No one's risking their life going in after him. We know what this stretch of river is like. Can one of you radio through for Underwater Search?"

"He'll be dead by then," one of the others says. Just as he says it, I see Ingham's head bobbing on the surface of the river. Chris slides off his jacket and dives in.

"Chris!" DI Jones yells after him.

Simon and Tom, two of the younger officers follow Chris into the river, both disappearing under the water at the same time. I hold my breath, waiting for them to come back up, letting a jagged breath slowly back out when they do. There's no sign of Chris though. They shouldn't have gone in, none of them, DI Jones was right. The undercurrents here aren't worth risking. After a few moments of ducking under the surface and coming back up, Simon and Tom make their way to the water's edge and are hauled out by their colleagues. I grip the stone wall of the bridge. "Where the hell is Chris?" I'm more pleading with, than asking DI Jones.

"Have we sent for the underwater team yet?" I hear the desperation in his raised voice.

"On their way, Sir," a voice calls amidst the spluttering of Simon and Tom who are being dragged up the muddy bank. "We called for their despatch when DCI Ingham climbed over the railing. Just in case."

"Oh shit. We've got to do something," I say to DI Jones. "We've got to get Chris out."

"You're not going in. If you do, I'll personally fire you."

"We can't just leave him in there."

"What's the ETA of the underwater team." DI Jones shouts again, down to the river bank. I can hear sirens in the distance.

"Over there!" Paula's voice rings out across the river and we all divert our attention to where she is pointing. At first, I expect the head of Chris to have emerged, and I once again hold my breath, looking for him. What we see, however, are security lights blinking on, and the retreating form of DCI Ingham, limping downriver along the embankment.

"Get after him!" I shout as the underwater search van screeches up beside us and four frogmen jump out. Several officers set off in Ingham's direction.

"Who are we looking for?" One commands.

"PC Chris Canvey," DI Jones yells. "He jumped in from here after DCI Ingham. He hasn't resurfaced." All four of them hurtle down to the water's edge, one dragging a canoe behind him.

"They're going to find his body." I feel like throwing myself in too. "He's got a young family. He's not going to make it out. He'd have come back up by now."

"Let them do their jobs Mark. He's young, and he's fit. In fact, he's as tough as old boots. He might have come up further downriver. Ingham did."

"We need the helicopter over there."

DI Jones tilts the radio towards his face. "Can the control room redirect the air search further north of the River Alder? We've got foot patrols after DCI Ingham. We need the helicopter over them."

Moments later, the helicopter is passing over us, and projects its beam further downriver. I run from the bridge down the banking. Three frogmen are submerged in the dark river already, the fourth is in the boat flashing his light around. I glance across at the entrance of the Yorkshire Arms; the windows are filled with rubber neckers and two Special Constables are holding back drinkers in the doorway.

"Any sign of him?" I shout to the officer in the boat. He shakes his head. Tears are rolling down my face. The tragedy that's taken place lately is beyond anything I could ever have imagined. "Please find him." I look up at the helicopter, watching it pass slowly along the length of the river, its beam reflecting from the surface of the water. I sink to my knees, sobbing. I can't take any more. "We were so close to catching Ingham. We nearly bloody had him. And now this. And we don't even know yet who else we're looking for."

The officers who gave chase after him come into view at the bend of the river. "He got away," one says over the radio. "We ran out of path. He seems to have disappeared into thin air."

DI Jones appears at my side. "We'll get him." His mouth is set in a thin, hard line. "The infrared will pick him up. You two and you two, get in the cars and join the units combing the locality. He can't get far on foot."

MARIA FRANKLAND

"Mark, come with me. You're shaking. Let's get you in the car."
DI Jones places his hand under my arm and pulls me to my feet.

"I'm not leaving Chris." I tug away.

"Mark. They'll find him. They've got all the equipment. They
know what they're doing."

"Yeah, but what are the chances of them pulling him out alive." I
wipe more tears and now snot away with the back of my sleeve and
helplessly follow him up the steps of the bridge to the roadside.
Torchlights and swirling blue lights illuminate the nearly dark sky
all around. There are crowds gathered at the roadblock in front of
me.

"Ghouls," I hiss as DI Jones opens the door to the car. "They're
just waiting to watch as a body is dragged out of the Alder. It
should've been Ingham, not Chris."

"There's a hell of a lot of public interest," DI Jones says as he
sits beside me in the car. "There was always bound to be.
Especially now."

"I just want him and whoever else is involved caught, and Chris
found alive." I take the hanky DI Jones passes me. "And my
Lauren back."

"Hopefully two of those wishes will be granted within the next
couple of minutes."

"I can't just sit here Sir. I need to be out there, helping my
colleagues."

DI Jones turns to face me. "Mark," he begins. "Against my
better judgement I let you stay on the investigation because I could
see how much you wanted it, needed it even, to keep going. And
I'm full of admiration for the professional way you've committed
yourself to your work and this team whilst you're going through
what you've been going through. However, you've incurred a
nasty head injury and you've been through enough. It would be
negligent of me to let you carry on." He puts his hand on my

shoulder. "Officers are crawling all over the place, looking for DCI Ingham. Once we've got him and spoken again to his wife, we can start piecing it all together."

"But Chris…"

"Leave it. There's a team of experienced divers searching for Chris. As your supervising officer, I am *ordering* you to stay here and wait."

"Yes Sir." My voice is small. I'm beat.

We sit here for what feels like an eternity, the tears in my eyes blurring the swirling blue of the lights that come and go all around me. I want to talk about what's happening, about who else could be involved. But I can't think straight. I close my eyes as if that will somehow shut out the pain.

CHAPTER FORTY SIX

Chris

I lie on the riverbank, shaking with fear and cold. I don't know how I've managed to get out of there. I'm not sure where I am or how far down river I've come. I just pray someone finds me before I freeze to death. I try to call out, but I can't seem to find my voice. I've swallowed so much water. I will not die *here,* in a pile of stinking river mud. I've never felt cold like this. Please find me. Someone, please, please find me. My wife's face floats into my mind.

I hear voices and try once again to make some noise. I can't move.

"I didn't think you were going to pick up. You let it bloody ring out three times. I gave you that phone so I could get hold of you."

"I couldn't answer straight away. I was arguing with the wife."

"Good job you did. Answer, I mean. If you think I'd go down without taking you with me."

"I see my brother's done a good number on you. You had it coming. You've gone too far. This wasn't part of the plan."

"We've no time for that now. Just get me away from here, or we're both finished."

"You can't prove my involvement in anything."

Both voices sound familiar, but I can't make them out. I'm too exhausted.

"I could have wrecked your whole precious career Ingham, and you know it."

Ingham. *It's Ingham!*

"If it wasn't for me, you wouldn't have had a career in the first place Potts." He's out of breath but now there's no mistaking whose voice that is. But who is *Potts?*

"You owed me. You killed Dean. You killed my brother."

Mark's surname is Potts. But that's not his voice. And the only brother he's got is Will in the traffic division.

"My wife killed your brother. Not me."

"You were with her. You let her drive in that state." It *is* Will Potts.

"I didn't realise. I wasn't well at the time." DCI Ingham sounds as cold as me. His teeth are chattering as he speaks. "And I don't feel well now. I need to get warm and dry, and get away from here."

"Like hell. *She* killed Dean. She was wrecked. You both left us there. My brother dead, and I could have been too for all you cared. You ruined our lives Ingham."

"It would have finished me if the truth had come out. My job was all I had. Why couldn't you have just been happy with having the chance to catch drunk drivers in your work?"

"Whilst you and your *wife* got away with it? All these years, you've been sitting pretty as a Detective Chief Inspector. Whilst I haven't gone any further than Sergeant."

"You wouldn't have even got there without me. You needed me. As much as I needed you to keep your bloody mouth shut."

"You had the chance to inform on me many times. Instead, you became some sort of psychopath."

"That's rich, coming from you, Will."

"Anyway, you were more use to me in other ways than just a promotion."

"I think I've more than repaid you, Will. Since I've known it was *you*, like you say, I've kept quiet. I've let you get on with it. To be honest, after the first two I started to agree with what you were doing. Ridding the world of out of control drunken women. Did you know my mother was a rotten drunk?"

"Spare me the psychological crap Ingham. Who else knows it was me?"

"No one. I actually admired your guts for doing what you were doing."

"How can I believe you? After what you did to Lauren? When did I agree to that?"

"She was taking us down, you idiot. Can't you see that? Another half an hour and she'd have known everything about me and you. And we both know what a mouth she had on her. Taking her out was actually easier than I thought it would be. And that Denise too - friends with Pat. Another dangerous one. She was on her way to Pat's house. It was a surprise to find I enjoyed ending her. Do you find it exciting Will?"

"Shut it."

"Why Will? You do. You do enjoy it, don't deny it, Will. You wouldn't keep doing it if you didn't." His teeth chatter between his words.

"What about Claire, my sister? She's not a drunk."

"Now, that wasn't planned. More that the opportunity presented itself. But she was sticking her nose into our business too, wasn' she?" I hear a smile in Ingham's voice. "Maybe you and I are more alike than we think, eh Will? Now are you going to help me get away from here, or…"

"Help," I finally manage to croak. As soon as the sound leaves my mouth, I know it's not my wisest move. Maybe I should've just laid here until they went away. Especially after what I've just heard. I try to stay positive, maybe they won't leave me here to die. I'm a copper, like them. They know I've got kids.

The helicopter flashes its beam, but at the other side of the river, further up. With all I have left, I try to wave to catch someone's attention - it will only be a matter of time. But just before the beam comes over us, it sweeps to the opposite bank of the river again. I could weep if I had the energy. "Help," I call out, louder this time.

"What the hell are you doing here? How much have you heard?" Will shouts through the darkness.

"Help me." I don't feel the cold anymore. I don't feel anything. But I can hear the helicopter, which sounds like it could be coming closer. Please. Please. Please.

Ingham and Potts are shouting at each other. I can no longer hear what they're saying above the noise of the helicopter. I'm sure the infrared will pick us up. I am not a religious man but say offer a silent prayer into the darkness.

I become aware of some tussling and scuffling going on next to me. I cry out as one of them lands on my legs. Only for whoever it is to be hauled straight back up again. I hear what sounds like a fist connecting with a face. Again and again. My confusion is replaced with fear as a scream is followed by a splash. The fear drives me and I manage to crawl up the bank away from the water.

Too late. I'm being dragged along the ground. I flail around, trying to muster up some fight. "No," I yell into the darkness, looking up into the grinning face of Will Potts. I'm at the water's edge. "Please. Will. I won't say a word. I promise. Not to anyone." I'm so cold that my voice does not sound like my own.

"That's not good enough, I'm afraid."

"Will. I'm begging you. Just run for it. The helicopter's over there. You've time to get away before it picks us up."

"Sorry mate. No can do. Wrong place. Wrong time and all that."

With every bit of strength I have left, I try to roll away from the edge of the water.

"It's nothing personal."

I cry out as I feel his boot dig into my side, shoving me over the edge of the banking. As I slide back into the water, I scrape at the riverbank's edge with my fingernails. I will not die. Not now. I'll go under and he'll think I have gone. He'll run for it then. As I fill my lungs with air, Will Pott's boot slams onto my face. And everything goes black.

Drowned Voices, the second book in The Dark Water Series is out in February 2022… Click here to pre-order. Emergence, the final part of the trilogy, will be out in August 2022.

Before you go…

Join my 'keep in touch' list to receive a free book, and to be kept posted of other freebies, special offers and new releases. Being in touch with you, my reader, is one of the best things about being an author.

If you want to read my next psychological thrillers, find out more about Hit and Run on Amazon.

Book Discussion Group Questions

1. Discuss the disparity that existed between Mark's job as a police sergeant and Lauren's as a press journalist?

2. What do you know about the role of a Detective Chief Inspector in the police force?

3. Which character did you care most about?

4. What do you think of Mark's decision to continue to work after Lauren's death?

5. How does making funeral arrangements assist, or not, with the grieving process?

6. Imagine the outcome if Ingham had <u>not</u> intercepted his ex-wife's phone call to Lauren?

7. Describe the process that Will has gone through – from being a victim of a drink driver to becoming a serial killer.

8. Why might Ingham have attacked Claire?

9. What might have tipped Will from ridding the roads of drink drivers to throwing his first victim into the river?

10. To what extent can people hide who they really are from others?

11. How might each character's lives continue after this?

12. Why might people have thought Ingham was the serial killer.

13. How could Will have been stopped? Why might he not have been challenged?

Hit and Run - Prologue

(The next psychological thriller - find out more on <u>Amazon</u>)

All couples have issues, don't they? Everyone has their ups and downs. That's life. I'll get through this. But how?

A bike ride usually calms me down. As I ride out of Otley towards Ilkley, I don't feel the hill that normally challenges me. Today I'm at the top before I notice that my breathing is laboured.

On any other day, I would enjoy the freewheel down the other side, the summer air whooshing in my ears, impressive scenery as far as the eye can see. I'm always grateful that I live around here. But today I don't feel grateful for anything. The demons that have been chasing me have finally caught up.

I pedal faster, as though trying to escape them, glancing over my shoulder to see how far away the approaching vehicle is. I've got time to get around the downhill, but narrow bend onto a straight and wider run. Give it room to get past me. I know this stretch well and enjoy getting my speed up.

My tracker normally clocks me at forty miles an hour here. As I take the corner, I glance around again to the roar of the engine, now right behind me, the sound feeling as though it's vibrating through my chest. The driver is not slowing and is not going around me.

I don't know whether the sickening crunch is caused at the point of impact or as my body lands. Agony shoots through me and the world turns black.

Acknowledgements

I'd like to say a huge thank you to my husband, Michael. Although my stories are born out of my dark imagination, he is the wind beneath my wings and helps me run my author business. Plus, his editing expertise is second to none. I am also grateful to my family and friends for continuing to support my author career.

Next, another thank you to my talented book cover designer Darran Holmes, who always manages to capture the design I have in my head from a simple cover brief, and also to Sue Coates, the photographer who took my 'author photo.'

A special acknowledgement goes to my two beta readers, Joan Emmerson and Andrew MacDonald for early feedback on the story and to my wonderful eagle-eyed Advance Reader Team for their later stage feedback.

I am forever grateful to Leeds Trinity University and my MA in Creative Writing Tutors there, Martyn, Amina and Oz. Without graduating from the Masters degree in 2015, I'm not sure I would have ever made the transition from an aspiring to a professional writer.

And finally, to you, the reader. Thank you for taking the time to read this story. I really hope you enjoyed it.

About the Author

The domestic thrillers I write shine a light into the darkness that can exist within marital and family relationships. I have been no stranger to turbulent times myself, and this has provided some of the raw material for my novels.

I am a born 'n' bred Yorkshirewoman, and a mum of two grown up sons. In my forties, I have been able to pursue a long-held ambition of gaining an MA in Creative Writing and make writing my full time occupation. Recently I have married for the second time and have found my 'happy ever after.'

This is not something you will find in my novels though! I think that we thriller writers are amongst the nicest people you could meet because we pour all our darkness into our books – it's the romance writers you've got to watch…

I plan to release four novels per year and if you'd like to be kept in the loop about new books and special offers, join my 'keep in touch list' or visit www.autonomypress.co.uk. You will receive a free book as a thank you for joining!

Also by Maria Frankland

Memoir

Don't Call me Mum!

Poetry

Poetry for the Newly Married 40 Something

How-to Books for Writers

Write your Life Story in a Year

Write a Novel in a Year

Write a Collection of Poetry in a Year

Write a Collection of Short Stories in a Year

Printed in Great Britain
by Amazon

75693049R00192